"What's involved in this deal?"

"Weapons," Mack Bolan replied, "from ____'s Texas armory. It's active again, and he'____ ____ __ up restricted pieces that are ex____ ___ ___nt to move them quick, so th__ ____ ____k. You'll be the go-be____ ____ ____ ll be flying in som__

Vreeland whistled. ____ ____ onto that?"

"Slater told us. He's ____ __ __w who walked out of there. He chose to co____ __e."

The pilot looked at the Executioner, then at the heavyset agent who was standing at the bar. The man raised a drink to him in a mock cheer. Finally Vreeland glanced toward the other two mercenary types who'd been watching him throughout his conversation with Bolan. "I imagine that's one way of staying alive."

"The only way."

*Other titles available in
this series:*

DON PENDLETON's
MACK BOLAN®

JUDGMENT
—in STONE—

A GOLD EAGLE BOOK FROM
W☉RLDWIDE®

TORONTO • NEW YORK • LONDON
AMSTERDAM • PARIS • SYDNEY • HAMBURG
STOCKHOLM • ATHENS • TOKYO • MILAN
MADRID • WARSAW • BUDAPEST • AUCKLAND

First edition December 1997

ISBN 0-373-61457-8

Special thanks and acknowledgment to
Rich Rainey for his contribution to this work.

JUDGMENT IN STONE

Printed in U.S.A.

Misery acquaints a man with strange bedfellows.
—William Shakespeare
The Tempest
Act II, scene ii

With the proliferation of heroin and its social seeming acceptance comes an increase in human misery, a greater number of souls lost to the allure of a demanding, merciless mistress. There are those of us who do what we can to stem the tide, ever hopeful to rescue those who fall victim to the drug lords. The war on drugs rages on.
—Mack Bolan

CHAPTER ONE

The Bahamas

A warm tropical wind danced across the white beach, caressing the cocoa-buttered skin of Melitta Caporra. She turned her head slightly to protect her eyes, but otherwise savored the gentle breeze that ghosted through her long black hair.

She was lying on her stomach in the late-afternoon sun, top down and eyes closed, her mind a million miles away from the deal that would go down later that night. Countless deaths would result from the bargain she'd made, but a fortune would also come her way, enough to ease her conscience. And in the greater scheme of things, that was all that mattered.

After seeing so many people in her profession come to sudden and violent ends—and sometimes helping them on their way—she was a firm believer in living in the moment. Right now that moment meant sun, sand and silence while she baked her well-contoured body a deeper shade of copper, oblivious to the occasional stares from the men gathered in the villa while waiting for their covert ship to come in.

THE SECLUDED STRETCH of Bahamian beach was Caporra's own private paradise. At least in theory. But through the telescopic sight of Mack Bolan's compound crossbow, nothing was private—or safe.

Shrouded by lush greenery that carpeted the sharp incline, the Executioner's profile was nearly invisible as he completed his scan of the distant pastel-colored villa.

His face was painted with jungle green camouflage, and his skin was coated with a strong-smelling insect repellent. Sometimes he wondered what was worse, the potent chemicals seeping into his system or the swarms of tropical insects that would otherwise feast upon him in the lush green aerie he'd been hiding in.

This time there was little doubt he needed the chemical bath. Bolan was there for the duration, however long it would take for the terror transaction to be made. Everything he needed was stowed away in the black waterproof gear bag at his feet.

The silent-running inflatable boat that had brought him to the Out Islands before dawn was safely hidden a half mile down the coast. In case he had to make a quick exit, he had his eye on one of the sleek black powerboats bobbing against the villa's elaborate dock. It was a souped-up go-fast with twin engines and a single hull, the kind of cigarette boat favored by gunrunners and cannabis catchers, designed for lightning-fast runs to and from mother ships laden with illegal cargo.

This time the cargo that Caporra's crew waited for was deadlier than any drug smuggled in from her Colombian brethren. It was a portable antinavigation device that could override the controls of most commercial aircraft when they were flying on autopilot.

Once lock-on was made, whoever controlled the device controlled the plane and could send it plummeting from the sky with a simple flick of a lever.

Terrorists could hijack planes without showing their faces. It was a simple equation. If airlines didn't pay ransom demands, their planes would fall. Terrorists could also carry out undetected assassinations, sending planeloads of innocent passengers to tragic deaths.

The high-tech hijacking gear was en route from Cuba aboard a cabin cruiser manned by a rogue coalition of Cuban Intelligence operatives who'd been collaborating with South American cartels for the past decade. Now that the Cuban government was increasing its cooperation with drug interdiction, the rogue cell was out to make one last score before retiring.

Bolan would make sure it was their *very* last operation.

He pivoted slowly from side to side, sighting through the dangling vines and undergrowth to make sure of his field of fire, mentally rehearsing the silent kills he would make when the time came.

Then he slowly rested the crossbow on the tangled mass of undergrowth and swept his gaze back to Melitta Caporra.

At first sight it was hard to imagine that such a demure-looking woman was behind such a lethal operation. But time and time again the Colombian beauty had proved herself a totally ruthless operator.

She'd shed blood just as often as she'd shed loyalty in her climb to the top. Caporra was almost in the upper echelons of the cartel, one of the very few women to make it that far.

This deal would put her over the top and allow

her to call the shots from a safe distance instead of getting personally involved.

But first she had to deal with the Executioner.

He raised the lightweight scope that hung from a strap around his neck and zoomed in on the site one more time, lingering on the thatched-roof terrace of the pastel-colored villa.

The hardmen who were clustered around the wrought-iron tables on the shaded terrace weren't quite as relaxed as the woman was, though they put on a good show of hiding whatever jitters they felt about the operation.

At one of the tables sat two Bahamian gunmen and a Miami-based free-lancer named Guy Monteras, who were working their way through a pitcher of Bahama Mamas. While Monteras did little more than lift his glass now and then for a brief sip, the islanders tossed down the alcohol and ice as if it was fruit juice and they were at a health spa.

The two Bahamians were middlemen with long-standing connections to local officials. Their presence was supposed to guarantee that no authorities would happen upon the deal, so they felt comfortably immune from danger.

With his tanned skin, expensive smile and stylishly cut sandy hair, Monteras looked more like a tennis pro than a mercenary. Except for the light brown underarm-holster rig worn over his sun yellow shirt, he could have passed for any other relaxed tourist who'd come down to the islands for an overdue holiday. He was perhaps the most dangerous person in the group.

A military veteran with a distinguished record, Monteras had worked the private security trade for several years, most recently with the highly regarded

International Security Services outfit in Boca Raton, before he drifted into this underworld triad of Cuban, Bahamian and Colombian traffickers.

Sitting at the table next to them was a quartet of Colombians who looked dressed for business in any Brickell Street bank in downtown Miami. They wore light summer suits and dark glasses that carefully shielded any emotions that might have flickered in their eyes. The Colombians sat in total silence, like cool, menacing statues who could move when they had to or sit patiently forever. Whatever Melitta Caporra called for, they would provide.

At the last table were two ex–Cuban Intelligence officers. Though they were no longer with the government, they still favored uniformlike khakis and affected a military bearing. For several years they had worked closely with their official Bahamian counterparts, coordinating smuggling operations. Eventually they had to flee their homeland because of one too many unsanctioned intrigues. Now they were the off-island representatives for rogue operatives who still held high positions in Cuban Intelligence.

The Cubans looked out at the sea now and then, shielding their eyes against the sun-struck waves as if they hoped to see their compatriots sailing into view.

The tension level was lower than Bolan expected. The members of this group had obviously worked together enough times and made enough money to be comfortable with one another. Though they were all well armed, there was no reason for any of them to expect that their underworld alliance was about to crash and burn.

Bolan could see a few more men inside the villa,

brief shadows that suddenly moved about or came to the doorway to look outside. Occasionally a two-man patrol appeared, dividing their time between watching over the high-end Jeeps on the other side of the villa and making a haphazard patrol of the grounds.

The patrollers were definitely not military, walking about the grounds in almost random circuits. They were careful not to wander too far from the sandy beach or the landscaped grounds where the brush had been cut back, confident that the appearance of a patrol was sufficient protection. They were street sweepers, enforcers who were used to indiscriminately firing on mostly innocent or unarmed people. They had no reason to believe they would ever find themselves engaged in actual warfare.

Who would dare to come against them?

Bolan took a head count. With the hardmen on the terrace, the men inside the villa and the two-man patrol, he estimated he was up against fifteen or sixteen men and one formidable woman.

It'd be easy enough to just take out the grenade launcher and arc a couple of loads into the villa. When the high-explosive rounds went off, he could take out the panic-stricken survivors who made it out of the inferno.

But this mission wasn't about killing a small cadre of terrorists.

Not yet anyway.

It was about stopping the transfer of terror technology that could paralyze a nation. Just like the armed force in the villa, Bolan had to wait out the flotilla en route from Cuba and make sure the operation went smoothly. If the traffickers got spooked for any reason and called off the delivery, Brognola's team at Stony Man Farm might not be able to find where the next transfer would be made.

And Bolan might not have a ringside seat.

But after the Cubans dropped off their cargo, anyone who was left at the villa was fair game. There *were* two particular targets he was supposed to try to keep alive—Melitta Caporra and Guy Monteras—but the Executioner's safety came first. If it was too risky, they went down.

Brognola wanted both of the targets questioned if possible. Caporra was the financier for her end of the operation, and Guy Monteras was the logistics man. He had worked with all of the parties to make it happen. He knew their capacities, and he knew their weak spots.

Either of them could possibly tie the operation to Thomas Quinn, the CEO of International Security Services, whose client list read like a who's who of Washington *and* the underworld. Due to Quinn's past service in covert operations, he had a lot of friends in high places who had provided him with contracts when he formed ISS.

He also had a lot of friends in low places. But the jury was still out on Quinn. Anyone in his line of work needed contacts in the underworld. Unfortunately the man seemed to have too many friends on the wrong side of the law.

A disproportionate number of former ISS operatives had ended up on the government's watch list for suspected involvement in underworld operations. So far there wasn't enough evidence to move against Quinn, but according to Brognola this operation seemed to have Quinn's signature all over it.

If Quinn *was* involved and he managed to set up this operation, who knew what he would try next?

Bolan shrugged. He would find out soon enough. He reached back slowly into the leafy cover and grabbed a set of headphones linked to a sand-colored microphone dart lodged in the terraced roof. He'd fired the dart with the crossbow earlier in the day when the Cubans were testing out one of the powerboats, loudly gunning the motors by the dock.

The dart hardly made a sound then, little more than a hornet buzzing in the air, but now it provided him with the relatively clear voices of the group on the terrace. The Cubans were talking guardedly among themselves. One of the Bahamians was complaining about Caporra, speaking loudly enough so that the Colombians would have no trouble hearing him.

"Look at the woman, man. I don't believe it."

"What's wrong?" Monteras asked.

"You'd think she had nothing going on, not a care in the world. She's lying down on the job while we—"

"While you sit here drinking yourself into a stupor," Monteras said, laughing. "Don't be so righteous. You worked with her before, and nothing ever went wrong."

"That was different. She was just a player before. This time she's dealing the cards. The woman's supposed to be in charge, not burning her bottom."

"What do you want her to do?" Monteras demanded. "The meet isn't going down for hours. Nothing happens until dark, you know that."

"Just the same, it doesn't feel right." Through the scope, Bolan watched him swirl the remnants of his drink, contemplating the chinking ice as if to read his future. "When a woman leads an operation, it gets kind of sloppy."

Monteras cocked his head and said, "Maybe you

should go." His voice hadn't changed. It still sounded friendly, as if he were acting like some kind of mentor to the other man, but there was a menace in it just the same. Bolan caught it, but the islander hadn't. Monteras was the logistics man. That meant if there was a problem he would take care of it immediately and finally.

"What you talking, man?"

"I said go. If you don't like it, walk away. Nothing's stopping you."

"Maybe we will—"

"We can't do that," the other Bahamian interrupted, speaking for the first time. He'd picked up on Monteras's cheerfully worded threat.

"Why not, man?" the first man asked. "This is our island. Our rules. I think we should..." His voice faltered, as if suddenly aware that the rules were determined by Monteras. Anyone who left now would be a target. No one walked away from a deal. Not at this stage. They either saw it through or they were cut out. Surgically. "All right, all right, man. The woman's golden. No problems. We're staying."

"How wonderful," Monteras said. "For you."

The Bahamians left the table then. Bolan noticed one of the Colombians nod slightly at Monteras and smile.

Monteras nodded back, then cradled his hands and rested his chin on his lean, capable hands. He looked out at Caporra, then looked farther out at sea, falling into a trancelike state of waiting.

Bolan was careful not to fall into that same trance. He kept his eyes moving, first tracking the two-man patrol that was stepping on the tiled path on the side of the villa, then watching the men on the terrace and the men within.

And then his eyes fell back on Caporra.

She stood and stretched her lithe golden frame in the sunlight and wrapped a long beach towel around her shoulders. The towel lifted in the breeze, trailing behind her like the brightly colored cape of a priestess as she regally walked through the sand toward the villa.

NIGHT CAME SLOWLY, heralded by streaks of lightning that seared across the darkening horizon, writhing white snakes of electricity that tapered into infinity. The storm rolled quickly across the Bahamian archipelago, soaking every square inch of the island. Whenever it seemed like the storm was passing, another barrage of heavy rain poured down on the thick green foliage that surrounded Bolan. The Executioner sat through it like a mud-slicked gargoyle, keeping his eyes on the villa and the choppy sea.

They came an hour after the storm passed.

A round white light burned a hole in the darkness from far out to sea. The signal light flashed once, then paused for a few beats before flashing two more times. After another pause the light flashed once again.

The lights in the villa went out briefly. A half minute later they returned the signal, flashing a bright light in the same sequence: once, twice, once, then the lights in the villa came back on.

After the all-clear signal, Bolan studied the seascape until gradually he could make out gray shadows on the sea. The shadows slowly morphed into the silhouettes of a cabin cruiser, an ocean-going sport fisher and two large powerboats.

The sound of engines whining and hulls smashing

against the heavy waves reached him. The transfer was going down.

Bolan moved to the edge of the brush as the cabin cruiser and the powerboats tied up at the dock. The sport-fishing boat, a charter-type vessel with a lot of custom firepower, stayed farther out to sea, ready to provide covering fire or to beat a rapid retreat.

The soldier studied the dock though a hand-held thermal imager and watched the villa's crew provide a tense greeting to the newcomers. Black-clad shapes with automatic weapons spilled from the boats onto the dock, quickly taking command of the operation. Some of the men carried bulky electronic gear wrapped in thick nylon straps, the remote-control components for the antinav station that was built into the bulwarks of the cabin cruiser.

The commandos carried their packages to the villa, escorted by a silent team of watchful guards. After a short time inside the building, the entire commando team came out and hurried back to the docks. They carried lighter packages with them this time, gleaming metal containers of American dollars, favored currency of the smuggling set.

The commando teams climbed back aboard the powerboats and roared out to sea, leaving behind the lethally packed cabin cruiser and Melitta Caporra's quietly jubilant crew. The deal had gone down without a hitch.

BOLAN EMERGED from the darkness.

His footsteps pushed silently into the sand as he kept to the edge of the foliage, moving in a crouch toward the light that spilled from the door of the villa.

He was carrying enough weapons for a small

army, or at least enough to sound like one. Inching away from the cover of brush, he headed for a white wooden chair anchored in the sand. He propped his M-16, with a grenade launcher mounted beneath its barrel, between the wooden slats, then moved on.

If he needed a fallback position, this was as good a landmark as any. It was close to the water and it gave him a good killing field.

He took another step and froze in place, sensing rather than seeing the two-man patrol just before it rounded the shadowed corner of the villa and headed toward him.

Voices from inside had covered the approach of the two men, but their excited pace and their unworried silhouettes gave them away. Now that delivery had been made, they were more interested in their payoff than in guarding the site.

Bolan was happy to oblige.

A split second after a strange hornetlike sound sliced through the air, a volcanic eruption of blood appeared in the middle of the man's chest. The dark river of red spouted from the wound and coursed into the sand like a fountain as he fell back without a word.

The impact of the razor-point crossbow bolt had knocked the man off his feet and tumbled him flat to the ground.

Only two seconds had passed, barely enough time for the second man to figure out that something had gone deathly wrong, but plenty of time for Bolan to recock the Barnett compound crossbow with a quick lever pull.

The man looked at his fallen partner, then jerked his head back toward the darkness where death had come.

It came once more as the Executioner triggered the crossbow and fired almost point-blank into the second man's skull.

The razor point cored through the hardman's forehead and knocked him back several yards. His feet skidded in the sand, and he spun like a blood-soaked weather vane. With the feathered shaft of the bolt protruding from his temple, he sagged down to the ground beside his partner.

Now that both of the men had been taken out of the play, Bolan stepped past them and headed toward the vehicles that were parked in the circular driveway on the other side of the villa. The gravel driveway led to a remote-controlled iron gate that provided the illusion of security.

Like many of the villas in the Caribbean, this one had elaborate walls and a gate built around the roadside. But it was impossible to wall off the beachfront from the ocean.

Now the gates made it a prison.

Bolan knelt by the gates and seeded the ground with compact high-explosive mines, pushing the spikes into the ground across the gateway. There was enough clearance for the gates to open, but anything that rolled across the mines would be destroyed in a powerful blast.

He jogged back to the side of the villa and went into a crouch as he rounded the corner of the villa below the terrace. He carefully leaned the crossbow against the latticework. The time for silence was past; it was time to announce his presence.

With a slight rasping sound, he tugged the Heckler & Koch MP-5 free from the quick-release Velcro strap on his chest. For backup he had a Colt automatic in a side holster, and the pouches in his combat belt carried an assortment of munitions—such as the flash-bang stun grenade he lifted from the pocket flap.

He sprinted across the sand, catching a brief glimpse of the people inside just as he passed the doorway. Some of them were looking his way, while some of them were caught up in examining their newfound cargo.

None of them expected what came sailing through the door—a 120 mm stun grenade that went off in the room about a foot from the floor, exploding like a magnesium nova.

The brilliant blast of fire temporarily blinded and concussed everyone caught in the shock wave, and a massive rectangle of light shot out through the door.

Bolan stepped into the doorway, his eyes protected by the flash goggles he wore.

Two of the Colombians instinctively looked his way as they reached for their weapons, knowing where the danger had come from, but unable to see a thing.

"The door—" one of them shouted.

The Executioner fired a controlled burst from the Heckler & Koch MP-5, its threaded sound suppressor resting comfortably in the palm of his left hand. He fired from left to right, catching them both in a 9 mm figure eight. They went down as if someone had chopped their legs out from under them.

He pivoted to his left and squeezed off another burst that caught two of the khaki-clad Cubans barreling toward the front door.

Four down, too many to go.

Some professionals could recover from a stun blast in enough time to return fire. Many of them had gone through extensive training for it.

Bolan quickly scanned the room for signs of Monteras, the most capable adversary. In the mass of screaming and falling bodies he saw the mercenary's lean shape staggering toward the opposite doorway.

Monteras had out his automatic and was pointing the barrel blindly over his shoulder, squeezing off rounds that drilled first into the ceiling, then into the wall just above Bolan's head.

One of the Bahamians took a bullet to the back and dropped heavily to the floor. Both of his arms flailed out wildly, like he could swim to safety. But the wound was fatal. All that waited for him on the far shore was death.

As far as Monteras was concerned, the operation was aborted and the only thing worth saving was *his* life. It didn't matter who got in the way.

"Fire," Monteras shouted. "Everyone fire!"

The command was unnecessary. After the first devastating shock, everyone left standing in the room was reaching for a weapon, ready to follow the example of Monteras, who ran toward a large plate-glass window, one arm shielding his face while the other arm twisted behind him, still firing wildly.

Bolan ducked and stepped farther into the room, hopping over the fallen Bahamian and squeezing off a burst toward Monteras.

The rounds from the Heckler & Koch crashed into the window just as Monteras flew through the air and pushed the shattering glass before him. He vanished into the darkness in a rain of falling glass shards.

That left Bolan dead center in a room full of panicky gunmen. He saw Melitta Caporra crawling toward safety in one corner of the room, diving under a table laden with the antinav components.

Then he saw the broad-shouldered Bahamian

looming in front of him with a revolver in his hand, eyes scorched from the blast. It was the rum-tinted gunman who hadn't trusted Caporra, and the thunderstruck look on his face told him how right he was.

Bolan swept his left arm in a circular motion that batted away the man's gun hand, then held it high over his head just as it went off in a deafening roar. He stepped in close, jammed the barrel into his chest and fired twice.

The two rounds pounded into the Bahamian like 9 mm rivets that drove him backward. He stared at Bolan for an instant, his unfocused eyes trying to look into the face of the man who stepped out of the brilliant light to take his life. Then he stared no more and crumpled to the floor.

Even before the man fell, the Executioner continued to move in a half circle, emptying the MP-5 subgun in a sustained burst. The tail end of the burst stitched a straight line across one of the Colombians, turning his white suit red.

Guns went off to his left and right, punching holes in the roof. But the main threat came from the smashed window. Monteras was crouched just outside, aiming his automatic at Bolan.

It was just a split-second glimpse of the mercenary that leaped out of the chaos and registered with Bolan's subconscious. He darted to the right as the heavy stream of lead singed the air just inches to his left.

He had to keep moving to stay breathing.

Bolan threw the subgun to the floor. There was no time to change magazines.

He slapped the Colt Government Model pistol free of its holster and laid down several rounds that helped him make it to the door and forced Monteras to back out of sight.

The Executioner had pushed his luck too far already. Staying there any longer was suicide.

But he hadn't made it out the door before his peripheral vision picked up a flash of cold steel moving toward him.

"Kill him!" Caporra shouted.

She punctuated her order with an accomplished knife slash that started high over her head and came down in a savage arc toward his shoulder.

Bolan dropped into a crouch and twisted his left arm outward, tightening his forearm at impact. The rigid-forearm block met her wrist with enough force that she cried out with pain. The momentum of her strike caused her hand to tilt downward, and she cut a shallow gash across Bolan's skin before the knife clattered to the floor.

Even while he fended off *her* attack, Bolan kept on firing into the room with the Colt .45 to keep the remaining survivors off balance.

It was hard to predict what anyone in the room would do. Stunned from the chaos, gunshots and death screams that echoed all around them, the hardmen were in a constant state of motion. Through the acrid fumes that drifted across the room, the Executioner could see several shapes erupting from cover, their weapons spitting fire.

And holding him up at the doorway was Melitta Caporra, who clung to his arm and kicked at his side while she screamed in rage.

"What's wrong with you cowards?" she shouted back into the room as she flailed away at Bolan. "There's only one of him, just one of him! And look what he's doing to you! To us!"

At the moment the soldier was keeping them back, but unless he dealt with the banshee clinging to him, they would eventually take him down. He yanked hard on her arm and lifted her off the floor, pinwheeling her feet in the air just before she slammed into the door.

A choking sound escaped from her throat.

Then she went limp, arms gripping the door sill behind her as she gasped for breath and tried to keep from crumpling. The maneuver had knocked the wind out of her and maybe some sense into her. The Executioner wanted her alive, but if she kept it up there was nothing he could do for her.

Still holding on to her arm, Bolan tugged her through the door after him and stepped out onto the terrace. With a quick jerking motion he flung her over the railing toward the sand, where she landed with a heavy sprawling thump.

Instinct told him to follow her.

He leaped backward over the railing, hands reaching skyward, eyes toward the stars as he tucked his knees in close and completed the flip. He landed on his feet in the sand just in time to see streaks of gunfire ripping through the night, searing through the spot where he'd stood just seconds earlier.

The fusillade came from Guy Monteras, who stood at the side of the villa, desperately squeezing the trigger of his automatic.

Monteras knew he missed his target and tracked his weapon across the sand, firing shot after shot into the darkness.

Bolan backpedaled across the sand, off balance from the unplanned leap. He whipped his Colt pistol to the right and fired his last round at Monteras's blurry image.

The .45 round whacked into the wooden railing and sent a shower of splinters into the mercenary's face, a momentary diversion that gave Bolan a few necessary seconds to escape.

He sprinted down the beach, guided by instinct and the survival program that was driven into his brain. Even before he consciously registered what he was doing, his hands yanked the M-16 free from the white beach chair.

He ripped off a sustained burst that disintegrated the terrace near Monteras. The mercenary cried out in pain, then turned and ran.

From the corner of his eye, Bolan saw Melitta Caporra scrambling across the sand and heading toward the brush. She was dazed, but she was determined to survive.

Bolan watched her for a split second, then picked up some motion inside the villa. He dropped to his knees, noticing how heavy the gun suddenly felt and how much blood was running down his arm. Maybe the cut was deeper then he thought. He swung the barrel to his left, firing a burst that tracked the full length of the villa.

All motion stopped.

Suddenly it was silent.

The enemy's return fire was replaced by the sounds of panicked footsteps.

Car doors slammed and an engine roared.

Bolan ran to the side of the villa. At the sound of his approach, Caporra sprawled face first into the sand, uttering a practiced cry of vulnerability that didn't have the desired effect.

The Executioner nosed the M-16's barrel toward her, scanning the ground to see if there was any weapon nearby. There wasn't, which was what saved her life, not the acting job.

He already knew she was a killer.

Bolan hurtled past her, a black-clad shadow drawn to the front of the villa, the M-16 leading him forward like a gun-metal dowsing wand. He kept to the edge of the brush, stopping only long enough to thump a 40 mm round into the launcher tube slung below the rifle barrel.

But when he saw the gate open, he knew he wouldn't need to trigger the launcher.

Monteras and two other men were inside one of the high-end Jeeps, screeching forward across the gravel. A spray of stones rained to the ground seconds before the heavy tires tripped the mines spiked into the ground.

The high explosives went off with a sustained roar. Aimed right up at the car engine, the blast sent twisted and smoldering shrapnel flying through the hood.

The front end of the Jeep went airborne, then came down with a loud crunch as it smashed into the stone gatepost.

Another mine roared up into the gas tank, enveloping the vehicle in a dragon's breath of flame. For a split second Bolan could see the passengers totally covered with fire.

A hideous scream echoed in the darkness as one of the men burst out of the fiery remnants of the Jeep. Bolan stepped forward and triggered a mercy round from the M-16. There were no more screams, no more survivors—except for Melitta Caporra, who crawled across the sand toward him.

She was still playing her game, as though this were the first time she'd encountered death on such a massive scale. "You killed them all," she cried. "All of them."

Bolan could play games, too, when he had to. Right now he needed her cooperation.

He turned back toward her, the M-16 barrel idly tracking her.

"Not all of them," he said. "Not yet."

CHAPTER TWO

The last flames of the Jeep's wreckage died down slowly. With the flickering shadows no longer dancing across the seaside villa, the building looked almost normal again, a low-slung silhouette on the horizon.

But up close the bullet-riddled walls and shattered windows made it look like a tombstone marking the death of the perfect deal that Melitta Caporra had engineered. And the bodies of all of her confederates in that deal were sprawled inside the villa and on the grounds.

She was the only survivor and that, possibly, was temporary.

Bolan let that point sink in as he interrogated her at one of the few unturned tables on the terrace, just inches from the tattered railing.

She shivered periodically, clasping her hands over the shoulders of her white cotton dress. But the chill didn't come from the air—a hot blanket of moist air had settled over the island once again. The chill came from the shock and the fear consuming her body.

At their feet lay the debris from the shattered tables: ashtrays, broken glasses, packs of cigarettes and empty beer bottles.

"I told you I don't know what any of this is

about," the woman protested, looking up at him with almost innocent eyes. "I was just here...for their pleasure. The men brought me here."

Even though it was an obvious lie, she had trouble with it just the same. She'd risen so far that it was impossible for her to play subordinate roles convincingly.

The Executioner leveled her with a look. So far he'd let her talk on and on about her role with the terrorist cadre, just to see what she might reveal. Not enough to keep up with the charade.

"Let's get down to it," Bolan said. "We both know you're the one who brought them here. *You* came up with the money. You were the end user of the tech toys, or you planned on selling them to someone else."

"That's not true," she said. "I don't know anything about the...equipment they brought in. All those electronic gadgets. What could I do with them?"

"You tell me," Bolan suggested.

"There's nothing to tell."

"Maybe this will help your memory," Bolan said. He gave her a brief description of the operation, from all ends—the former agents of Cuban Intelligence, the Bahamians, the Colombians who worked with her and the role of Guy Monteras.

He left out the details about Brognola's DEA contacts who first picked up on the operation, as well as their counterparts in Cuban Intelligence who corroborated that some rogue elements of their agency were making a deal. But he spelled out the design and the purpose of the antinav gear, sophisticated devices developed by all of the world's major intelligence services for potential use against low-tech enemies.

"Am I right so far?" Bolan asked.

Startled at how much he knew and how much he guessed, she slowly nodded. Then she looked up at the man with the weathered face and stony eyes, as if she were seeing him for the first time. He wasn't the usual type of man she faced as an adversary or accomplice. Not just a mercenary or fast-talking drug dealer. This man knew how to command.

"Add the fact that you tried to kill me in there—almost professionally at that—and your story just doesn't wash."

"Listen to me," she said, leaning over the table, reaching for his hand. "I don't know how you know about all this, or who told it to you. But I do know we have to get out of here before the authorities come. If they find us here..." She looked around at the ruins of the villa and gestured at the bodies inside.

"They're already on their way," Bolan replied, tapping the small slim transceiver that protruded from a shirt pocket. "They were waiting for my call."

"From Nassau?"

"That's hundreds of miles away," Bolan said. "And I don't think anyone else around here heard anything."

The transformation of the placid villa into a war zone had been sudden and violent, but it had ended almost as quickly as it started. The private island they were on was remote, one of hundreds of small islands in the Atlantic known as the Out Islands, or as some people called them because of their distance from civilization, the Far Out Islands. There was little chance of attracting any official attention.

"Then what authorities are you talking about?" she snapped, pushing off from the table.

Bolan grabbed her wrist and yanked her back down. "The *final* authorities," he said, leaning over the table toward her. "And before they get here, you'd better convince me you're worth keeping alive."

"What?"

"They don't believe in taking prisoners," Bolan told her. "Neither do I. Unless you can help me out, your time's up."

The soldier dropped a cold mask across his eyes as he touched the reloaded Colt that was flat on the table by his right hand. He would never kill a woman in cold blood. If a woman was a direct threat to him, in battle or ambush, then all bets were off. But they were past battle now. At least the physical. Now it was a battle of the minds, and he was going to win it.

Caporra looked at the Colt, then at her adversary's emotionless eyes. She'd traveled with people who would kill innocents for just walking into the wrong place at the wrong time. And she had plenty of blood on her own hands. There was no reason to expect he wouldn't carry out the threat, especially after she'd seen him in action against the men she'd considered invulnerable.

"Who are you?" she asked. "Who are you working with?"

"It's obvious, isn't it? I'm working with the people who are shutting you and your kind down. Whatever it takes. And right now that's only going to take about five more minutes. That's all the time you got left."

Caporra nodded. She was ready to cooperate. Or at least pretend to cooperate. "I'll help you."

"Start with Thomas Quinn," Bolan demanded.

"Who?"

He sighed. "We already played this game. Just answers. No questions."

"I don't know any Quinn," she insisted.

"Thomas Quinn. He runs the ISS outfit in Boca Raton, Florida. It's a large private security company with worldwide clients."

"Good for him. I still don't know him."

"Guy Monteras used to work for him," Bolan said. "The man who helped arranged this deal for you. That help your memory any?"

The woman shrugged. "Guy worked for a lot of people. Lately he happened to work for me."

The Executioner shook his head. "Don't kid yourself. Monteras played a lot of roles, but he never worked for anyone but himself or Thomas Quinn."

"Maybe," Caporra conceded. "But if I don't know this Quinn, how can I get in touch with him, let alone hand him over to you?"

"We'll work together on that," Bolan said. "Right now all I need to know is that I can trust you."

She smiled. "You have my word."

"Your word means nothing. But your voice, that's something I can work with." He reached into his pocket, took out a microcassette recorder and placed it on the table. "Go ahead," he said. "I want your words. Start with who you're working for and tell me everyone you've worked with." He slid it across the table and started to press down on the Record button.

"What's that for?" she asked, staring at the recorder as if it were a loaded weapon as dangerous to her as the Colt .45.

"Insurance," Bolan said, holding his finger just above the button. "In case you happen to forget our agreement after I let you walk away from this."

"It's just a tape," she said. "I can say you forced me to make it."

"You could," Bolan agreed. "Matter of fact we don't even *have* to release the tape to your cartel friends. Might be better if I just spread the word to a few people in the right places. Before long your own people will start to wonder why you're the only one who walked away from here."

Bolan let it sink in for a second, then added, "You're going back to them without the money and without the goods." He gestured toward the villa where the Colombians lay. "And you left some of their people behind. Maybe they'll trust you. Maybe they'll think you're a mistake that should be erased—however they do it these days."

The Colombian cartel executions were notorious for their brutality. Dispatching traitors in the most gruesome and public ways had become an art form to some of their specialists.

Her eyes told him she knew it was the truth. Caporra already had a fine line to walk when she returned to her people without risking any complications Bolan could throw into the mix.

"Okay," she said.

Bolan pressed the Record button of the small recorder and slid it across the table.

THE SQUADRON of Black Hawk helicopters droned above the dark water, their black shapes nothing more than occasional silhouettes against the moon.

Three of them turned toward the Bahamas while the rest banked toward Cuba and followed the same path as the small renegade fleet.

They flew low across the water, the dark thrumming of the turbines and the whirring rotors sounding like a high-tech growl of a predator getting ready to strike.

There was little chance of losing their prey.

AWACS aircraft and high-altitude TARS surveillance balloons were tracking the covert fleet even before it left Cuban waters to make the Bahamas run.

A pair of E-2C spy planes had also taken to the skies, crisscrossing the corridor between the Bahamas and Cuba and keeping a lock on the signatures of the renegade vessels. The high-tech air umbrella fed the information to the sophisticated gear on board the Black Hawks, which had enough fuel to stay in action for six hours.

As a backup intercept force, U.S. customs had five twin-hulled Blue Thunder speedboats patrolling the sea lane, ready to cut off the rogue fleet before they reached Cuban waters. With 575 hp engines, the water-borne rockets had enough speed to deal with anything the opposition had.

The men piloting the boats and the Black Hawks were handpicked combat veterans who'd been on these kind of high-seas operations before.

Altogether a half-dozen U.S. agencies were involved in the mission that was coordinated by Hal Brognola, head of the Justice Department's Special Operations Group, who used his access to the highest levels of government to cut through the usual intra-agency red tape.

The rogue fleet was totally unaware of the invisible armada bearing down on them. They wouldn't reach home port this night.

MELITTA CAPORRA STOOD on the sand where just hours before she had been sunning herself and looked up at the sky at the omens of destruction.

It seemed to be full of helicopters, high-tech birds circling like carrion hunters above the paradise that had been turned into a cemetery.

Her plans had also died here, she realized. Until now she had a fast ascent in the hidden hierarchy that ruled Colombia and most of South America: cartels, syndicates, floating governments run by money and murder. She would have been set for life if this operation had gone off.

"Time to go—your escort's here," said the man beside her, who'd only given his name as Belasko. He tightened his grip around her arm and led her toward the dock where two dark blue powerboats were knifing through the water, spotlights piercing the waves.

He had only been the advance force, pointman for an island invasion. Now the cavalry was coming. If one man could do so much damage, she shuddered at the thought of what all of them could do together.

Caporra walked briskly next to him in an effort to keep up with his rapid, almost effortless pace. He guided her across the sand as if she were weightless, practically lifting her off her toes.

Her future was no longer in her hands. The tape of her "confession" was in his pocket now, and so was she. She had little doubt he would come after her if she failed to report in as he'd demanded or if she missed too many calls to her homes in Colombia.

There was also his threat of tipping off the cartels

about her confession if she didn't keep her part of the bargain. The cartels would hunt her down for him. One way or another they'd meet again, he'd told her, and after that guaranteed rendezvous, she'd either be working for him or she'd be dead.

He helped her into the cartel boat she was most familiar with and told her the escort would follow her down to the Exuma Islands to make sure she reached there safely. From that point she would have to make her own arrangements to get back to Colombia, complete with the genuine story that she'd barely made it out of the ambush with her life.

As she switched on the motor, blood pumping inside her in cadence with the throbbing engine, she looked back at the beach that now had the look of a military base.

One of the helicopters was landing on a flat stretch of sand, rotors kicking up a dust storm as the heavy struts descended in a gentle rocking motion.

Another chopper had landed on the road outside the villa gate. Splashes of artificial daylight from the aircraft's beacons illuminated the villa's husk.

A third chopper hovered near the terrace, rotor wash battering the remnants of the thatched roof as a half-dozen commandos glided to the ground from black nylon ropes like spiders. They ran into the house in single file, footsteps rapidly beating across the floorboards.

The house was no longer hers, nor was the "ransom machine" she had worked so hard to get. Along with the cabin cruiser—which was now filling with men from the landed helicopter—it would be taken back to the United States, a country she thought was fighting a toothless war.

Until now.

Caporra flicked on the running lights of the blood-red cigarette boat, boosted the throttle, then rocketed into the bay. The hull smashed down hard on the water several times, drumming the full force of the ocean into her feet. But then she built up enough speed for the sharp-nosed boat to cut through the waves like a whining metal scythe.

But no matter how fast she went, she never gained on the pair of gun metal blue powerboats that kept her company. They maintained the same distance behind her effortlessly as they fanned out to the right and left, wardens who would make sure no harm would come to her.

She was a prisoner of war with no chance of escape. But at least for now, with the wind and sea spray whipping into her face, she was running free on the high seas.

And there *was* a chance she might be truly free again. She'd sensed that the man called Belasko, whoever or whatever he really was, had a strict code of honor. If he struck a bargain with her, he would keep his end of it as long as she delivered.

All she had to deliver was Thomas Quinn.

THE COVERT FLEET WAS almost home free.

Luis Santana, the white-haired but still wiry commander of the operation, smiled as he stood in the wheelhouse of the sport-fishing boat and watched the pilot lean forward at the helm like a man about to win a race.

They already had the trophies, packed tightly in the waterproof metal currency cases. Now all they had to do was complete the course.

Santana exhaled a 'stream of smoke from his half-smoked cigar and watched it swirl in the breeze that sifted through the open window. He bit down hard on the aromatic wrapped leaf and sucked in another harsh blast of smoke. The embers burned brightly in the wheelhouse, which was lit only by the dim red-and-green glows of the pilot's control panel.

Outside the wheelhouse Santana's men were dressed in black, sitting on fishing chairs with automatic weapons anchored in the fishing-pole slots. One hard-eyed gunner was positioned in a body-contoured trench at the bow, his machine gun ready to cut down anything in its way.

It was a smooth operation from start to finish, cloaked in tight security.

They were running fast across the Atlantic, lights out, navigating by the green screens. The pilot handled the boat expertly, as if it had been his own private property for years. In a way it had. Santana had confiscated the sleek charter boat in the eighties from a pair of American college students who majored in smuggling coke and smoke from Colombia. They'd committed the crime of not paying off Cuban "guardians" before their transit of Cuban waters.

Using his position as a high-ranking officer in Cuban Intelligence, Santana attached the boat to *his* covert teams, which specialized in counterintelligence, drug interdiction...and smuggling.

This particular crew had previously carried off several operations, and Santana trusted every man. Many of them had been with him since his soldiering days in high-casualty hot zones throughout Africa, where they fought as mercenaries for Soviet or socialist-backed armies. Ideology had nothing to do with it, but economics did. Santana and the others were fighting for money to bring back home to Cuba.

That money-making attitude stayed with him when

he made the transition from battlefield combat to Cuban Intelligence covert operations. He still served his country well, but he also served himself and the military veterans he brought into the intelligence organization with him.

Santana stubbed out his cigar and scanned the dark horizon with a growing sense of satisfaction. He could just barely make out the shadows of the powerboats flanking the charter boat, but he knew they would stay in formation all the way to the Cuban shore.

It was a good team, and a good life loomed ahead of them.

But so did a huge metal wasp that suddenly buzzed the decks of the charter boat. It took a few seconds for Santana to decipher what had just swooped out of the darkness at him.

The Americans!

The Cuban swore. He knew what was coming next. There would be no way they could escape from the aircraft.

With a heavy droning sound, the dark helicopter made another pass. This time a blinding spotlight erupted from the heavens and streamed down into the wheelhouse.

Santana's pilot shielded his eyes from the dazzling light and eased up on the throttle. The powerboats experienced the same burst of light as dazzling strobes poured from a droning light-ship that paced alongside them.

As his dazed eyes tried to recover from the assault, Luis Santana recalled what he'd seen on the edge of that pool of brilliance—a sky full of assault helicopters.

Even now Santana heard the metallic voice that

boomed out of the loudspeaker attached to the helicopter. It was an American voice speaking Spanish, demanding surrender.

The Cuban shook his head. Until now he hadn't considered the enormity of the smuggling operation, the means of mass destruction that he'd placed in the hands of terrorists. But the Americans would definitely consider it, just as his own people would. Luis Santana knew that one way or another, he would never be a free man again.

Santana barreled through the wheelhouse door onto the deck and gave his answer in a language everyone understood. The language of war. He pointed his automatic rifle skyward and triggered a blast at what he hoped wasn't an afterimage, but one of the helicopters.

As soon as Santana fired, the rest of his crewmen opened up, firing as they rocketed on into the darkness, an exodus of desperate and dangerous men.

CAPTAIN JACK PARSONS, known as Jack the Preacher to his crew, gave his sermon of the evening the instant the charter-boat bandits raised their weapons. It was short and sweet. "Light them up," he said into the wraparound mike attached to his helmet, the command to unleash hellfire and brimstone on the enemy below.

Parsons's crew chief opened up with the 7.62 mm minigun on the door mount and stitched the wheelhouse with machine-gun fire, moving the barrel in a figure-eight pattern that covered every inch inside. Then he strafed the decks of the powerboat closest to the charter boat.

A second helicopter carried out the same maneuver on the opposite flank, chopping into the charter boat and the remaining powerboat with an endless barrage of machine-gun fire.

Glass crashed and men ducked for cover. But there was no shelter to be had. As the first two helicopters banked off to right and left, another chopper came up behind and opened up with two GECAL Gatling guns that swept through the remnants of the crews.

The machine-gun volleys sprayed the decks like metal rain, saturating the few men left standing, knocking them flat on their backs or tumbling their bodies overboard, freshly weighted down with heavy .50-caliber rounds.

A second wave of attack aircraft unleashed heavy ordnance on the traffickers' small fleet.

A Hellfire missile burrowed into the charter boat, blasting the bow and machine-gun emplacement into the air while nearly disintegrating the man who was still lying behind it.

Other rockets streaked through the air and thumped into the powerboats. One ripped like a tin can and pinwheeled across the water when its extra gas tanks blew. The second powerboat was cut in two, with dark waters rushing in to claim the human and metal wreckage.

The choppers circled for another pass, illuminating the ocean below with huge floodlights that gave the water a ghostly and menacing hue.

There was no return fire this time. It was over.

The only signs that an assault had taken place were bullet-ridden planks rising and falling on the crests of the waves, sinking metal husks dragging bodies with them to the bottom of the ocean.

The last part of the alliance was destroyed.

CHAPTER THREE

Fort Lauderdale, Florida

The silver Ford Probe rocketed up Interstate 95, an air-conditioned cocoon sealed off from the 104-degree heat wave that had settled over the Fort Lauderdale area.

As blasts of chilled air filled the car, Bolan hit the Scan button on the stereo until it picked up an all-news station from Miami. He listened once again for any reports of unusual incidents in the southernmost Bahamas.

So far there'd been only the usual reports of some charter boats and weekend sailors that were feared lost in the storm that pounded the Bahamas and the Florida coast.

Nothing out of the ordinary. Good, Bolan thought. The cleanup crew had done its job well, erasing signs of the covert raid on the villa. If they followed usual procedure, the soldier figured a couple of the bodies would have been left around to be eventually found by the authorities.

The others had probably been carted off the island and given a quick, anonymous burial. The inflatable boat he'd used had been hoisted into one of the helicopters along with the small arms and crossbow he'd brought along for the operation. The antinav gear was safely in U.S. hands, and the members of the task force Brognola had assembled for the mission had been sent back to their regular details in customs, Coast Guard and the other military services they'd been seconded from.

And Bolan was on vacation.

At least that's what it looked like from all outward appearances. He was dressed in light summer slacks, a V-neck sports shirt and wraparound shades. His lean yet muscular arms were more tanned than usual, as was his face. He looked like someone unfamiliar with the southern Florida climate who'd spent too much time on the beach, though his coloring had come from hours of surveillance beneath Out Island palms.

All in all he had a carefree look about him, right down to the high-octane sports car that Hal Brognola had waiting for him when he touched down on U.S. soil.

It was outfitted with sun roof, stereo, retractable lights and a 9 mm parabellum Smith & Wesson Model 469 automatic pistol built into a compartment in the door panel. The 12-round magazine made it a good backup to the .357 Derringer rigged into the windbreaker clumped on the passenger seat.

There was more armament in the trunk.

Like most of the other vehicles in the covert fleet available to Brognola and other Feds, the car was fully operational. It was armored and laden with sophisticated surveillance and communications gear.

Everything you needed to drive through southern Florida.

When the news started to repeat itself, Bolan hit the Scan button again until a jazz station piped a mix of Brazilian and African rhythms into the car. It was as much a part of the atmosphere as the heat.

As he drove north toward Boca Raton, Bolan drifted into an almost trancelike state, giving his mind a chance to rest while he scanned the landscape and studied the phalanx of dark blue clouds rolling overhead.

Rain was coming to wash away the heat.

He'd been on alert ever since Brognola brought him in for the first stage of the operation. Soon he'd be moving into the second stage, waging a covert campaign that would either flush ISS into the open or prove they were innocent.

In the meantime it was important to wind down a bit.

If you were on edge all the time, always ready to go, then sooner or later you were gone, just one more burned-out fighter pushed over the brink. Sometimes that was the hardest part of being a warrior—knowing when to pull back and let the mind and body do its thing.

Right now the part of his mind that was constantly planning and preparing him for battle was playing a much more sedate role in going over the details of the next few hours: check into the hotel in Boko, make contact with Brognola for a fuller briefing on Thomas Quinn and ISS. There hadn't been time earlier. The intel had come in with just enough time for Brognola to summon his teams and point Bolan in the right direction.

Another part of his mind was concentrating on the scenery. It'd been a while since Bolan had been in southern Florida, but just like last time everything was constantly changing. All along the interstate new communities were springing up, following twisting roads that led east toward the coast or west toward the Everglades.

But everything moved fast in Florida: construction, jobs, cars, boats, music, drugs, money—especially money. It came pouring in from both legal and illegal sources, laying foundations for corporate and criminal empires. And sometimes the two were combined.

About ten miles south of Boca Raton, the dark clouds that were moving overhead suddenly unleashed a blinding screen of water. Torrents of rain dropped fast and heavy, turning the interstate into a slick ribbon of road.

Cars all around him turned on their headlights in a futile effort to penetrate the sheets of water that overwhelmed windshield wipers and drummed hard on the rooftops. Some slowed down, some sped up and some pulled off onto the shoulders to wait out the storm with their red flashers blinking on and off, hoping that no half-blind driver would crash into them.

Bolan turned off the air-conditioning, and rolled down the window to let some fresh air whip into the car. He eased up on the accelerator and rode out the storm, continuing toward Boca Raton.

It was over in five minutes, and once again the sun beat down mercilessly through the muggy haze.

By the time he got to the Glades Road exit for Boca Raton, Bolan had the air-conditioning back on and the radio turned low.

His vacation was about to come to an end.

He drove east for a few miles on Glades Road, which was lined with palm trees and corporate towers, country clubs, restaurants, new malls and resort complexes. Off in the distance were the gatehouse communities that were becoming so common in Florida. Expensive homes were walled off from the outside world in varying degrees, some with guards at the gates to monitor anyone who drove into the area.

Boca Raton was rapidly becoming the place to be in Florida, an upscale address for publishing and film companies, headquarters for Fortune 500 corporations, and home for plush international hotel chains that were sprinkled all throughout the town and along the oceanfront.

As Miami grew more crowded, more people and more money moved north into Boca Raton. That made it a perfect location for ISS headquarters, which had been there for almost a decade now, ever since Thomas Quinn left covert agencies for covert enterprises. Within that time he'd become a respectable businessman and had membership in all the right clubs. On the surface he was a pillar of the community.

Now Bolan and Brognola were here to do some heavy digging and, if necessary, topple that pillar.

The Executioner swung onto Federal Highway, driving a short distance north to the Sovereign Hotel, a multilayered and pastel-colored hybrid of Spanish architecture and high-tech towers. It looked out onto the Intracoastal Waterway, parallel to Ocean Boulevard.

The hotel was home to well-heeled tourists and even more affluent permanent residents who'd grown accustomed to the luxury accommodations. It was also the latest command base for an operation against ISS. That meant that many of the hotel "guests" and probably some of the newest staff members were actually top investigators and military specialists drawn from government agencies.

Bolan drove around a tree-lined loop that ran past hotel shops, a restaurant and nightclub and ground-floor offices, then pulled into the shadows of the two-tiered parking garage.

A parking attendant came out of his booth. "Welcome to the Sovereign." He reached toward the driver's window. "You can leave your keys with me—"

"Actually I can't," Bolan replied, driving past him and pulling into an empty parking spot close to the exit. He wasn't about to leave the keys to a rolling armory in the hands of someone he didn't know.

He slipped on the designer windbreaker, complete with its holster pocket sewn into the inside lining for the small but devastating .357 Derringer. Then he pressed the trunk release and stepped out into a warm sea breeze that blew through the open-air garage and stirred the palms near the entrance.

Bolan reached inside to scoop up the black carryall that held a change of clothes and his Beretta 93-R shoulder rig. He locked the car and walked over to the attendant's booth.

"Sorry, but the car's brand-new," Bolan said, acting like a true blue gear-head totally in love with his wheels. "No one drives it but me. You know how it is."

The attendant shrugged. "Not yet."

"Do me a favor, though," Bolan said, pulling out a handful of twenties and handing them to the attendant. "Keep an eye on it for me. Make sure it doesn't get scratched and no one parks near it if you can."

The attendant smiled. "For a hundred bucks I can," he replied, folding the twenties and stuffing them into his pocket. "Enjoy your stay at the Sovereign."

"MICHAEL BARRON," Bolan said when he stood in front of the registration desk, using one of several identities Hal Brognola had prepared for him. "My company reserved a room for me."

The Barron name was an identity that he could assume whenever he was on an assignment that called for him to have a past—in case someone did some serious checking on his background. If anyone bothered to check, they would find that Barron was from Baltimore, Maryland, and was a consultant for ComNet Communications, a major supplier of communications technology. The company was real and actually did a lot of business with government and civilian clients.

The few people who knew of the false name would speak highly of Barron to anyone who asked.

It took just a couple of minutes for the desk clerk to key in the Barron name on a small computer to verify the arrangements and hand him a computer-coded access card for his room.

"Enjoy your stay at the Sovereign," she said.

"Thanks," Bolan said, nodding slightly, then heading toward the elevators.

His room on the second floor faced the waterway, where a number of pleasure boats were cruising toward the inlet that would take them to the ocean. He gave the room a quick once-over, unpacked the carryall, then sat on one of the beds near the phone stand. The red message light had been blinking on and off ever since he'd arrived in the room.

He grabbed the remote control and clicked on the large-screen television in the corner of the room, turning up the volume just enough to create difficulty for anyone trying to monitor their conversation. The Executioner doubted there was a risk of being bugged. Before they set up camp in the hotel, one of Brognola's electronic exterminator teams would have detected and subverted any type of surveillance gadgets in place.

If anyone was doing the bugging, it would be Brognola's people.

But it was habit, and habit was what had kept him alive so far, so he turned up the volume until it was loud enough to obscure any conversation. Then he picked up the phone and played back the message.

It was from Hal Brognola, and though it sounded like one old friend to another, it was really a call to a briefing. "Welcome to the Sovereign," the big Fed's voice said. "We're having a little get-together in the hospitality suite in room 402. It starts as soon as you get here."

Short and sweet, Bolan thought. No names mentioned. No complicated codes used. Typical Hal Brognola. They were waiting for him.

Bolan locked his room, then headed up to the fourth floor, where he would meet any other "ComNet consultants" Brognola invited to the party.

The suite was at the end of a long corridor with rooms on both sides that were probably occupied by other deep-cover operatives. In the event any hostiles made a move on the hospitality suite, they would have to make it past a gauntlet.

Someone was obviously watching Bolan from the security peephole in suite 402. As soon as he reached for the door, it opened inward to reveal a Secret Service type—black hair, black suit, black mood—who impassively watched him.

Hal Brognola stood beyond the guard, cigar in hand. "Come on in, Barron," Brognola said, waving his arm toward another room in the suite where Bolan could see one more man. "The party's already started."

Bolan shook hands and followed the Justice man into the adjoining room, which had no windows. It was a standard precaution that Brognola always took for secure conversations. No windows meant that a laser mike couldn't read their voice vibrations bouncing off the glass and convert them into speech.

There was a long and narrow coffee table in the center of the room, positioned between two wing chairs and a leather sofa. The other man who'd been called for the briefing sat on the sofa, his leather boots resting on the edge of the glass.

The table held all the ingredients for a party, at least where Hal Brognola was concerned: two insulated carafes of coffee—enough for Brognola to get through an all-day planning session or two—a couple of bottles of soda and a plate full of crumbs, a glass ashtray with a few half-chewed cigar butts in them.

"Hell of a spread," Bolan said dryly, looking at the table.

Brognola grinned. "Help yourself," he invited, pointing first toward one carafe, then the other. "Hi-test and decaf."

At the moment Bolan was more interested in studying the man on the couch, who was obviously going to be part of the operation. He looked like a blond-haired and full-bearded Viking who'd been hauled through time and deposited at the hotel.

He wore faded jeans, and his loose gray sweatshirt with the arms cut off revealed well-muscled shoulders and lean, heavily veined arms. It was the kind of shirt that could easily conceal a holster inside the waistband of the jeans.

His hair hung halfway down his back, wrapped in a ponytail with a leather thong. There was a tattoo of a black crow on his left bicep. He looked like a biker or a boat captain or a doper. His eyes regarded Bolan with neither meanness nor kindness, just a pure, objective look of a man taking his measure.

"This is Armand Cane," Brognola said.

Cane stood to shake hands with Bolan, and he had a firm, no-nonsense handshake.

"Michael Barron," Bolan stated.

Right after the introductions the bodyguard drifted into the room. "Call for you, Mr. Brognola."

"Not now," the big Fed replied, looking over his shoulder and raising his hand to halt the man's approach. "I've got a briefing to run—"

"Afraid it has to be now, sir. The call's from Washington." Brognola sighed. "All right." He turned to Bolan and Cane. "I have to take this in the other room. I'll keep it short."

"We'll be here," Bolan said. He grabbed a ceramic mug and poured it full of black coffee. He dropped into a chair facing Cane and took a long sip before setting the mug on the table.

Cane leaned back onto the couch, arms sprawled over the back of cushions, his fingers tapping a beat. "So I guess you're with the ComNet sales department," he said.

"That's right."

Cane smiled. "How's business?"

"Booming. How about you? You in sales, too?"

"I'm kind of in the insurance department," Cane replied. "I make sure things come out all right."

Bolan smiled. Cane did seem like the kind of man to have standing behind you when an operation blew up, someone who knew how to handle himself in a hopeless situation. He also seemed like the kind of guy who could get you into those situations, Bolan thought.

A few minutes passed before Brognola finished his call and came back into the room. He closed the door behind him and sat in the remaining chair. Then he leaned forward with his hands clasped in front of him, intermediary for the interdepartmental team he was putting together.

"Sorry about the interruption," Brognola said. "But it was from Washington, pretty high up, and it concerns our operation here."

"What's up?" Bolan asked.

"Prime minister's office in the Bahamas just called the White House. Tried to get through to the Man himself, but they had to settle for one of our Justice Department people. It appears there's been some kind of incident on one of their islands." He glanced toward the Executioner.

"Imagine that," Bolan said.

"For some reason they suspect our government's involvement. They're raising the roof about foreign intervention on their shores. They mentioned that some civil servants had been killed, but they stopped talking about that when we told them we heard it was a drug deal with the Colombians."

Cane shook his head. "They're not mad because of intervention. They're mad because they didn't get their cut from hosting the deal."

"Could be," Brognola said. "But we still need their cooperation. You know the players on both sides over there. Make peace with them. Make some promises to the people we can count on and see what they can do to smooth things over."

"Will do," Cane said, though it obviously pained him.

Bolan couldn't blame him. At one time half of the Bahamian cabinet had been indicted or forced to resign for providing assistance and occasionally outright protection to cartel traffickers. Things had improved over the years, and there *were* a few elite Bahamian strike forces that really went after the traffickers, but they were outnumbered by the opposition...and by collaborators in their own government.

"Anyone else making waves?" Bolan asked.

"No," Brognola said, "Not yet. We've received back-channel contacts from the Cubans. Officially they're pleased that some outlaw elements are no longer in their service."

"They would have taken care of it themselves if they had to," Cane said. "Lately we've been getting more cooperation from them than we could ever dream of. They saw the writing on the Berlin Wall when it fell. Since then a lot of Cuban Intel operatives have been making the right moves."

"All right," Brognola said. "Let's deal with *our* situation and why we're here. I know you both prefer to work alone whenever possible. Each of you is tops in your own arena. There's no denying that." He looked hard at each man. "But this is one of those times when it's not remotely possible to go it alone. One man isn't enough. Hell, one agency isn't enough. We're facing something so big here that unless we go after it with maximum force, it might get the better of us. Worse, we might not even know it got the better of us until it's too late. We're up against a sophisticated outfit with long arms, deep pockets and big plans."

Bolan had seen that for himself up close. If the

Cuban and Colombian teams had somehow managed to rendezvous at a different time or place, they might have succeeded in handing off the antinav gear. And it wouldn't have taken long for the fallout to hit the U.S. or any other target the terrorists chose. That was just one operation. Who knew what else was coming along the pipeline?

"First let's get the issue of trust out in the open," Brognola said. "I know where both of you stand when it comes to large-scale operations with a lot of desk-bound chiefs trying to throw their weight around."

"Same old story," Cane agreed. "Field agents get screwed and the suits get promoted."

Brognola agreed. "Most of them don't remember what it's like to be on the front lines—if they ever were there in the first place. But I've worked beside both of you men on several occasions where our lives were on the line. We came through it because we trusted each other totally. Unconditionally." Brognola pointed at each man with his cigar. "I'm asking you to extend that same trust to each other. It'll be a while before we know who our friends and enemies are. Until then, all we've got is each other. Do either of you have a problem with that?"

Bolan shook his head. "You wouldn't have brought us here if you didn't have faith in both of us being able to work together. That's enough for me."

"Same here, Hal," Cane agreed.

"Good," Brognola said. "In a way you already *have* been working together, though in a compartmentalized approach."

Turning to Bolan, he said, "Cane worked the Cuban and Bahamian contacts that clued us into Melitta Caporra's operation.''

Then he turned to Cane and said, "Barron relied on that information to take them down.''

Brognola gave each of them a brief résumé so they knew the kind of expertise they could draw upon.

Cane was on loan from the DEA, the longer the better in the eyes of his superiors. Over the years as a specialist in the Florida, Mexico and Latin American theaters, he'd made a lot of waves with the higher-ups. He was about to be exiled to some desk jockey Siberia in D.C. to make drug-bust charts for dog-and-pony shows for the media. But Cane got a reprieve when he tumbled onto Melitta Caporra's operation. Instead of only passing the information to superiors who might bury it or ignore it because it came from him, Cane tipped off Brognola.

From then on things moved at lightning speed. Brognola cut through channels and requested Cane as his special assistant. With the big Fed's backing, Cane had carte blanche to marshal DEA resources wherever and whenever he needed. That meant access to DEA fleets, undercover hit squads and raw intelligence. Whatever they might need to call into play.

"Guess that makes me king for a day," Cane said. "Might as well enjoy it while I can. When this is over, I'm in the doghouse.''

"Nothing's set in stone," Brognola said. "When the smoke clears, I'll do what I can do to straighten things out with your people." He gave Cane a brief and somewhat sanitized version of Bolan's career. "Belasko has been with me from the beginning," he said, using the cover name often attached to Bolan. "*Before* the beginning, actually." Without naming specific missions, Brognola covered part of Bolan's career as the "execution" arm for covert missions, enough to let Cane know that he was working with a man who was equally at home in military, paramilitary and spook operations.

When they had sufficient background, Brognola asked for Bolan's summary of the Bahamian operation.

The Executioner gave his assessment of the operation—the body count, the military level of the participants and ended with his impression of Melitta Caporra and her status as a likely collaborator.

"When the time comes," Brognola said, "she might be the key."

"Think you *can* find her if you have to?" Cane asked.

Bolan shrugged. "Important thing is, she thinks I can. That'll keep her on the hook for a while."

"Until then, we've got a few other dragons to slay," Brognola said. "A good number of them are connected to our friend Thomas Quinn and ISS." The Justice man pulled open his briefcase and set it on the table. "Cane gathered some background for you, Belasko."

Bolan scanned the materials that Brognola spread out on the table: military jacket, intelligence reports on Quinn's questionable activities while working for the government, charges brought against him and dismissed for lack of evidence—or sudden disappearance of witnesses.

There was a list of operatives who worked for him and conducted operations in line with U.S. interests. And it was balanced by another list of ISS operatives who went to work for the underworld.

It was a mosaic of the intelligence and underworld

communities. Quinn had been involved in several U.S. operations south of the border: Costa Rica, Nicaragua, Colombia, Guatemala, Argentina.

Practically everywhere the U.S. had run covert operations, Thomas Quinn was there. Sometimes in an official capacity as an intelligence officer. Other times as a "private" citizen providing men and matériel. He'd been one of the "guns for drugs" couriers during the Nicaraguan quagmire, sending planes full of weapons to Costa Rica for transfer to Contras. And many of those same planes came back loaded with cartel cocaine. Despite the testimony of some of Quinn's pilots that he knew of their smuggling activities, the drug shipments were dismissed as isolated instances, aberrations initiated by a few cowboy pilots.

Quinn's defense was that he had to work with shady characters to get the job done. Some managed to get the better of him, while some didn't.

There was a mountain of information to go through, most of it connected to Quinn's current ventures as a civilian. Because of his past dealings, he had access to the kind of skilled operatives who could do the necessary work, as well as to the kind of customers who needed him. U.S. government agencies used him as a cutout for quasiofficial operations, senators and congressmen used him as a private intelligence gatherer and corporate CEOs used him for industrial espionage and protection. And traffickers used him as conduit for safe passage.

Then there were the foreign operations. ISS had dispatched mercenary teams to Sierra Leone and other trouble spots across Africa. He also sent trainers and advisers to Croatia.

Mingled with all of his hush-hush work were the

security services he provided to celebrity clients in Florida and California. All in all, Quinn had his hand in a lot of pies.

The Executioner riffled through the materials, then stacked them on a corner of the table. "This'll take about a century to get through," he said. "Any chance of getting a condensed version?"

"No problem," Cane said. He made a thumbs-down gesture. "He's dirty and we should take him down."

"We need proof," Brognola said.

"It's a gut feeling."

"If we went on your gut feelings, we'd take down half of the Colombian government," Brognola commented.

"Don't forget Mexico," Cane said. "And Bolivia, Panama..." He leaned forward and made a half fist, then ticked off his fingers one by one as he named other countries he'd worked in. "Take your pick," he said, reciting the impossible conditions the DEA faced outside U.S. borders.

For years the U.S. drug-interdiction effort involved multimillion-dollar contributions to the antidrug forces in the source countries that provided cocaine, heroin and cannabis to the U.S.

Most of that money passed through several government middlemen, each of them taking his cut before the money ultimately made its way to the cartels to finance more drug deals, buy off a few more statesmen or bankroll their elections.

There was no shortage of high-ranking officials who sold out their countries to the cartels: attorneys general, presidents, prime ministers, secretaries of defense. The list was endless. So were the crimes.

At times the antidrug forces openly attacked DEA

officers they supposedly were working with. Instead of helping them, they had kidnapped and murdered several of them. When the DEA managed to mount joint raids on cocaine-processing labs with the help of the host country, more often than not the cartels were tipped off to the raid ahead of time. The strike forces would come out of the sky or the jungle only to capture a ghost town of deserted labs with maybe just a few peasant workers.

Or the DEA would land in the middle of an ambush—attacked by rebels, cartel gunmen, crooked *federales,* or army death squads that hired themselves out to the cartels.

Cane's dim view of his so-called allies was colored by all of the treachery he'd seen, treachery that had now come home to roost in the guise of ISS.

"Now we're starting to see the same thing here," Cane said. For several years he'd been keeping an eye on ISS operations and was able to associate the organization with several underworld figures. But there was nothing that could concretely prove Quinn's guilt.

Brognola listened carefully, nodding as Cane made his points. "I'm not saying your instinct is wrong," the big Fed said when the DEA man finished. "We wouldn't be here if there wasn't strong suspicion that Quinn is on the wrong side. But he's got powerful backers in our government and the intelligence community. If we just go in there and whack him, then it could put us out of business. Everything we built up over the years will be gone."

Bolan knew what he meant. If they conducted a large-scale operation to take down Quinn and ISS without hard proof, then Brognola's critics could paint him as out of control. Then it would be the end of Stony Man Farm, the end of Hal Brognola's White House connection.

"Okay," Bolan said. "We have to dot the i's and cross all the t's before we put him in the cross hairs. But what's the game plan, Hal? You didn't bring me down here to play detective."

Brognola glanced at Bolan. "You're right. That's going to be my job, Belasko. In fact, it's already started. I've got people on the Hill looking into Quinn's political connections. Investigators for intelligence oversight committees in the Senate and Congress are quietly taking a look at his escapades. And some DOD friends are going to unravel his legend as a war hero."

Bolan took one last sip of the now cold coffee before sliding the empty mug across the table. "Whatever skeletons Quinn has in his closet will take a while to reveal."

"It will," Brognola said. "In the meantime that's where you both come in. Cane has been watching another trafficking circle taking shape. It's got all the marks of an ISS operation. Someone has put together a regular doper's air force in Puerto Rico, the latest staging area for the cartels."

"Lot of these pilots worked for Quinn in his Contra days," Cane said. "They're bringing in coke and smoke to Florida."

"Where?" Bolan asked.

"Everglades," Cane replied. "Getting ready to make an air drop practically in Quinn's backyard. Might even try to land to off-load this stuff."

"So who's working the ground crew?" Bolan asked. "Some mercs who used to work for Quinn?"

"Worse than that," Cane said. "According to my

sources, they're using the Cracker Corps for this one.''

"That some kind of militia?" Bolan said.

"Hell, no," Cane said, smiling at Bolan's suggestion. "They're the most disorganized bunch of redneck rangers you could ever meet—except when they're on a boat or when they're waiting for a shipment to come in.''

"How many?"

"Let me put it this way," Cane said. "We are going to be facing an army of good ol' boys—actually, bad ol' boys—who do not take kindly to strangers mucking about in their swamp. Especially strangers who plan on taking their livelihood away. A real tough-hided bunch.''

"They immune to bullets?" Bolan said. "I faced off a group recently, and they bled like anyone else.''

"Wait'll you see them."

"Somehow I don't think I'll be waiting too long," Bolan said.

Brognola reached for his briefcase and started to put his papers back in order, signaling an end to the meeting. "That's our game plan for now, Belasko. I'm heading back to D.C. to put some more pressure on Quinn's political front. You and Cane cover the war front. If we hit him hard enough on both fronts, sooner or later he'll be out of friends and money. He won't have anyone left to hide behind.''

The head of the Justice Department SOG picked up his briefcase and headed for the door, a businessman on his way to strike some hard bargains on Capitol Hill. "That's it, gentlemen," he said, looking back at them. "Let's go to war.''

CHAPTER FOUR

The Everglades, Florida

Claude LeBrun cut the outboard motor and eased the small wooden boat into the mouth of the narrow channel. From here on in he would go quiet.

As the arrow-shaped bow glided soundlessly across the water, he listened for the sound of intruders disturbing the natural rhythm of the Everglades, before deciding *he* was the only intruder in this stretch of water.

Then he quietly slipped the long wooden pole into the water and speared it into the muck on the bottom of the channel.

He poled the boat beneath a leafy canopy of mangrove branches, home to hawklike kites and needle-beaked nake birds who chattered briefly at his approach.

The intertwining branches formed a vinelike cave overhead, narrowing the strip of water even more as it shielded him from the hot afternoon sun.

Skeletal mangrove roots reached down into the water from both sides of the channel and clung together in a spiderweb pattern that bumped against the boat every ten yards or so.

Another month, and this strip of water would be impassable.

That was fine with LeBrun. By then, he'd be able to retire for a while. A big payday was coming, and all he had to do was live through that day.

A patch of sunlight shone down at the end of the mangrove corridor about forty yards ahead. Soon he'd be out in the open again.

When the boat neared the edge of the hidden channel, LeBrun leaned forward and jammed the pole deep into the bottom, anchoring it in place until the boat came to a stop.

As he floated in the still water, he carefully unwrapped the gun cloth at his feet. He lifted the Ilarco SR/SB 180 submachine gun and idly swept the barrel across the swampy terrain, savoring the hefty feel of metal in his hands. It was a solidly built piece of war-making machinery.

He rested the weapon across his knees and calmly sat there like someone with all the time in the world, trolling for a catch.

The select-fire weapon looked like a tommy gun with its drum magazine on top and its capacity of 165 rounds. He'd taken it from a dead man who'd tried to cheat him out of a truckload of rolled-up gator hides several years back.

Since the man wouldn't pay, LeBrun took his life, his gun and his money, then took the hides to a more honest—and still living—buyer. It still amazed LeBrun how the man tried to cheat him like that, thinking he had nothing to fear just because he was connected to the Mob.

LeBrun had dispatched him quickly, slashing a hunting knife across his throat before he even knew what happened, before he could even fire a burst from his tommy gun. Maybe it was the way that LeBrun was relaxed in any situation that caught the man off guard.

LeBrun was *always* relaxed because he knew he could take out anyone he came up against man to man, knife to knife, gun to gun. He'd proved that more times than he could count.

After his stint as an Army Ranger, LeBrun had gone back to his native Louisiana bayous, where he got on the wrong side of a crooked game warden who was running several teams of poachers. When the warden sent a few of his men after LeBrun's hide, the former Ranger sent them all to the great beyond, then headed down to Florida and looked up some of his old connections.

LeBrun followed a simple rule—look out for yourself because no one else would. He'd killed some people for the government and he'd killed some people for himself. There wasn't much difference as far as he was concerned. They all bled the same color.

And that was how it would be until someone took him out. Everyone was fair game.

He scanned the swampy terrain, looking for anything that didn't seem right to the naked eye. Then he held up a pair of binoculars and peered through the glass. He did a slow prowl of the mangroves and cypress trees ahead, pausing at the telltale mound of a gator nest before scanning the rest of the wide creek where patches of saw grass rose several feet out of the water.

For a moment he thought he saw some motion, but it was just the swaying of the saw grass as it bent from the breeze that slinked through the swamp. There was no sign of anyone from the Cracker Corps.

But they were out there somewhere, heading toward the hammock LeBrun had chosen for the rendezvous, a small island of tall grass and willows that could serve as a landing strip with a bit of preparation.

LeBrun started to move out into the open, still on guard. When deals like this were going down, he had just as much to fear from friends as from enemies. Everybody was quick on the trigger, and there'd already been several battles over turf. Just like the government had mapped off the Everglades into conservation areas, the local dealers had sectioned it off into cocaine corridors.

You dealt in someone else's territory, you paid the price.

LeBrun reached the southern edge of the hammock an hour later, after going around the long way. He pulled his boat ashore, then walked through the woods to the rendezvous point.

He stayed in the shadows at the edge of the woods while he looked over the gathering.

About fifteen men were already at work, maybe half of the hard-core members of the Cracker Corps. They were sweating in the hot sun as they chopped a swath through tall grass and brush.

Machetes gleamed as they rose and fell through the lush undergrowth. Chain saws buzzed with a metallic whine as they splintered through sun-bleached butterwood branches to gouge out a landing strip for the bush planes that would come in.

A couple of six-seater airboats and a few outboards were clustered beneath a large willow at the western rim of the hammock. They resembled the airboat he kept at his place, maybe with a little less horsepower.

The Cracker Corps had come directly from their

canal-side homes in the swamps, all of them on the outskirts of the cities near Everglade Parkway, the east-west Alligator Alley that cut the Glades in two. They'd moved deep into the swamp on waterways that few people knew about.

And that made them a bit too lax when it came to security, LeBrun thought. They figured no one would be crazy enough to follow these invisible highways deep into the wilderness.

After waiting for another minute, LeBrun stepped out of the woods and stood there with his submachine gun nosing in front of him like a dowsing wand. He studied the field of fire.

Fifteen men.

One hundred and sixty-five rounds.

Six seconds, and he could wipe them all out.

LeBrun smiled and walked forward through the tall grass.

Moses Creedy, the patriarch of the clan, was the first one to look his way. He broke off from the crew he was supervising and walked forward to meet him. Creedy moved quickly, like someone in a hurry to get it over with. All six foot seven inches of him was on edge.

He was a broad-shouldered man with skin as leathery as the gators he used to poach before he moved onto bigger game. Cocaine paid a lot more than the hides.

Creedy was a good man to have on your side, but he wasn't the smartest man in the world. He needed direction, and that could only come from someone who dared to direct him.

Like Claude LeBrun.

When Creedy first tried to get into the smuggling game, there had been several other bands of crackers testing the waters. With a little prodding from Le-Brun, Creedy got the idea to organize his clan and a bunch of other hard cases into the Cracker Corps, a moonshine militia who would form whenever there was a drop from the sky—or whenever another group of smugglers dared to enter their territory.

"Almost thought you weren't coming," Creedy said, pushing his way through the tall grass.

"Took the long way around on a slow boat."

"Why in hell'd you do that?"

"I'm a cautious man, Creedy. That's what keeps us alive and well."

"Maybe. But some of the men've been here for hours. They're starting to grumble about you not showing up—"

LeBrun shook his head and glanced at the group of hard-muscled and hard-eyed men wielding machetes, shovels and chain saws. Some of them looked his way, curses on their lips in French, Spanish and English. LeBrun met their eyes until they looked away. Then he laughed. "That's how it's supposed to be, Creedy. You and me get paid to think. Those boys get paid to dig. And they get paid damn well, don't they?"

"True enough," Creedy admitted.

"Besides," LeBrun added, waving the barrel of the subgun, "I shoot better than I shovel. That's my part."

Creedy shrugged. He was used to LeBrun's indifference. While most men trod carefully around Creedy and his crew, LeBrun acted as if he was ready to kill or be killed at a moment's notice and the outcome wouldn't make much difference to him.

His men recognized that quality. Most of them had

it to some degree, but it had never been refined the way it was in LeBrun.

"We're cutting a strip long enough to land most any bush plane they can send in here," Creedy said. "And I got the boys working on those damn bunkers you asked for. Don't know why we need them that deep. It's not like we're going to have to hide anything in them. Or are we?"

LeBrun lifted his binoculars and scanned the trenches the men were cutting into the earth, zooming in on the branches they were using to prop up the foot-thick sod. They were digging out bunkers large enough to conceal five or six men or hold some waterproofed packages of cocaine until delivery was made.

"They'll do just fine," LeBrun said. "Long as you cover them with enough brush so no one can see them from the air or ground."

"Kind of figured that," Creedy said. "But I haven't figured out why. Who we got to hide them from?"

"That's what you and me got to talk about," LeBrun replied, treading through the grass as he headed toward the embryonic air strip.

Creedy fell in step beside him, his heavy boots crushing the grass and undergrowth. "You planning to rip off the Bank?" he asked, his voice falling into hushed tones when he mentioned the name that LeBrun used for the suppliers.

"Hell, no. Why ruin a good thing?"

"Right," Creedy said. "No sense in trying to break the Bank. Besides, from what I saw, their pilots are a touch crazier than you are. Crazy enough to come after us if we pop a few of them."

"Half past crazy," LeBrun agreed, smiling at the

image that came to mind. "They'd napalm your house if you cross them. Or me."

"Never happen. You and me are partners," Creedy said, though it was obvious he wouldn't mind seeing LeBrun out of the way. The leader of the Cracker Corps didn't like taking orders from anyone, even someone like LeBrun, who was careful never to show that he was the one calling the shots.

But Creedy liked making the kind of money LeBrun's connections brought in. It kept up the life-style he'd grown accustomed to—fast boats and women and satellite TV. He had built up quite a respectable Everglades empire for himself, thanks to LeBrun. As long as that money kept falling from the sky, LeBrun had nothing to worry about.

LeBrun had purposely kept the operation compartmentalized, acting as the go-between for suppliers and the off-loaders. Creedy and his crew would off-load the cargo, then filter out through the swamps and up the canals, transferring the catch to other safehouses or safe houseboats along the waterways.

Once the operation was completed, LeBrun would pay Creedy his share. In turn Creedy would pay off his Cracker Corps. It was a good system that kept everyone wealthy and kept LeBrun alive.

That system was about to change.

"There's a bit more to this one, Creedy," LeBrun said as he walked toward one of the bunkers to watch the men work. "We're all going to earn our money this time. Getting double our usual rate."

"Why's that?"

"Combat pay," LeBrun said.

Creedy stared hard at him. "You best explain, Claude," he said, not bothering to hide the menace in his voice. His gaze swept up and down the line of men he'd brought to transform the hammock into an air strip. Men who trusted in him, and men he was about to put at risk.

"There may be some heat attached to this load," LeBrun said.

"Now's a good time to tell me."

"Well, hell, Creedy," LeBrun said. "If I told you before, you might not have gone through with it."

"What kind of heat are we talking, Claude? Customs people? DEA? Some of the Game boys?"

"No wardens on this one," LeBrun said. "Probably not any legit heat, either. According to my people, someone's trying to put them out of business. Someone who doesn't take prisoners."

"Another outfit moving in on them?"

"Looks like," LeBrun said, figuring it was better to let the man think it was an outlaw force instead of a covert team. His ISS cutout had told LeBrun they were facing some kind of commando team that had wiped out one of the Bank's Bahamian accounts.

But it was minimum risk, the cutout told LeBrun. As long as the Cracker Corps had enough manpower to deal with a few unexpected guests, the operation would be a success on two fronts. The deal would go down.

And Quinn's opponents would go down.

It was a typical Quinn operation, LeBrun thought.

Quinn still used cutouts to distance himself and ISS from his smuggling operations the same way he had when he hid behind Uncle Sam's coattails.

And he still downplayed the risks, just as he had when he'd first recruited LeBrun and a handful of other Rangers for one of his Central American operations. The first one was a legitimate operation to sound out LeBrun and see what boundaries he would cross. The rest of the operations were lucrative. Since then, LeBrun had maintained an on-and-off relationship with Quinn.

It was *on* whenever LeBrun needed money and whenever Quinn needed something taken care of. They'd worked out a simple way of making contact. All LeBrun had to do was call up a detective agency in Miami and leave a message. It would be forwarded to the right person, who would in turn leave a message for LeBrun. Just like that, he was back in business.

"What are we supposed to do?" Creedy asked. "If they think someone's wise to the drop, why don't they just do it somewhere else? Or do it some other time? Hell, we can wait. It's not like any of us are starving."

"You're missing the point," LeBrun said. "They *want* to be followed here, and they want us to make sure whoever follows them stays here forever."

"Shit," Creedy said. "Some of these boys aren't ready for a pitched battle. Fighting's one thing, killing's another—"

"Look, nothing's definite," LeBrun said. "I'm just telling you what may happen. You get paid double no matter what. The competition might not even show up. But if they do, make sure you got enough firepower to turn them into gator bait. Otherwise, the Bank's going to foreclose on us."

CHAPTER FIVE

The ISS complex on Glades Road rose like a granite-and-glass pyramid in the heart of Boca Raton, with several levels of rooftop courtyards and atriums connected by Azteclike steps. Palm trees and sculpted gardens adorned the walkways that connected the different wings.

A garage on the main level held a fleet of armored sedans, Hummers and surveillance vehicles that were used to shepherd ISS clients or conduct surveillance on ISS targets.

Offices on the lower floors handled security for corporate and entertainment clients. Higher-level offices dealt with the more secretive aspects of modern security agencies—arms brokering and mercenary recruitment. There was even a high-tech dirty tricks unit that ISS's Washington backers would periodically sic on their opponents.

Though the long walkways, shade trees and stone benches gave the complex the atmosphere of a college campus, it was more of an invisible college. And the man who set the covert curriculum was Thomas Quinn, who had whitish blond hair and an aura of latent menace that stemmed from cool blue eyes that overlooked nothing and overcame everything.

Though his lean and rangy frame came from decades of slogging through jungles and storming strongholds of every description, he had the easy-going look of an athlete who still kept on top of his game.

His current game was staying alive and in control.

He was sitting alone in his top-floor office, reflecting on the best way to deal with the leader of the Mescone cartel, who was calling for his head.

The Colombians were pressing hard. They lost people, and they lost the payoff money Melitta Caporra gave to the Cubans. Caporra was one of the ranking members of the Mescone cartel, and she'd barely escaped with her life. That in itself was an embarrassment. Even worse, the Mescone leadership lost face with the other cartels. They'd made much of the high-tech capability they were buying from the Cubans. Now it, too, was gone.

Since Quinn's man had made the arrangements, the Colombians said it was up to him to make things right.

Quinn had two alternatives.

He could make reparations by using some of the money from the Everglades operation to bankroll a bigger deal that would eventually let him pay off the Mescone cartel in full, or he could kill everyone in the cartel, maybe make it look like an antidrug initiative from one of the covert agencies.

At the moment the path of least resistance was to come up with money to soothe their egos and their pocketbooks. But at the same time he liked the idea of making a preemptive strike against them. And maybe he could even make a profit in the bargain if he approached one of the Mescone competitors who would like to see them dead.

All it would take was a surgical-strike team: a land

force to keep tabs of the cartel leadership, an air team to launch a strike and take out their soldiers, an exfiltration squad to cover any retreat...

Quinn's invasion reverie was interrupted by the apple-butter voice of Lisa Kincaid, the executive assistant he'd recruited from Langley's propaganda and psychological-warfare department.

"Call from the Capitol, Mr. Quinn. Senator Ritenour on line six."

Quinn pressed down the intercom and said, "I'll take it." Then he clicked on the flashing light.

"Yes, Senator."

"Ah, Thomas. It's good to hear your voice."

"Yours, too, Senator. It's been a while."

"Yes, uh, not since that, uh, campaign thing."

Quinn smiled. The campaign thing had been a break-and-entry operation to recover incriminating tapes of Senator Ritenour and an attractive lobbyist who had been buying access for years.

"What can I do for you, Senator?"

"Actually, Thomas, it's something I can do for you this time."

"Oh?"

"Don't be so surprised. I do look out for you, son."

"What is it, Senator?"

"Hold on a second, Thomas. I think there's some trouble on the line here. I'm calling from a car phone. Seems to be breaking up."

"This end's clear," Quinn said, knowing the room was regularly swept for monitoring devices. "I can hear you just fine."

"Yes, well," the senator said, "maybe you'd better call me back in a few minutes just the same. You can call me on my home line. Things'll be a *lot* clearer then.''

"Will do," Quinn said. He waited until enough time had passed, then called the senator's home number, using the scrambler unit that matched the one he'd installed at Senator Ritenour's Georgetown home. The high-end unit altered the speech spectrum, splintering into several different sound bands and continually changing the transmission code. It was as secure as any phone system could be.

Senator Ritenour picked up the phone on the first ring as if he'd been waiting urgently for the call. That in itself was a sign that something was up. Ritenour was usually unflappable. He'd been through so many scandals that very little could spook him these days.

"It's me," Quinn said. "What's the problem?"

"You are."

"Can you be a bit more exact?"

"Something's in the wind here, Thomas. Your name's been floating around the Senate and the Congressional intelligence oversight committees."

"I've got a lot of friends on the hill."

"They might not be your friends much longer," the senator warned. "Apparently someone is digging into your background, dredging up some of the South American things, defense contracts, rumors of money laundering connected to ISS."

"I can weather the rumors," Quinn said.

"Maybe not. The Senate has a lot of capable investigators. Many of them come from spook agencies themselves. They know how to look and they know where to look. Some of your past associates, for instance."

"Senator, this is old news. People have been trying to take me down for years, and I'm still standing. What is it you want me to do?''

Senator Ritenour laughed. ''Sounds like you're already doing it, son. I want you to fight back. I'll do what I can to help you up here. Call in some chits, find out who's gunning for you.''

''Got any leads?'' Quinn probed.

''Not yet. But it's somebody, something big…with a wide reach. Getting a lot of cooperation up here. Pretty soon the rabbits'll start running and you'll find out who your real friends are.''

''I don't need friends,'' Quinn said. ''I just need people who will do what I say. Spread the word, Senator—in your own tactful way, of course—that if people get a bit too talkative about me, well, I can get pretty talkative about them. To newspapers, networks…wives.''

''You wouldn't be threatening me now, would you, Quinn?''

''Senator!'' Quinn said with mock horror. ''You and I go back a long time. We've stolen horses together and we'll hang together. You have my word I won't harm you.''

''That's a real comfort, son,'' Senator Ritenour said. ''And I'll see what I can do about making a case for you. And reminding everyone just how deep your roots go.''

Quinn's political intelligence was legendary on the Hill. Both Republicans and Democrats knew his private security agency contained enough explosive material to clean House and Senate if it ever saw the light of day. They also knew Quinn was discreet—for a price.

Quinn debated about telling the senator about the overt attacks he was experiencing on his operation.

But that might spook him. Despite their mutual vows of allegiance, both men would sell each other out if it came down to that. The only question was how much they could get.

He decided to wait until after the Everglades drop was made and the dogs of war were brought to heel. Then he could let the senator know he was taking care of things on his front.

"All right, Thomas," the senator said. "Seems we understand what we have to do. Other than that, how's business?"

It wasn't an idle question, since Quinn's company was working on a number of projects steered his way by Ritenour's office. That meant he would have to make substantial contributions to Ritenour's favorite charity—himself. "Business is good, Senator," Quinn said. And it was good. But not good enough to survive many more losses from the covert end of his business. That was the lifeblood of his empire, and if he didn't stop whoever was after him, they'd bleed him to death.

After a few more pleasantries, Quinn hung up and immediately made a series of phone calls.

The first call was to Venezuela to an American expatriate in the banking business who happened to be an old friend of Quinn's. It was a brief call and, to anyone listening in, a purely social one that invited the banker to visit Quinn sometime for a cruise.

That call set in motion a flurry of activity in a dockside warehouse in Maracaibo. A team of workers used barrel clamps and forklifts to move pallets and fake floorboards from a ground-level bay at one end of the warehouse.

A short time later an elevator system brought crates of cocaine up to the main floor and the crates were transferred to a cargo ship making several legitimate stops in the Caribbean.

The Venezuelan port was one of Quinn's preferred shipping points, thanks to its strategic location on the Guajira Peninsula where the border with Colombia was easily crossed.

In recent years the port had become a major disembarkation point for cocaine, heroine and cannabis from several South American cartels. And it had the added advantage that Quinn didn't have to deal directly with the Colombians.

It was all part of a global shell game.

Whenever the heat was on in one country, there were several others that could pick up the slack: Venezuela, Panama, Costa Rica, Belize, Peru—all were places where the drug-processing laboratories were always in season and there was seldom a shortage of cooperative government officials.

The main reason Quinn liked using Venezuela for this operation was its direct line northeast to Puerto Rico.

His newest cargo ship would have several ports of call in the Caribbean, but its first stop would be out at sea, where a crew of cigarette boats, fishing yachts and any other craft at hand would off-load the clandestine cargo and bring it to Puerto Rico.

With its status as a commonwealth of the United States, there were no customs inspections to interfere with the reloading of the cargo onto private planes that would fly it to the mainland.

QUINN'S SECOND CALL was to an exclusive resort hotel in San Juan. He spoke with the owner—another old friend who had put his profits from arms sales into the real-estate business.

The hotel owner went down to the nightclub and made a call to another hotel and bar he owned in Manati, just west of San Juan.

The waterfront haunt was as far removed from the luxury hotel as the group of "guests" he'd been harboring there, a gathering of pilots who'd flown arms and armies, rice, sugarcane, opium, heroin and cocaine around the globe.

The group of pilots had transported the cargos for themselves, the agency, Quinn, ISS and whatever country cared to hire them.

Eddy Scofield, the nominal captain of the crew for this operation, took the call at the bar and listened to some barely disguised code words that told him he and the crew would be going into action soon. Within two days they had to be ready to fly fresh loads to the mainland.

After he hung up the phone and slid it across the bar top, Scofield signaled the bartender, who reached into an ice chest beneath the bar and fished out a bottle of beer for him.

Scofield weaved his way back through the empty tables at the deserted bar, which had been deserted lately because of the pilots who'd been staying there for several days while they waited for the go-ahead.

The disheveled crew didn't look like they regularly handled cargos worth millions of dollars. They were dressed mostly in jeans, baseball caps, khaki shorts and boat shoes, and a lot of them wore impenetrable shades that hid their eyes.

They shared an easy camaraderie that stemmed from working together on previous operations. The crazies and suicidal among them had been weeded out through a smugglers' process of natural selection and now were either doing time in jail or were planted deep beneath the ground.

That left a tight-knit group of irregulars who were getting ready to go into battle. A quick scan showed some barely concealed weapons, mostly pistols outlined beneath long shirt tails and knives sheathed on belts. Every man was armed and every man knew how to use his weapons, a good skill to have in the small coastal town. During the past few years, it had acquired a Wild West atmosphere, with many people dependent on the drug trade.

Killings and gunfights were as common as the cocaine that flooded the area.

Scofield dropped into a chair at the nest of tables they'd pulled toward the waterfront window. It was covered with cards, cigarettes and bottles, the fuel that most of them ran on between flights. During the days, they turned the bar into a clubhouse and at night it became a bordello.

"Last call!" Scofield said, rapping his ice-beaded bottle of beer onto the table and calling for order. "One more drink and then we're officially on alert. Got to be ready to fly."

There were some gripes from the men, but it was just routine. They were used to the drill. What they were about to pull off required men who were stone-cold sober and clearheaded enough to see who their friends and enemies were. Some of them would be flying on decoy routes. Others would be flying into the real landing zone.

From the way they'd been drinking, it would take some drying-out time before they were fit to fly.

They drifted to the bar in ones and twos, then sauntered back with their drinks and gathered around Scofield.

"This one's going to be a bit different," Scofield said in the soft, low voice he always used when he got serious. It was the kind of voice that made people lean forward to catch what he was saying. "We might run into some resistance on the ground. Not from the Cracker Corps. We can trust them."

Scofield's words sobered up the men quickly. Making a dope run was one thing. Making a dope run into a combat zone was another.

"Who we looking out for?" one of the men asked.

"That's the problem. We don't know. But if people start shooting when we get there, don't waste time figuring out who's coming at us. Just unload on them with everything you got."

"That could take out some of the friendlies."

"There are plenty more friends to be had," Scofield said. "Important thing is, we make our delivery, take out whoever's laying in wait for us and then get out of this in one piece."

QUINN'S NEXT CALL was to Gilberto Vicente in the principality of Andorra, a small landlocked state between France and Spain where ISS maintained one of its European satellite offices.

Unlike the high-tech headquarters in Boca Raton, Vicente's offices were located in a three-story gabled building in the university quarter of Zaragoza, the alternately medieval and modern capital of the Aragon region.

From the sedate structure, Vicente handled mercenary recruitment and other delicate operations for a worldwide clientele, relying on contacts from his service in the Spanish antiterrorist force Grupo Especial de Operaciónes. During his stint with GEO, he'd led hostage-rescue operations against the left-

and right-wing extremist groups targeting banks, large corporations and media figures throughout Spain. His mastery of languages also made him a prime candidate for security details with foreign VIPs and liaison with allied intelligence services. Vicente gradually built up a covert client list that extended far beyond Spanish borders, a roster of influential members who never forgot the services or favors he provided them.

Nor did the Guardia Civil forget the scandal stemming from one of Vicente's rescue operations in the countryside. The botched operation led to the death of two undercover police officers and four civilians, along with every member of the kidnapping cell. The ransom money vanished under suspicious circumstances.

Gilberto Vicente vanished from the public eye a short time later, leaving the service and the country. He moved to Panama for a while and soon had business deals in Colombia and throughout South America.

It was in Panama where he first encountered Thomas Quinn. After several joint ventures, they became business partners and Vicente set up his office in Andorra. Though in some official quarters Vicente was still regarded with suspicion, he had managed to rehabilitate his reputation with people who counted—the firms and agencies that needed his services and didn't mind a cloud or two hanging over him.

Vicente's offices were isolated from the world at large, thanks to Andorra's traditional mode of transportation. No railroad cut through the country, and there were no airlines. It kept the European office transactions removed from the public eye just as the front companies Vicente ran from the small building kept his transactions removed from ISS and Thomas Quinn.

The two men had complete trust in each other. Not only had they become comrades in arms and business partners, but they both knew where all the skeletons were buried.

Which was why Vicente agreed to go to the States at Quinn's request. If Quinn went down in flames, he would go with him.

But he continued to argue with Quinn as a matter of form.

"I really think I should stay," Vicente said. "We may lose out on some proposals I've been floating around. Croatia. Bosnia. Macedonia. They're all buying, and a lot of it is legal now—rockets, mortars, comm gear. Radar installations." Vicente always spoke of his business affairs like an engineer. Proposals. Site visits. Installations.

Vicente was an accomplished engineer of war, which was exactly why Quinn needed him on the home front.

"Understood," Quinn said. "You've opened a lot of markets, but without a foundation here what can we do? Someone is trying to rock our foundation— that's why I need you here to attend to our business interests. There's a certain business agent that needs looking after."

At the moment Quinn's most pressing business interest was a DEA special agent in Miami who had been selling information to ISS intermediaries. For several years he'd been a fount of reliable information about drug-interdiction tactics, location of DEA personnel and names of informants the DEA had cultivated. Lately the agent had cut off contact.

It was time to show the agent that it wasn't up to him to decide when to cooperate. The agent was bought and sold, and it was time to collect.

Vicente would do the collecting.

"Very well," Vicente said after making a few more protests at leaving his affairs in Andorra. "I'll drive across the border and catch the first flight out."

CHAPTER SIX

Hal Brognola had cleared the way ahead of time for Mack Bolan and Armand Cane. When they arrived at the Marco Island customs base after a hundred-mile drive across Everglades Parkway and down Route 951, a team of blue-jacketed agents was waiting for them in a small office that looked out on the Gulf Coast.

Several detailed maps of the Everglades hung on the wall, showing strategic waterways, preferred smuggling routes and a number of towns that had been the home bases of known Cracker traffickers.

Since Armand Cane had worked with customs several times in the past, the DEA agent made the introductions, referring to the Executioner as a specialist from Washington. Instead of the Mike Barron identity, he used Bolan's nom de guerre, Michael Belasko. In case any government agency checked him out, they would find out that Belasko had government bona fides.

Bolan was welcomed with a wary appraisal and strong handshake from the head of the team, Customs Investigator Patrick Fergus, a man with a crew cut that was sheared so close to the scalp you could barely make out the reddish tint of his hair. He also had a stubble of beard that was nearing goatee stage, which gave him the look of a beatnik.

A heavily armed one at that. Over his regulation jacket with shoulder patch and customs badge, Fergus wore a spring-loaded quick-draw shoulder holster with a .357 Smith & Wesson.

The half-dozen other customs agents also carried similar holster rigs and had access to heavier firepower from a wall-length gun rack full of standard-issue Colt AR-15 assault rifles.

After they all sat down at a long conference table, the leader of the customs squad gave Bolan a hard look. "What exactly *is* your specialty, Mr. Belasko?" Fergus asked, using the skeptical tone field agents always adopted when visited by strangers from Washington.

"Whatever the mission requires," Bolan said in a no-nonsense tone. "Right now that requires your cooperation. Have I got it?"

Fergus nodded. "Yes, you do. In a big way." He looked at Armand Cane, whose long hair and biker boots gave him the image of someone they usually tried to catch. "Can't say it's a pleasure to see *you* again, Armand," Fergus said. "But my orders say I have to cooperate with you."

"Mine, too," Cane replied. "This is part of an inter—"

"Spare the hurrahs," Fergus said. "I heard that speech before. Just tell me what you want and I'll tell you what you can have."

"Fair enough. I want to take down the Cracker Corps."

"Who doesn't?" said one of the agents sitting across from Cane. "Trouble is getting them all in one place."

Customs had a special interest when it came to Cracker smugglers who prided themselves on outrunning and outthinking the customs agents all across southern Florida. Crackers in the dope trade worked from the Gulf to the Florida Keys, as well as out to the Bahamas and the Caribbean Islands. They were old hands when it came to running shrimping boats or mother ships toward southern Florida, where they would off-load onto cigarette boats and make the dash up into the Everglades.

There were several Cracker outfits working the smuggling game, but none of them as elusive and formidable as the Cracker Corps, who had recently become a thorny problem for customs.

"Then I've got good news, gentlemen," Bolan said. "It looks like the Cracker Corps is coming out in full force this time around."

"So that's what this day trip's all about," Fergus said. "You want to ride along with us."

"Actually," Bolan said, "we want *you* to ride along with us. We'll lead the way into the hot zone. But we'll need some heavy backup once the deal goes down."

"You sound like you've done this before," Fergus said, wondering if he was dealing with one more Washington hotdog playing undercover games or if Bolan was the genuine item.

"A few times," Bolan said.

"From a desk or from the field?" Fergus asked.

"Both," Bolan answered. "Like I said before, I do whatever the mission requires...to whoever needs it."

"Good," Fergus said. "Nice to know you won't be needing a chaperon. Anyone else invited to the dance that I should know about?'' he asked, a skeptical look clouding his face.

Bolan understood the man's concern. The more agencies involved, the less control Fergus would personally have over the operation. And that meant the more unknowns his men would have to face.

''There'll be some air support, but the key to the operation is a fast-moving strike team on water,'' Bolan said. ''In case anyone gets away.''

Fergus looked intrigued. ''Tell us about the deal. Everything you can, and we'll see what we can do.''

Bolan nodded toward Cane. ''He's got the intel.''

The DEA agent sketched in the intelligence he'd received from his contacts on the periphery of the Cracker Corps and from DEA sources in Puerto Rico. So far they had a good idea of the general location for the off-load and the number of men involved. More intelligence was coming in every minute from a network of DEA agents that tracked the movement of suspect ships and planes and plotted their courses.

''When's all this supposed to happen?'' Fergus asked.

The DEA agent shrugged. ''Could be starting right now.''

''Thanks for the advance notice.''

''Hey, I don't make the schedule,'' Cane said. ''You've got to catch them when you can. We'll be there whenever they get there.''

Fergus looked around the table at his men. Though they tried to remain passive, they all had the look of the chase about them. This was what they were trained to do. Most of them had come from military services: SEALs, Coast Guard, Marines.

"What are we waiting for?" Fergus asked. "Let's go storm the beach."

TWO HOURS LATER the Executioner was knifing across a wide corridor of water in the southernmost section of Big Cypress Swamp at fifty miles per hour. A steady spray of water misted the air as the silvery torpedo blurred past cypress and mangrove bars.

The airboat moved like an extension of Bolan's hand, guided by the steering lever he gripped like a ski pole as he followed the twisting lane of water, slaloming through a young mangrove patch of watery saplings that were just starting to sprout up above the surface.

A caged aircraft propeller on the rear of the boat whipped the wind behind him, powered by a 350 hp engine.

The air felt cool on his face as it buffeted against the thin, slanted goggles that protected his eyes.

The advantage of the airboats was their maneuverability. Instead of having to go around the marsh and saw-grass fields that protruded from the water, they could go through them or over them.

The disadvantage was the loudness.

The airboats made good chase vehicles, and with a six-man armed crew they were dead serious strike craft. But the problem was getting in range without being heard and scaring off the smugglers, or worse, running at full speed into an ambush.

That was why the customs fleet that wound through the southern edges of Big Cypress Swamp also had a pair of silent-running Zodiac inflatables loaded with special ordnance and sophisticated communications gear. Enough compact equipment and weaponry had been fitted into the motorized water-craft to turn them into floating command posts.

Right now the customs crews were spread out in other airboats, wearing their plainclothes gear and tooling around like pleasure boaters who were taking rented airboats for a spin. Their regulation colors and Kevlar body armor would come on when they went into battle.

Bolan, Cane and a couple of other men would move in well ahead of the main strike force, keeping in touch with the airboat armada that would hang back until the deal went down or contact was made with the Crackers.

The Cracker Corps would also have airboats at their disposal, and they knew every one of the myriad waterways that coursed through the Everglades. This was their turf, and Bolan had to be ready for what-ever came his way.

He took the airboat on one more run, boosting the throttle and cutting through a patch of saw grass like a silver mower, with the tall, razor-sharp strands whacking against the aluminum before flattening out beneath the boat.

Bolan made a quick foray into the thickening swamp, cutting the throttle and moving the steering lever to the right. The nose of the airboat lifted out of the water and came down in a gentle splash as it came to a stop. He made one more practice run, keeping one hand on the steering lever and one hand on the 93-R Beretta.

Ideally there would be at least two people working this kind of boat. One to pilot it, one to hose down the opposition with automatic fire from the AR-15s. But there was no telling what would happen once they went into battle in the swamp.

A QUARTET OF DOLPHINS paced the thirty-five-foot cabin cruiser as it drifted toward the causeway. Sometimes they swam in front or on the sides, now and then dropping behind so they could catch up in a mad dash of spirited leaps and splashes that sent them rocketing in and out of the water.

Special Agent Lawrence Savidge lost sight of them for a moment as he sailed beneath the causeway, his attention drawn by several men fishing on one of the concrete bases where they'd had a small fire to cook their catch. To some, the causeway was home away from home. To others, it *was* home. Periodically the homeless fishers were chased out, but they always came back.

Where else could they go?

At times Savidge felt sorry for them. It would last for about three seconds, then he would continue on his way.

Everybody made his own bed and had to lie in it. And these days the DEA agent wasn't sleeping so comfortably himself.

He looked for the dolphins again and saw them cavorting a short distance ahead. He increased speed to catch up to them. After all, they were one of the reasons he came out here.

Savidge had seen the sleek dolphins for several nights running and had come to expect them almost as if they were his own private marine escort. They'd been waiting for him every evening when he went out into Biscayne Bay to catch the sunsets.

He'd been out in the bay for an hour now. It was totally dark now, magic time in Miami.

The skyline was lit up by the towers and resorts that lined the coastline like neon stalagmites painted against the dark sky. And looming out from the shore was the huge guitar from the Hard Rock Café like a beacon in the night dropped by some giant alien rocker.

The only happiness he had these days came when he was on the boat looking on the shore. At least out here he was away from everything. He was safe, unreachable.

Lately people had been trying to reach him, people who weren't used to being ignored.

But Savidge had decided the best way to deal with them was to cut off all communications. Unfortunately they didn't see it that way. There had been several phone calls made to his house late at night. Sometimes the voices demanded meetings. Other times the voices were silent, and the unknown party stayed on the line just to let him know they were still out there.

Sometimes he felt like just staying on the boat and seeing how far it took him. Far enough to start a new life perhaps, so he wouldn't have to deal with them ever again. But that was impossible. The people he dealt with had a long reach, both lawful and unlawful.

He was no longer the master of his fate.

Savidge stayed out in the bay for another hour, keeping close to the coastline and savoring the breeze that eased across the calm water. The boat was his refuge, but it was also a reminder of what he had done to earn it. Selling names of DEA informants who would subsequently disappear. Sometimes they'd reappear in bits and pieces.

It wasn't that they didn't deserve it, most of them anyway. They were all players in the game whether they knew it or not, playing with cards shuffled by unseen dealers.

There were other crimes. He'd crossed the border a step at a time: information on task forces, names of DEA personnel in Central and South America, bases they operated from.

One thing led to the next.

But eventually he grew afraid of what would come next. Getting rid of informants was one thing. He hardly had to think about that at all.

It was a bit harder when it came to revealing information on DEA agents and associates outside the U.S., but Savidge came through for his cartel callers. He rationalized it by convincing himself he wasn't telling them anything they didn't already know. Foreign stations were notorious in their failure to conceal identities and ranks of their operators. Since the host governments sold that information to the cartels as soon as it was available to *them,* Savidge really wasn't giving anything away.

But lately the "requests" made of him had become more serious.

His contacts wanted the names and ranks of DEA agents operating in the U.S. That would place them in the direct line of fire.

It was a line Savidge couldn't cross. He'd adamantly refused the requests and then, when the demands kept coming, simply stopped talking to his contacts.

There was no one he could turn to. He was an enemy now, to both sides.

All he had left was his time on the boat, and even that was losing some of its luster. It was getting so there was no escape. His conscience, which had lain buried for so long, was emerging from the depths.

Even the sea was no longer a sanctuary.

He docked the cabin cruiser at his slip in Miamarina and drove his BMW to his Collins Avenue condo, a place he might have been able to afford without any underworld assistance if he'd saved well and wisely throughout his career.

Savidge lived on the fifth floor with a moderately sized balcony that looked out onto the bay and onto hundreds of other similar balconies on neighboring condos. There was a swimming pool, tennis court and sizable garden pond that served home to a variety of fish, ducks and now and then an alligator or two.

It was the kind of place where the residents felt secure, thanks to the neighborly attitude they felt toward one another and the presence of a two-man security detail around the clock.

Definitely one of the more secure condos in the area.

Which made it all the more surprising when Savidge unlocked his door and saw the man sitting on his leather sofa with his feet on his glass-topped table. He was well dressed and at first glance looked like a successful business executive. But the barely hidden feral look in his eye hinted that his business could also include murder. He was sipping a glass of wine while he listened to Schubert's *Winterreise* on Savidge's five-thousand-dollar stereo unit. A bottle of wine stood on the table, a most expensive vintage Savidge had been saving for a special occasion.

Savidge stood there as if he were hypnotized, a creature of prey who'd seen a snake coiled to strike.

The man was waving the wineglass gently in cadence with the somber music, almost as if he were conducting.

"Come in, come in," the man said, playing the perfect host. "Close the door behind you." He spoke softly and pleasantly, with a slight European accent that Savidge couldn't place.

Savidge closed the door quietly, dismissing the split-second urge to bolt out the door and run for his life. There was nowhere to run anymore.

But he wasn't totally powerless. He unzipped his windbreaker to reveal his holstered pistol, more for show than intent.

The show had little effect.

"No guns," the man said, quite unconcerned at the sight of the weapon. "We have not come to that point yet. Hopefully we never will."

The stranger seemed perfectly at ease as he spoke to the DEA agent. But there was something about him that compelled Savidge to follow instructions. He closed the door behind him and dropped his keys on the table near the door.

"Who are you?" Savidge demanded.

The man took another sip of wine before putting the glass back down on the table and nodding his head at such a reasonable request.

"My name is Gilberto, and I am here to solve all of your problems."

"What are you talking about?" Savidge said.

"I am talking about our business arrangement."

"I have no arrangement with you," Savidge said. "Or anyone."

The man who identified himself as Gilberto nodded sagely and sadly, as if the matter weighed greatly on his mind. "That is true," he said. "You have severed your contact with our mutual friends. It is a regretful situation that I am sure has caused a great deal of worry on both sides."

Savidge felt himself pale. Dizzy. It had been years

since he'd had an actual confrontation with the other side.

"But that is settled now," the man continued. "You will either cooperate with me or you will be dead. Either way, you will have no more worries."

Savidge took a couple of steps toward the stranger, then froze in his place when he heard sounds coming from another room in the condo. Someone was in his bedroom. Opening drawers, closing them. He wondered what they were searching for. Savidge stared at the hallway at the sound of approaching footsteps, looking like a condemned man, expecting Gilberto's enforcer to come out into the open.

Instead, he saw a woman, a beautiful woman in blue jeans and a half shirt that rose above her smooth, flat stomach. Her hair hung down to her shoulders in torrents of bright yellow tresses that came from a bottle.

The casual but calculated look appealed to him. Though the woman was obviously a fake blonde, her body was real. The soft, clinging top left little doubt of that. She was well tanned and had aggressive blue eyes that painted a canvas of intriguing possibilities in front of him.

"She is also one of our mutual friends," the man explained.

"You got a lot of friends," Savidge said.

"We are all friends in this business."

Despite the situation, Savidge couldn't keep his eyes off her for very long. His gaze flicked back and forth from the blonde to the strangely comfortable intruder. She was obviously a lure, a diversion thrown into the mix to keep him off balance.

"She will stay here with you," Gilberto said.

"What for?" he asked. And now he acted like a

man who'd just been reprieved. Only this time the reprieve came from the lawless, not the law.

"She will serve as a reminder to make sure that you fulfill your responsibilities to us, and a reminder of the good life it is still possible for you to lead."

Savidge shook his head. It was like winning the lottery and stepping in front of a speeding truck at the same time. The woman was a dream come true; the man was a nightmare from which he would never wake.

"You will find her a most pleasant taskmaster," the man said.

Savidge looked from the blonde to the man who continued speaking in the tones of a professor to a novice student. "Any unpleasantness, well, that will be my department." He slid one hand over the other as if he were washing his hands of the matter. "Come. Let's talk this over."

The woman vanished into the bedroom, moving quickly and silently, as if she'd been conditioned to make herself invisible when it came to business matters. It wasn't a matter of tradition or chauvinism. It was simply a matter of survival. The less she knew, the longer she lived.

Savidge walked over and sat on the far end of the couch, feeling like he'd stepped into a surreal tableau, a trap that had been constructed for him year after year. It was sprung the first time he took money for selling out, but only now was it snaring him.

Still, it wasn't anything like what he'd imagined. Gilberto was so pleasant and so apparently honest that Savidge was disarmed. He was also embarrassed that he hadn't even made a single gesture at self-defense.

Perhaps it was fear that made him accept the

man's presence. Or perhaps Savidge simply recognized that, at least in matters of killing or command, Gilberto was a natural leader and it was up to him to accept his role in the pack.

And that meant Savidge was either a follower, or a corpse.

Gilberto wasted no more time in pleasantries. The mask was removed, and he was in command.

"Our association has been in effect for many years," he said, "ever since your unfortunate encounter in South Beach."

"You know about that?"

"We know about everything," Gilberto assured him. He then proceeded to offer a detailed profile of Savidge's career that could have been compiled by someone in the agency, and probably had.

Gilberto knew all about the South Beach incident where Savidge had orchestrated a raid on a cartel safehouse several years back. An informant had given Savidge's crew all the information they needed.

But moments before the bust went down, for whatever insane reason took control of his tattered mind, the informant clued the traffickers that a bust was imminent.

Savidge was the first one through the door. He was also the first one hit. Even before the pain registered, he knew what had happened. His feet went out from under him, and his back slammed down to the floor. He'd been hit in the chest and in the stomach, and bullets were flying all around him but he couldn't even move.

The informant and a cartel gunman were killed in a cross fire, another DEA agent was wounded and the quarry they were after got away.

It took nearly a year for Savidge's rehabilitation.

Though the physical wounds eventually healed, the mental ones stayed with him forever. Savidge tried to go back in the field, but every time he went on an operation one question weighed on him. Was he willing to trade his life for some mindless, soulless, low-life bottom-feeder in the drug trade?

The answer was no.

He couldn't go on street operations anymore. Savidge was promoted. He moved up into a desk position that mostly involved gathering and analyzing intelligence on cartels and local talent in the drug trade. He still planned operations but now he was removed from the day-to-day activities. It was almost like a chess game. He made his moves, and the pawns lived or fell.

One thing stayed the same. The rulers never fell. They just went on getting richer and richer, and the war would never be won.

That was the attitude that made him a candidate for a cartel approach.

Someone in the DEA itself, another cartel confederate, had probably passed on the information that he was ripe for a bribe.

It took a while for Savidge to realize he wasn't ripe back then, but that he was rotten. And now it was harvest time.

After he concluded the dossier of Savidge's descent into the underworld, Gilberto leaned toward him as if he were an old friend to whom Savidge had confessed his sins. "Your life has not been easy. And so I can understand how this crisis of conscience led to a lapse in good judgment. After all, it is very foolish to try and break all ties with us." He put his hand on Savidge's shoulder.

Savidge tensed at the touch of the man's hand. Despite the mock friendship, he sensed it could just as easily close around his throat.

"But we are satisfied it was a temporary matter," Gilberto went on. "You made the decision and now you must live with it or die from it."

Savidge nodded. "What do you want from me?"

Gilberto smiled. "That's the easy part. Nothing much. Just some information on something that is going to happen very soon."

"Which is?"

"Are you aware of a corporation called ISS?" Gilberto asked.

"I've heard the name," Savidge said.

"In what context?"

Savidge laughed. "The worst possible context. ISS is on a watch list because of possible involvement in drug trafficking, money laundering and murder—to name just a few things."

"A full-service corporation," Gilberto agreed. "As a matter of fact, ISS, or a group that some people believe is connected to ISS, is planning a major operation even as we speak."

"And you want me to divert attention from it?" Savidge asked.

Gilberto shook his head. "Quite the opposite," he said. "I am sure it already has the attention of a number of people. Normal precautions will be taken—decoy operations will be launched at the same time—but this certain group will follow the ISS angle. Apparently they have a mania about it."

"So what do you want from me?"

"Names," Gilberto said. "After this operation is over, there's bound to be fallout. A lot of pressure will come down. Not from small-timers, but from the people who call the shots. I want to know who is doing the asking."

"Why?" Savidge asked, though he suspected he knew the answer.

"So we can put their minds at rest. And their bodies."

Savidge nodded, aware that he'd reached the end of the line. He was being asked to provide names of insiders in the agency, a hit list for an assassination bureau.

Gilberto stood and nodded curtly before heading to the door. The discussion was finished. There was no question about Savidge's compliance.

The cartel negotiator nodded toward the other room where the woman had vanished. "She'll keep you happy," he said. "And if you keep us informed, we'll keep you alive."

He closed the door. His footsteps rapidly receded on the outside walkway, the sound of a man in a hurry to collect some more souls.

CHAPTER SEVEN

The skies were right for smuggling.

Dusk was approaching, and so was the makeshift landing zone on the edge of Big Cypress Swamp.

The Brazilian Embraer twin-engine plane was less than ten minutes away from the rendezvous, a heavy metal workhorse droning through the sky. Even with all the fuel spent on the zigzag route from Puerto Rico, Eddy Scofield thought the plane still felt heavy.

The Embraer was weighted down with a gun-ready crew and a cargo to kill for.

But soon everything would be back to normal.

With a bit of luck, he would land his customized commuter plane in the waning moments of daylight, off-load the cargo and take off again under cover of darkness.

Scofield brought his plane down low, soaring over a patchwork mosaic of green forest and wheat-colored saw grass.

He was as familiar as any pilot could be with the Everglades, an ever-shifting map of wilderness swampland carved up by a slow-moving river that was fifty miles wide at times, a shallow freshwater sea that swept down through the southern part of Florida. Tropical storms and floodwaters periodically ripped through the swamps, leveling forests, creating new channels and choice sites for clandestine landing strips.

To an outsider it was an impenetrable, forbidding jungle, steamy nesting grounds for alligators, poisonous snakes and two-legged, heavily armed predators.

To a smuggler like Scofield it was a big backyard with limitless possibilities.

Fortunes could be made here, and death could be found here. But Scofield had made so many runs now he considered it part of his own private preserve where nothing could happen to him.

His eyes were alert and his senses were soothed by the blues music that bounced around the cockpit. It was business as usual, and his business was making money the fast way.

"Looking good," Scofield said, nodding in cadence to the music. "We're right on schedule."

"Too good," said the man sitting next to him. Robert Slater, a scarecrow of a man with a gaunt face, had plane-crash scars that ran parallel to the part in his hair, giving his spiky blond hair an eccentric look, like furrows in a field of yellow corn. Slater always saw death and destruction lurking where Scofield saw a good time waiting.

They were the perfect complement to each other. Their contradictory natures had kept them alive during their years in the drug trade. "If you ask me," Slater said, "it just looks too damn good."

"I didn't ask you, I told you. It looks good and it feels good and it's going to stay good. We're going to sail through whatever comes our way. Just as long as you don't jinx us, man."

Slater shook his head and fell into a moody silence.

"Okay," Scofield said. "What is it?" He clicked

off the music and looked hard at Slater, sensing that the man was bothered by more than the normal pre-operation jitters.

Slater just shrugged.

"Come on, Slate, what could be wrong?" Scofield asked. "There's no one around us except us, man. Clear skies all around."

"That's what I'm afraid of." Slater looked out the cockpit window, scanning the greenery below, as if he could detect danger with the naked eye and find enemies waiting in the mangrove forests. "We haven't seen any traffic up here."

"Give it up, man," Scofield said. "There's not supposed to be traffic up here, not if everybody's doing their job." Scofield didn't know all the details, just that several decoy flights had been launched throughout the Caribbean the same time they were making their run.

At the end of their runs the decoy planes would jet through airspace over the Turks and Caicos Islands before heading toward Miami. Flights through those outlaw islands always caught the attention of customs and the DEA and would help deplete the heat's already thin resources.

It seemed to be working.

For the past half hour Scofield had seen few planes in the southern Florida air corridors. Most of them were private planes or passenger jets returning from playgrounds in the Bahamas or Caribbean. They'd turned off toward Miami International or the airport in Fort Lauderdale.

Right now that left the sky over the Everglades pretty much to Scofield and the two other small planes traveling with him. They were spread out about five miles apart, flying low over the swamp.

Each plane was packed with extra fuel tanks, small arms, bricks of cocaine and bales of square grouper, the carefully wrapped cannabis containers that would float in the water in case Scofield had to air-drop the cargo instead of landing on the hammock.

The problem with making an airdrop was trying to ensure that it hit the right zone. His crew could only push so much so fast out the bay doors. With a limited drop zone, that meant a lot of error.

Those expensive bundles could get snagged in trees, rip open in the water, or even land on the people who were waiting on the ground below. Ground crews could always claim that half of the load was lost in the airdrop. These "lost loads" had made many a fortune in the past.

Adding to the risk was the amount of time the ground crew needed to track down the dropped cargo, time enough to get caught by the law.

But this time the law was going to get caught. If anyone was waiting for them below, the Cracker Corps would take care of them. And the plane crews weren't flying blindly into this. They had some fireworks of their own to bring to the party.

"ALPHA BIRD to Belasko."

The helicopter pilot's voice came loud and clear through Bolan's miniature headset. "This is Alpha Bird to Belasko. Acknowledge."

Bolan responded with a single click from his handset to acknowledge the contact from the lead scout chopper.

The Executioner's magnolia-and-moss-shrouded observation post was situated on the edge of a muddy green strip of water a good distance from the Cracker Corps landing zone, but he kept radio silence out of habit. There was no need for verbal confirmation and no guarantee that his presence was undiscovered.

After all, if Bolan had made it this far into the swamp undetected, then one of the Cracker scouts might be doing the very same thing, moving quietly on the outer perimeter of the zone.

"Alpha Bird to Biker," the pilot said. "Acknowledge."

A few seconds later Bolan heard two clicks from Armand Cane, responding with the agreed-upon signal from his post on the other side of the hammock.

"Triple-header's in the park," the pilot continued, using the code name for the three planes that the DEA had been tracking even before they neared Florida airspace. "We are going black. We'll be back at show time. You roger that?"

Bolan clicked again.

A moment later he heard two clicks from Cane, acknowledging that the helicopters that had led them through the swamp to the landing zone would temporarily fade away from the kill zone, hovering in some sheltered patch of forest until it was time to make their presence known.

The pair of quiet-rotor choppers had been making wide circuits of the swamp for the past few hours, downloading electronic intelligence—ELINT—to the dimly lit green screens built into the electronics package in the front of the Zodiac.

Both of the angular, low-signature stealth helicopters had been flying wide recon patterns, keeping their distance to avoid being spotted by the Cracker Corps or the incoming crews of the doper airline.

Chances were small that either of the aircraft would be detected. Along with the stealth-plated design, computerized vibration sensors instantly made adjustments to quiet the thrumming sound of the turbine.

The sound and sight reductions made the scout and attack helicopters formidable vehicles for insertion and exfiltration of covert troops, as well as Medevac in case the operation went bust.

For now the pilots were taking no chances. They were hanging back, waiting for the right time to come in—nightfall—when the risk of being detected was closer to zero and it was too late for the detectors to do anything about the warbirds.

But even at that distance the helicopters were still able to transmit intelligence from the satellite and high-altitude recon planes Hal Brognola had tasked to the Everglades mission.

The high-resolution images on Bolan's screen showed a landing strip carved out of the hammock in the middle of two strips of waterway. And moving along the landing strip were several man-size signatures furiously working away at last-minute preparations. The Cracker Corps soldiers were moving away the last bit of brush they had used to camouflage the strip from above.

Bolan studied the screen, checking the spiderweb of waterways to see if any hostile craft were moving their way. But the smugglers' boats were still beached near the end of the runway, waiting for cargo.

There were two major waterways that split around the hammocks, making it easy for the strike team to get there, and just as easy to be spotted by the Crackers if they went in too early.

The wider stretch of water was on the southeast side of the landing zone. Armand Cane and a couple of black-clad customs agents were encamped on the far side of the water, waiting for a chance to move into the hammock.

Bolan was on the western perimeter, separated from the hammock by a serpentine waterway that wound toward a saw-grass-splintered expanse of water near the hammock.

It wouldn't take him long to get there when the time came. The dull green Zodiac raft was up on the bank beneath the heavy green brush. Its nose was slanted toward the water, just like the gators that had taken up sentry duty along the banks, sitting there and waiting until the right prey came along.

Hopefully that prey wouldn't include anyone from the strike team.

Bolan kept his eyes moving around the swamp, partly to check for signs of Cracker intruders and partly for any sign of gators moving. That was the eeriest part about waiting out in the swamp. He'd seen several eight- or nine-footers already and couldn't help wondering how many he *hadn't* seen.

Under these circumstances the swamp was definitely not a pleasant place to be, Bolan thought. But it was the only place to be if they were going to take down the Cracker Corps.

Bolan looked up when he heard the unmistakable sound of an airplane flying into the zone.

Its drone grew louder as it approached the rendezvous point. And then it came into view, a small, solidly built cargo plane that flew almost directly overhead before veering toward the landing strip.

The plane skimmed over the tops of the trees and made a quick pass over the landing strip, cutting its speed to scout out the terrain below.

The sound of the struggling engine diminished as

it banked to the right and circled over the swamp-land, moving slow and wide.

From his sheltered observation post, Bolan watched the silvery bird make two more passes, sil-houetted against the darkening sky, before it came in for its final approach.

Plumes of smoke trailed behind the plane as it slowed and vanished from sight, heading toward the strip of level ground hacked out from the trees.

Bolan dug his feet into the bank and pushed the Zodiac raft forward, jumping into it as the nose dropped into the water. The heavy thrumming of the plane would provide enough cover for him to get nearer to the hammock.

The inflatable glided silently across the water, bringing the Executioner almost within striking dis-tance.

"HOLD TIGHT," Scofield shouted as the wheels of the aircraft touched down on the erratic landing strip.

"No shit," Slater said, teeth snapping shut as the plane took a hard bounce. The lush green hammock that looked so inviting from up above had suddenly turned into a blur of chopped-down trees and a gauntlet of panicked men waving their beacon flash-lights wildly as they scattered out of the way, trip-ping over one another and the brush that flanked the strip.

One of the wheels clunked hard against a dip in the ground and temporarily snagged on some branches.

But the plane had enough weight to maintain its balance. That plus Scofield's calm grip of the con-trols kept them from flipping end over end. He'd landed in far worse and managed to arrive all in one piece.

The cargo plane zigged and zagged down the runway, bearing to the right of the strip where one of the wings almost beheaded a heavyset man who was waving his flashlight.

Scofield gradually slowed the plane and continued heading toward the end of the hammocks where the airboats were gathered.

Slater kept his eyes on the groups of rough-looking men moving along both sides of the strip. The irregulars from the Cracker Corps carried a variety of hunting rifles, pistols and automatic weapons. Even without the firepower, they were a scary bunch.

But Slater was more concerned with men he couldn't see. He looked past the men into the woods, searching for signs of a force deadlier than the Cracker Corps.

They were vulnerable now. If an attack was going to come, this would be an ideal time.

"How's it look?" Scofield said.

"Can't see a thing," he said, "yet..."

THE EXECUTIONER PUSHED the oar silently through the water and guided the raft through the tree-lined slough. Clouds of insects settled over the water, dancing in chaotic whirlpools.

He passed through the stinging mist, keeping his head low and listening for any unusual sounds in the woods.

But he heard nothing other than the usual scurrying of four-legged night creatures making their rounds through the swamps.

It was safe—at least for the moment.

He'd used the silent-running motor to power the

Zodiac raft halfway toward the hammock, sure that no one would hear the quiet engine while the first plane was thrashing its way through the landing strip.

But he cut the engine as he grew closer to the encampment. Silence was relative when it came to these engines.

When an inflatable was making a coastal sortie, the engine could barely be heard over the waves and pounding surf that provided steady cover. But out here in a swamp with its occasional lulls, even at relatively low speeds the engine could be detected. At high speeds it would be a dead giveaway, especially combined with the sound of the wake it cut through the water.

Bolan continued on his way, making steady progress toward his destination.

Dusk was giving way to twilight.

As Bolan wound closer to the hammock the trees all around him took on a gnarled and ghostly hue. They were full of shadows at first, but gradually the forest became an impenetrable darkness.

Night had come at last.

And with it came the recon helicopters, which were airborne once again, sending real-time video to the unit in the front of the raft. Bolan looked down at the green screen.

It was almost like looking at a video game, he thought, but here the players were flesh and blood and the end of the game usually meant the end of life. With the screen mapping out the terrain, the Executioner avoided the risk of stumbling blindly into an outpost.

The night-vision cameras on the choppers were gyro-stabilized and provided television-news-quality pictures to Bolan's monitor, which showed the strip and several glowing man-size images clustering around the plane.

Bolan could also see the position of Armand Cane on the far side of the hammock. He, too, was waiting for the right moment to strike.

There were several strange images on both sides of the landing strip that immediately attracted Bolan's attention. The images also attracted the attention of the pilot of the Bravo helicopter, who raised the Executioner and Cane on the radio.

"We're picking up additional signatures in the target zone," the pilot said.

The voice in Bolan's headset drew his attention to some infrared signatures flanking the landing strip. "Signatures are shifting from body paint to rat scans. Looks like we've got some extra company on the ground—make that *underground.* Do you copy?"

Bolan clicked his response and studied the screen, focusing on the shifting images. Sometimes the human-sized electronic signatures were clearly painted on the screen, as the pilot indicated. Other times the signatures seemed to shrink to the size of muskrat or other small creatures.

That meant they were moving in and out of cover. However many men appeared on the screen, there were obviously a lot more hidden away in some type of bunker. The Cracker Corps had prepared an ambush for them.

A good one, too, Bolan thought, if they walked right down the middle and opened fire on the Crackers. But a frontal assault would be a suicidal one. They had another entrance planned.

Darkness provided the perfect screen for the smuggling operation. But it also provided the perfect backdrop for a night attack. With every second that passed, the night fighters were getting closer to their target.

CREEDY'S MEN POURED out of the woods like wolves as the plane taxied across the high grass and angled toward the boats that were lined up along the shore of the hammock.

The half-dozen airboats were hidden by green foliage that draped them from view as they bobbed lazily in the water.

There was enough room at the end of the T-shaped hammock for two small cargo planes to be off-loaded. But there was also too much forest at this end of the strip to take off safely.

Scofield pulled sharply on the control yoke to swing the tail around and get the plane in position in case they had to make a rapid exit. The twin-engine Embraer turned slowly as the wheels sliced through the clutching high grass. Finally the nose of the plane was facing the opposite direction from when it landed.

Scofield relaxed a bit. Even in the twilight he could see the far end of the strip where the hammock ended in a dropoff. Bordered by a wide strip of water, the swampland runway had enough free space for the plane to make its climb.

"Look at them all," Slater said, trying to count the armed men who were running towards them across the field.

And then Slater noticed a few of them who were climbing halfway out of some jagged trenches cut into the ground. Brush and freshly cut trees had been carefully arranged to cover the trenches. And now through the foliage, several heads were poking out to get the plane in sight...and maybe in their sights.

"Christ!" Slater said. "It's like an anthill. They're all over the place."

"Just what the man ordered," Scofield said. "Enough good ol' boys to do some real damage."

"To who?" Slater asked. "What if this is some kind of rip-off? Trying to make a quick score. I don't like the odds."

Scofield laughed. "You don't like anything. Besides, it's not like we came here empty-handed. They move against us, they're dead."

"So are we," Slater said. "Man, we get paid to fly, not to die."

"Then stay alive," Scofield said, looking out the windscreen as a dozen men split up on both sides of the plane.

The Cracker Corps swarmed all around the plane, alternately carrying weapons, ropes and crowbars. Some of them dragged plastic skids that slid easily across the high grass.

A few of the men rapped on the doors on the side of the plane, eager to off-load the cargo they'd been waiting for.

But Scofield was being cautious.

He pushed open the cabin door and leaned out of the doorway to look over the reception committee. The first man he recognized was a beefy-looking giant in jeans, sweat-stained T-shirt and a sleeveless denim vest with enough hooked pockets and flaps to carry an arsenal.

It was Creedy, the leader of the Cracker Corps, and he was on edge, a few hundred pounds of energy about to explode.

"Come on, let's get moving," Creedy bellowed. The cry was immediately taken up by several of his men.

"Not yet," Scofield shouted, gesturing with his hand for them to calm down as he scanned the crowd for another familiar face. But the man he was looking for was nowhere in sight. Not a good sign. "Where's LeBrun?"

"We don't need *him* to unload," Creedy said.

"Maybe you don't," Scofield said, "but we do. This thing just isn't going to happen until we see our boy."

Slater stood behind the pilot, gun hand by his side as he looked out at the off-loading crew. He was moving from side to side, cursing under his breath and ready to fire at the slightest provocation.

In the back of the plane four of Scofield's men also stood by the cargo doors, holding their weapons, ready to open the doors and spring into action if they had to.

"You never needed him before," Creedy said. "What's the matter? Don't you trust us?"

"Sure, I do," Scofield said. "Most of the time. But this run's special. We both know that. Need's special handling."

Creedy swore and looked all around him, upset at the challenge to his authority in front of his men. In the past LeBrun had let him handle the contacts for the off-loads. He was equally upset that there was no sign of LeBrun. He'd lost track of him during the landing.

"Let's do them," Slater urged. "Before they do us." His voice was meant to be a whisper, but it came off louder than he'd expected and didn't quite hide the panic he was feeling. Slater was always like this before a deal went down, feeling like a target in a shooting gallery, with Scofield handing out free rifles to anyone who wanted to take a shot. "This doesn't feel right. Where the hell is Claude?"

"That's what I'm going to find out," Scofield said. "Just sit tight." He could sense the man's growing tension. It almost matched his own. Scofield just managed it better.

Acting unconcerned, Scofield turned back toward the broad-shouldered and grim-eyed leader of the Cracker Corps. "Well?" he said. "Where the hell is LeBrun?"

"Right here," LeBrun replied. His voice came from the shadows as he walked into the open, waving an automatic rifle in front of him. He was dressed in woodland camouflage, jungle green khaki with tree-bark patterns around it.

Same color as the swamp.

He'd probably been standing near them all along, Scofield thought, shaking his head. "We were getting worried, Claude. Sure took your sweet time."

"Always do," LeBrun said. "Just making one last recon of the area."

"How's it look?" Scofield said.

"Safe as milk."

"All right, then let's do it!" he shouted to the rest of his crew in the back of the plane.

A few seconds later the cargo door slid open, revealing a four-man squad with automatic rifles cradled in their arms. One of the men flipped a ramp to the ground. It landed in the grass with a loud whump that echoed over the hammock before digging into the soil.

Scofield's crew began to toss and slide crates down the ramp. The cocaine bricks were packed into small wooden lockers, and the bales of marijuana were wrapped and taped in waterproof plastic sheets.

In recent years the price of smoke had climbed to where it was worthwhile to bring it in again, keeping the ultimate customers satisfied and keeping the distribution network in place.

LeBrun and Scofield watched from the side as the ground team did its work, scrambling back and forth from the plane in well-practiced motions. Creedy's men carried some of the crates and snagged others with hooks and crowbars as they dragged them toward the skids.

Three men then pulled the weighted-down skids toward the airboats, where a two-man crew stacked them into the flat-bottomed hull.

As the unloading continued, LeBrun stepped away from the plane, idly looking around him. He walked past the trenches where the backup squad waited.

It was easy for him to spot the ambush sites, mainly because he knew their location. Someone new to the area might not be so lucky, he thought. The entrenched gunmen could present a fatal surprise to any attacking force. As long as they were ready.

From his past experience, LeBrun suspected that the ambushers had probably lost their edge. They'd been waiting for someone to come in firing. But now that there was no one for them to spring their trap on, they were falling into a dangerous state.

In their minds the danger had passed.

LeBrun drifted toward the trench on his right where there was enough moonlight for him to make out the shapes gathered below ground level. He leaned over and said, "Keep alive."

Some brush rustled near the edge of the trench as one of the men cursed and another one shouted back up at him. "Good advice, Claude. See if you can do the same."

Creedy's rank and file had no special regard for him. In fact, he could imagine that one or two rifles might even be pointed at him in idle threat.

That was the problem, LeBrun thought. They weren't professionals and had allowed themselves to become idle spectators, maybe even congratulating themselves for getting out of the hard work of off-loading the drugs.

"It's not over yet," LeBrun cautioned. "Unless you stay on your guard it will be all over *for you.*"

LeBrun continued down the grassy runway to where a handful of Creedy's men were stationed. They were holding their long flashlights at their sides, ready to turn on the beacons when the next plane arrived.

Scofield's flights always came in threes.

Two of the planes would be loaded with cargo. In case one of them crashed and burned or was taken by the DEA, the other one might still make it through.

The third plane would act as a decoy or, if necessary, carry whatever cargo didn't fit in the first two planes. But its main task was to ferry reinforcements in case the lead planes ran into trouble.

LeBrun walked around the perimeter, stepping softly through the woods. The swamp seemed welcoming, a refuge where nothing could go wrong. But the night was still young, and he still expected something to happen.

He had a feeling, the kind he used to have when he went into enemy-occupied territory.

But this night, he was the enemy. This was his territory. If any intruders dared to trespass, they weren't going to make it out.

LeBrun was about to make another quick tour of

the hammock when one of the men behind him shouted, "There it is."

LeBrun looked behind him and saw several men running through the field to take up their positions. Seconds later a half-dozen flashlight beams sliced through the night, marking both sides of the landing strip.

And up above came the second plane, a dark silhouette painted against an even darker sky. LeBrun could just about make out its shape as it whined above the field.

The pilot was making a test run to check out the strip to see if there was any trouble below and to get radio confirmation from Scofield.

The sound of the plane's engines receded as it banked to the right, making another pass before coming in for a landing.

THE EXECUTIONER WAITED in the shadows at the western edge of the hammock as the second plane rolled across the grass toward the far end of the airstrip.

The first plane was almost empty now, and the second aircraft was rolling into position at the end of the T-shaped hammock.

It was time to strike.

If Bolan waited much longer, his luck might not hold out. Under cover of the second plane's engines, he had moved up and down the edge of the hammock, reconning the enemy's positions and unloading his ordnance along the jagged and murky shoreline.

The inflatable had more than accomplished its original purpose, serving as a floating weapons platform that got the Executioner and his gear in place.

Now it was time for the craft to play an even greater role.

Bolan locked the steering lever in place, kicked up the throttle, then lifted off the brake as he dived into the high grass.

His feet splashed into the water before he scrambled totally onto the land. By then the inflatable was roaring down the waterway, its engine sounding loud and clear as it plowed through the water, running parallel to the hammock.

The pilot of the second plane had killed the engines, and the inflatable was the only thing moving or making a sound.

All activity had stopped for a few seconds, time enough for the Cracker Corps to realize that something was coming for them after all.

Then all hell broke loose.

Even before Creedy and LeBrun gave the order to fire, the gunmen nearest the edge of the hammock had dropped into kneeling positions and trained their weapons toward the sound.

A stream of autofire ripped across the field and over the water. The first volleys flew high in the air, striking the forest on the other side of the water.

By then, more men were running across the hammock, opening up with everything that they had.

Several machine-gun bursts chopped into the swamp, and a shotgun blast echoed across the water like a cannon.

Confused by their own fire and the inflatable coursing through the water, the traffickers fought a pitched battle with the unknown.

Sheer numbers and angles of attack finally produced a result, bullets ripping into the dark inflatable and blowing it out of the water. The gas tanks erupted, and a fireball rolled out over the water, reflecting on the faces of the irregular army.

Most of them had cycled through several clips and had to reload, while others hurried to the edge of the hammock, searching for their vanquished foe.

The Executioner was ready to commence firing.

CHAPTER EIGHT

The boat was dead, but the explosive charges Mack Bolan had planted in the ground were live as soon as he pressed the button on the pocket-sized remote-control device in his palm.

The first string of radio-activated C-4 plastique charges went off like mortars at the feet of the Cracker Corps.

Streams of white-hot fire ripped through the men who were closest to the edge of the hammock, turning their momentary cries of triumph into cries of death as they fell back from the blasts and landed in the tall grass.

The concussive force of the shaped explosives sent a shock wave through the underworld army, rolling across the field with a loud, rumbling echo.

The second line of gunmen was standing in the field in a state of shock. One moment they'd been hypnotized by the inflatable going up in flames, not realizing that they'd shot up a decoy. The next moment they were watching their friends shredded by white-hot bits of metal.

Bolan keyed in the next sequence on the remote detonator, then pressed the blast button a second time.

Another explosion lit up the swamp and poured streams of flame into the remaining line of gunmen.

One man was lifted off the ground, screaming from the sudden agony that ripped through him. But by the time he landed in the tall grass, his voice had stopped. Death had claimed him before he could even register what was happening.

Several other gunners were caught in the open, some of them escaping the full force of the blast because they'd staggered backward after the first explosion had been triggered. Others already stood outside of the immediate blast area.

The sudden wall of flame that gusted across the swamp produced a chain reaction throughout the surviving members of the Cracker Corps. Their first instinct was to run for cover; their second was to reload and open fire as fast as they could on the imagined source of destruction.

Once again there were no human targets, but there were plenty of bullets flying through the swamp.

Bolan kept his head down. He was lying low about fifty yards down the hammock on a small incline. Any gunfire that came his way burned the air above him. For now he was safe. But if they came closer, he was out of luck. The numbers on the other side were still too great.

From the opposite side of the field near the planes, he heard several men shouting commands.

"Over there, over there. By the water!"

"Go, go, go. Move now!"

The Executioner pocketed the remote detonator. There was still one string of explosives set on another frequency, but that could serve as a last line of defense in case he got hemmed in. He could always make a last stand behind the picket line of hellfire.

A grasping halo of brush rustled around the soldier's shoulders as he inched forward. Damp and disintegrating leaves clung to his face as he moved slowly and carefully, like some primordial creature rising from the swamp to study the predators in its domain.

From that angle Bolan couldn't see all of the action. It meant exposing himself to more risk, but he had to know what was coming so he moved forward, hugging the ground.

Sharp stalks of saw grass slashed at his skin as he moved up to level ground where he could scan the field through the hand-held thermal imager.

Several shapes were lit up in the green screen.

On the opposite side of the hammock, two groups of men trampled through the grass, sprinting from the off-loading area near the planes. While part of the flight crew supervised the off-loading, this part was responsible for securing the landing zone or, in this case, preparing a counterattack.

The first group ran parallel to the tree line. They had an assortment of automatic weapons, and they looked like they knew how to use them. Maybe they weren't in their prime, but they'd obviously had considerable training in the past.

Bolan could tell by the way they moved that they were professionals, but what they were doing was so logical that he guessed their plan immediately.

They would run down the side of the forest, then fan out and move toward the water's edge where Bolan was hidden, safely spacing themselves behind the second group that was already starting to fan out across the airstrip.

It was a good plan except for one thing. They hadn't taken into consideration the possibility of more than one point of attack. The explosions had focused all of their attention on this side of the hammock.

Soon there would be a lot more than one man for them to deal with.

The second group moved like glowing apparitions through the tall grass, crouching behind cover, lying low and aiming low, ready to cut down anything in their path.

At least a dozen rifle barrels pushed back the stalks of grass and nosed through the briar patches, like hunters beating the brush for prey.

The prey was busy watching the predators, figuring how much time he had before his situation was critical. These were dangerous men, Bolan realized, experienced fighters who had come here expecting to make contact.

Almost as dangerous, but in a different manner, were the Cracker Corps gunmen who were still doing their shooting, seeing enemies everywhere and firing their weapons nowhere in particular. It was a lead-filled lottery, with bursts of full-auto fire that could accidentally hit something.

Bolan swept the imager slowly across the field, moving back and forth until he located the bunkers he'd seen highlighted on the monitor. He could make out some shapes but not many.

They were still in the shelters, probably thanking their stars that they missed the action and were being held in reserve.

Their luck would change soon, Bolan thought as he held the pistol grip of the M-16 against his shoulder. Equipped with the underslung M-203 40 mm grenade launcher, the multipurpose combat weapon offered a variety of strategic explosive rounds: air burst, high explosive, armor piercing, riot control, smoke and illumination.

In the right hands the combination assault rifle and grenade launcher could turn a soldier into a one-man army.

It was in the right hands now.

Bolan flipped up the quadrant sight, adjusted it for the nearest bunker, then pulled the launch-tube trigger.

The low-velocity air-burst round thumped out of the M-203 and sailed across the hammock toward the bunker.

And suddenly the safe haven turned into an inferno. The high-explosive round went off just as it sailed above the trench.

A cloudburst of fiery rain streamed down onto the bunker, immediately flushing out any survivors. The wounded gunmen erupted from the dugout like hornets, but this time they were the ones who were stung.

Bolan rolled over to his right, moving down the bank once again in case anyone zeroed in on the direction the air-burst round had come from.

The Executioner slid the launch barrel forward, then slapped it back to lock in another 40 mm round. Using his bearings from before, he rose to a crouch just long enough to fire another air-burst round toward the second bunker. He kept on moving, rolling down the bank again after catching a brief glimpse of the grenade going off near its target.

The second round had struck home, but it also attracted the attention of the hunting parties that were moving across the landing strip. With an almost simultaneous movement, the crews from the plane swung toward Bolan's position and concentrated their fire.

Lead singed the air over his head and whipped through the saw grass.

He could hear the grass thwacking from the onslaught all around him, cut into pieces by full autofire. Some of the rounds pounded into the ground just in front of his position and sent up volcanic clumps of dirt.

The gunfire grew closer as the marchers hurried to cover the distance toward their enemy.

But the smuggling crew had a lot more to worry about than the Executioner as two quiet-rotor helicopters streamed down from the sky.

They'd been lying low until now, waiting to carry out their choreographed moves. The helicopters split left and right as they approached the hammock, the drumbeats of the rotors stirring the grass at the edge of the water.

"Alpha Bird to Belasko, stay low, stay low—we're coming in."

The voice from the lead pilot in Bolan's headset was immediately followed by a voice from the second helicopter on the far side of the hammock, which was coming in just over Armand Cane's position.

"Bravo Bird to Biker, stay low. We're commencing the light show."

Each chopper unleashed a stream of rockets toward the field as they followed the waterways like a road map.

Twin SNEB rocket launchers were mounted on each side of the aircrafts' weapons platform, holding up to twenty-two 68 mm rockets.

The multidart rockets poured down into the middle of the field like lightning bolts. Row after row of explosions scythed through the grass, finding targets in every direction.

The whooshing rocket fire decimated the men in the bunkers as it ripped right down through the earthworks.

The helicopters continued on their maneuvers, flying low over the treetops with their lights out. Each attack craft flew in a half loop that took them to the opposite side of the field.

As soon as they were in position, the choppers fired illumination rockets at the battlefield.

The fire-spitting missiles streaked across the sky before dropping daylight onto the swamplands.

The darkness retreated instantaneously as artificial incandescence painted the sky a brilliant and blinding white. It looked like a high-powered sun had fallen into the midst of the traffickers, silhouetting their shapes against the light like pop-up targets.

Stunned first by the rockets and then by the light, they were unprepared for any kind of firefight—especially one that came out of the darkness at the southeastern edge of the hammock.

Sudden flashes of flame punctured the night as Armand Cane rose from the brush like a grim reaper and triggered a full-auto blast from his CAR-15 rifle. The veteran undercover man dropped back out of sight long enough to slap another magazine into the assault rifle.

The customs agents who came in with him picked up the slack and unloosed a burst at the sun-struck targets. The synthetic daylight added to their panic, making them realize how vulnerable they were.

After the opening volleys, Cane's small rifle team staggered their fire. There was always someone from their team firing a sweeping burst across the field while others had to change their magazines.

The sustained fusillade cut into the standing men like scythes through dry grass. Caught in the wide-open killing field, the smugglers could barely return fire as their ranks were thinned yet again.

Cane and his men emptied several more magazines before dropping back down out of sight.

And then the Cracker Corps poured hundreds of rounds through the woods toward Cane's position, creating havoc for a minute before they realized no one was firing back at them.

Their quarry was either dead, or they would soon face an attack from another quarter.

SCOFIELD STEPPED AWAY from the water's edge, where a thicket of mangrove trees had offered the airboats some cover.

The cocaine flier had been with LeBrun and Creedy when the helicopters struck. He'd been figuring the best way to get out of there if things got close—airboat or airplane—when the choppers had made their run.

After the brutal pounding from above, Scofield couldn't help thinking that maybe there was no way out of there.

Slow-motion shock had taken over the survivors of the attack, dazed by the destruction that had been visited upon them.

The air assault was over almost as quickly as it had begun, but then came the high-wattage rockets and the sudden ground attack from the south. That had also ended suddenly—after doing its damage to the men stalking through the field. Now smoke and embers drifted over the landing strip, which had become a cemetery in progress.

It was like almost every action had been anticipated. Whoever was moving against them had every inch of war ground covered.

Scofield's army wasn't outnumbered, but it certainly was outmaneuvered. And judging from the skittish quality of the Cracker Corps, he couldn't expect things to get much better.

It took every inch of Creedy's mammoth frame to keep his men in line. They wanted to make a run for it in the airboats and get out while they could. Creedy made them stay, convincing them the only way out was to dig in and take care of the attackers.

Two of Creedy's men refused to leave the boats and looked up at him as if he'd gone insane.

"What are we supposed to kill?" one of them said. "Ghosts?" The man had a long bushlike beard, massive arms that hauled crate after crate from the plane—and a thick hand that held a sawed-off shotgun as if it were a toy. "Can't see them, can't shoot them, Creedy. We're going."

LeBrun stepped to the edge of the hammock and looked down at the men in the boat with cold eyes and his 165-round Ilarco subgun. Then he nodded his head toward the waterway where the nose of the airboat was pointed. "How far do you think you'd get if you went now?"

"He's right," Creedy said. "They've got the water covered."

"I'm not talking about *them*," LeBrun explained, waving the barrel of the rifle. "I'm talking about me."

The man with the customized shotgun looked enraged, but he carefully pointed the barrel away from

LeBrun. "You going to let him talk to me like that?" he shouted up to Creedy.

"Out of the boat," Creedy said. "Talking's better than dying."

The men got out. The revolt was over. For now.

Scofield glanced over the hammock toward the Embraer aircraft, wondering if he'd have a revolt of his own on his hand. It was impossible to tell what men would do when they came under fire.

As Scofield headed toward the plane where his copilot waited, he heard several men calling out to one another to see who was still in one piece and who was gone for good.

There were a lot of unanswered cries to the deathly roll call.

A few men called out Scofield's name as he passed by, men he'd brought with him and men from the Cracker Corps who'd seen him deliver the goods on several other runs. They were looking to him for guidance.

And for confidence. He didn't have any left, but he still had to fake it if he wanted to make it out of here.

Scofield was the pilot, the battle-seasoned pro, the man with the swagger and the man with the swag. And most of all, he was the one who had led them into this maelstrom.

But Scofield didn't know what to do. Not yet.

For this run, not only was he supposed to make the drop, but he was supposed to make the kill. It was up to him and LeBrun to take out whoever was dogging Quinn's operations.

Both LeBrun and Scofield had been instructed to bring enough men and matériel to pull it off.

But now half of the men were gone, and the ones

who were left standing had burned off most of their ammunition.

The smart thing to do would be to run, but then Scofield would be on the run forever. Not just from men he left behind, but from the man who'd been calling the shots all these years.

Scofield had to stick it out, but first he had to figure it out.

The helicopters had vanished into the darkness, and there were no telltale sounds of their rotors, so it was impossible to tell how far away they'd gone or when they were coming back.

And it was just as difficult to figure out how many men were somewhere out there in the darkness.

But he knew what was out there—stone-cold soldiers who could conduct an operation.

Even now Scofield could be in someone's sights.

He swore and kept on moving toward the plane where Slater was pacing like a guard dog ready to lash out at the enemy, except the enemy wasn't co-operating. The enemy was staying in hiding, killing them long-distance.

"Come on," he shouted to Slater.

"Jumping Christ Incarnated!" Slater shouted as he looked over the rocket-strafed swampland and the clusters of machine-gunned men. "Where the hell do you want to go?"

"There," Scofield said, pointing toward the field. "We can't wait for them to come and get us."

Slater followed the direction of Scofield's hand. Grass was smoldering and men lay dying. Out there was no-man's-land, and Scofield wanted to be his personal guide through it.

Slater leaned back against the empty cargo plane, supporting himself against the fuselage. He knew the plane made too good a target for whoever launched the attack against them. But Slater couldn't abandon it just like that.

The plane had flown them in and out of tight situations before, and in his mind it had become a gargantuan good-luck piece.

Like most pilots he had certain superstitions about flying and surviving. As long as he stayed faithful to the plane, it would stay faithful to him.

Scofield saw him hanging back. "Move it, Slater," he shouted. "You've got to stick close to me. In case we have to bail, I want you with me."

"What about the others?" Slater asked. "We can't leave without them." He and Scofield went by the same simple rule—you went in together and you went out together. That's why all of the men had been willing to fly with Scofield run after run. He'd taken care of them.

Until now.

"So help me find them," Scofield said.

"Who's going to guard the plane?"

Scofield shook his head and looked back at the two men who had just helped off-load the cargo. They were in a rigid stance, gripping weapons and staring into the night.

"I don't think we can guard it now. Not until we find out what's out there."

"Death's out there, Scofield," Slater said, looking at the field. "And lots of it."

But both men headed into the field.

It was hard for Scofield to tell, but it seemed as if most of the wounded men were part of the Cracker Corps, not the men he'd brought with him from Puerto Rico. He stepped across a body sprawled out on the ground, and paused to look down at the man's face.

It was Leo Garmancia, one of Scofield's hand-picked men. He'd been blown to pieces during the rocket attack, and now his smooth-shaved face and his neck were about the only part of his body not covered by blood.

The rockets had shredded him.

Scofield continued to move forward with a Heckler & Koch submachine gun at his hip. He wanted a target to fire at, but his training kept him in check. Wasting ammo was a good way to get wasted.

Besides, it was quiet now. Uneasily so. After the furious attack, the lull played on everyone's nerves, making them wonder what was coming next and where it was coming from.

Scofield looked up at the sky for signs of another helicopter attack, but they were out of sight. The stealth aircraft were never out of mind, however.

"See anything?" Slater asked as he rustled through the grass beside him.

"Nothing good," Scofield replied. "Too many casualties."

"Whose?"

"Ours. Half the men we sent out here didn't make it. The other half—who knows?"

Slater nodded. Though he seemed nervous as his scarecrow shape wandered through the brush, he was still ready to strike.

The holster flap to his automatic pistol was open, and a 9 mm Spectre submachine gun was clutched firmly in his hand.

The solidly built weapon had a large 50-round stick magazine and was a serious piece of well-machined metal that worked like a jackhammer, steadily pounding away until the target broke.

The maneuverable and reliable Spectre was another good-luck piece for Slater. Fifty rounds bought a lot of time in a firefight, enough to keep alive if the other man couldn't keep up the rapid-fire exchange.

Scofield stopped suddenly and turned in a half circle. So far they'd been heading toward the southern edge of the hammock, which made him think that perhaps the attackers had moved into the woods on the east. By now they had plenty of time to move out.

Unless they were hit in the last brief exchange.

"Wish the bastards would show themselves," Scofield said.

"Don't count on it," Slater replied as his eyes pierced the gloom. "This isn't a cop shop we're fighting."

"Right," Scofield agreed. "This is military."

"Paramilitary, military. It's all the same," Slater said. "They're not here to arrest us. And we're not going to roll over them like they're some band of peasants with pistols."

Scofield nodded. In the drug wars they'd had their share of run-ins with competing cartel outfits, many of them little more than farmers-turned-fighters or perhaps criminals turned commandos. But in those encounters Scofield's people had always come out on top.

It had been a matter of training and skill in those cases.

Most of Scofield's people had military backgrounds and had seen a lot of combat. When that kind of experience was pitted against untrained enemies, the cohesive fighting force easily outguessed and maneuvered them.

But right now it was Scofield's people who didn't know what to expect. The alliance hadn't been thought out well. Other than showing up with a lot of guns, the Cracker Corps and the drug-running air force hadn't figured out a plan of attack.

As he stepped deeper into the tall grass, Scofield had a feeling that this time *he* was the one who was outclassed and outthought.

And out of luck. The feeling was reinforced seconds later by another unwelcome sound permeating the swamp.

The whine of high-speed airboats cut through the night. From the sound that seemed to echo from all directions, Scofield knew there were several boats moving fast on both sides of the hammock.

Others heard the sound of the airboats surging through the water, and it was like a siren that warned the traffickers the end was near. More nails in the coffin were coming their way.

The first attack had come from land, the second from air and now the third and possibly last attack was coming from water.

They were coming in for the kill.

Scofield pointed toward a clump of brush that covered a small rise close to the waterway. "Let's get over toward the water."

"Let's get the hell out of here," Slater countered, but he was already moving toward the edge of the hammock.

By now several other gunmen were weaving through the tall grass. If nothing else, they'd finally have a chance to see the enemy.

But just before the airboats came into view, another brace of illumination rockets seared through the night. The brilliant flares bombarded them with daylight once again.

Before Scofield and his men could concentrate on the assault force, several high-explosive rounds thumped into the hammock. The grenade-launched explosives came sailing in from the strips of woodland on the east and from the southern tip of the hammock, landing with ground-shaking force.

A trio of airboats materialized out of the smoke and mist, drifting over the water. Scofield recognized the thunderous blasts from an M-60 machine gun just before he saw the heavy weapon spitting fire from the starboard bow of the first airboat.

There was another M-60 mounted on the other side of the boat, making it a formidable double threat.

Two dark figures with assault rifles stood behind the machine gunners. Blue-jacketed customs agents loosed burst after burst from their automatic weapons, following a pattern established by the machine guns.

The first airboat veered toward the shoreline with telling effect as it pounded rivers of lead into the hammock. Scofield returned fire as best as he could, and heard his bullets plunking into the metal hull of the airboat, immediately followed by a scream. But there were so many people screaming and shouting, it was hard to tell which side had just lost a man.

Then he heard Slater cry out and thump into the brush.

"Slater! You hit?"

"Just parted my hair."

"That's some trick, man," Scofield told him. "It's short enough as it is. Let's pay the bastards back."

With one of the boats diverted from their counter-fire, Scofield and Slater had some more killing time of their own. They rose from their positions long enough to take aim at a second airboat.

Both men concentrated their fire at the speeding airboat just long enough to burn off the rest of their clips, the sustained bursts forcing the airboat to turn away, momentarily halting their attack.

The two drug runners dropped to the ground in tandem, elbows and knees digging into the soft, wet earth as they scuttled away from their position.

The response from the airboats was immediate. Tracer rounds climbed across the hammock toward the position Scofield and Slater had just vacated.

Then the airboat autofire swept across the hammock, seeking out remaining pockets of resistance as they made their strafing run.

For a few seconds both pilots had some breathing room, and they used the time to throw in fresh magazines.

Scofield had a few more clips, but Slater was down to his last fifty rounds. They couldn't hold much longer, not with the kind of firepower that was concentrating on them now.

Scofield's head jerked to the left when he heard another line of explosives going off, right where two of the braver men from Creedy's group had charged toward the water.

The men were firing with everything they had when they walked into the middle of a minefield.

They'd been after someone, Scofield realized. They'd probably spotted the enemy and saw a chance to get even. But instead, they ended up making a suicide run.

As the smoke and flame cleared, Scofield saw a black shape at the edge of the hammock—the man who'd initiated the attack. The drug runner triggered several rounds his way but had to dive to the ground again as a burst from an M-60 burned the air above his head.

Scofield rapped Slater on the shoulder, then gestured with his thumb toward the plane.

"It's time," he said. "Round up whoever's left."

"It's past time," Slater muttered as he backed away and looked over the battlefield. "No one's left by now, man. No one."

"We've got to look."

RIGHT AFTER HE HAD set off the last explosion, Mack Bolan dropped the remote detonator into a vest pocket and dived into the air just as the airboat driver maneuvered the craft within several feet of the hammock.

Subgun rounds had pounded into the water all around him while he was airborne, stretched out flat as a ladder.

As a wave of side spray from the airboat drenched him, the Executioner landed in the middle of the boat with his legs trailing in the water. He took a hard shot to the ribs from hitting the side of the boat, but with the adrenaline pumping he hardly noticed it.

Two pairs of hands caught him, then hauled him inside. The boat surged out into the water again and continued its assault.

CLAUDE LEBRUN EMERGED from the mangrove thicket like an apparition. He stood perfectly still, knowing his already camouflaged silhouette was made even more difficult to see by the hardwood trees that flanked him.

He waited until the airboat was almost coming on him before he fired the Ilarco.

The first thirty rounds chopped into the water and sliced harmlessly down into the muck at the bottom.

The second thirty rounds climbed up the boat, riddling the front hull in a deadly metal cadence and ripping into the man behind the M-60 machine gun, knocking him flat on his back.

LeBrun angled the weapon slightly and caught the second machine gunner, who fired several rounds high into the air as he fell away from his weapon. But the gunner managed to keep one hand on the trigger and still fired at the hammock.

Safely ensconced between the trees, LeBrun continued to spray lead, tracking the stream of lead until it chunked into the mounted M-60, finally knocking the gunner down for good.

With a slight pivoting motion LeBrun triggered a short burst that caught another of the raiders who crouched in the boat.

As the man fell back into the boat, LeBrun returned to cover.

He saw Creedy and a few of his other men firing at the airboats with unrelenting bursts. They'd taken a terrible pounding in their home territory. Now that they had a chance to strike back, they gave everything that had.

It was enough to temporarily hold off the airboat raiders and give the Cracker Corps some hope—until the second string of strike craft roared around from the far side of the hammock and charged at the drug-laden boats.

The first attack craft raced past the moored boats of the smugglers and raked the shoreline with autofire.

A heavyset smuggler sprawled flat in the boat and fired a sawed-off shotgun that lit the night with bright explosive flash. Other hardmen joined in, pouring rifle fire, pistol shots and subgun bursts into the attacking boats. Whatever Creedy's men had at hand was unloaded during the initial exchange.

By then, all the boats were in the water, slaloming around one another as the engines roared. Traffickers and their attackers found themselves in a race for survival.

Amid the confusion some of the drug runners slipped away into the spidery streams of water. The battlefield was shifting, expanding.

So was the chaos.

LeBrun saw one of the planes rolling across the field, lights out as it tried to build up speed.

All around him there was panic and death.

LeBrun kept low as he cut across the hammock and headed for the tree line and safety.

THE BOAT NO LONGER had a pilot.

A stream of autofire had knocked the customs agent who'd been steering the airboat off his perch in front of the propeller.

Bolan grabbed the lever and vaulted into the seat. He looked down at the fallen man and saw that he was still alive. The customs agent was most likely concussed, and hurting from the fusillade that had thwacked into his antiballistic vest, but he wasn't bleeding.

Bolan revved the engine as he pushed hard on the steering lever and rocketed the boat into the middle of the water.

Cold wind blasted against his face, and hot lead ripped through the air around him. Two customs agents were sitting in the boat, reloading their CAR-15s, and one gunner knelt behind the M-60.

The belt-fed machine gun had used up almost all of the ammo, but there was still a strip of metal left, enough to do some quick and serious damage.

Bolan scanned the swamp ahead. With the naked eye he could see flashes of metal and churning wakes of water, but it looked like a free-for-all from that distance. He eased up on the throttle so the boat could cruise along at a speed slow enough to allow him to lift the thermal imager hanging from his neck.

The small green screen swept quickly across the chaotic small-boat sea battle and gave Bolan a chance to pick out a target no one else had engaged yet.

He zoomed in on a crate-filled airboat with three heavyset figures aboard. The men were obviously part of the Cracker Corps, and they were bent on slipping through the net, crouching low as the airboat slashed through the patches of saw grass jutting from the water.

The tall stalks flattened beneath the airboat, then closed in around it after it passed. Only a narrow furrow remained to show the direction that the fugitives had taken.

"Over there!" Bolan shouted over the loud drone of the engine.

"Where?" roared the man closest to him.

Bolan pointed out the boat vanishing into the saw grass.

"Got him," the agent said, then tapped the man next to him several times and indicated their target.

In turn the other raider passed the signal to the gunner behind the M-60.

Now that they were all focused on the same

quarry, Bolan gunned the engine once more. Behind him the huge propeller fanned the hot, fetid air of the swamp as the airboat crashed through a floating field of saw grass.

Stalks slashed at their faces and broke all around them as they closed in on the fleeing traffickers, who were running low in the water.

Abruptly the saw grass fell away.

Both airboats rocketed into a widening stretch of water. Without any brush holding them back, the metal-hulled boats skimmed across the swamp as if they'd been fired from slingshots.

The fugitive boat was about thirty yards ahead, a bulky silhouette against the moonlit water. It was angling toward a spidery offshoot of the main waterway, but Bolan hung back on their left flank while his crew fired at the fleeing boat.

If the other boat cut in front of Bolan, it was dead.

The watercraft kept going straight, engine straining with the weight from the cargo and from the heavy men who were guarding it.

When streams of subgun fire came Bolan's way, he steered his craft over to the right and trailed in the wake of the airboat. The huge caged propeller of the fugitive vessel served as a bulky shield that prevented the enemy gunners from getting off clear shots.

The M-60 opened up, sending a spray of bullets climbing toward the back of the boat, but before it could strike home, the wide channel suddenly grew narrower. And the terrain grew wilder.

Mangrove roots coiled up out the dark water like fingers that grasped at the boats.

The high-speed hulls had no trouble skimming over or around the splintery wooden obstacles at first, but then the strip of water narrowed even more as it coursed around a sharp bend.

A tall, shadowy field of saw grass cordoned off the waterway.

It was a dead end.

The lead boat roared straight toward the landfall, cutting sharply at the last instant so the boat swung around and the gunners could catch Bolan's crew with a broadside volley.

Shotguns and subguns erupted from the traffickers' boat.

Instead of turning away from the attack and getting caught out in the open, Bolan gunned the airboat straight ahead and used the cushion of air to launch the craft onto the landfall. It was a split-second decision that the Executioner made without being consciously aware of it. Instinct that had been honed from years of battle took over.

The traffickers had decided to make their stand with a highly skilled maneuver that brought their boat to a dead stop.

But now they had to stand and die.

The nose of Bolan's airboat soared past the back of the trafficker's boat at a right angle, leaving them with nothing to shoot.

Bolan's crew chopped them down with sustained bursts as they hurtled by. Bullets ripped through the crates, into the hull and into the traffickers, knocking them toward the front of the boat. One mammoth-shouldered man with a pistol-grip shotgun had managed to turn slightly and fire a blast over Bolan's head.

But it was a futile maneuver.

The heavyset man was already dead, and the shotgun spun like a trinket from his large hands as he fell into the water.

It all happened in an instant, barely enough time for the man piloting the other boat to realize they were dead in the water unless he made some kind of move. He gunned the engine but then fell away, riddled by bullets.

The boat tipped over on its side from his awkward motion, dropping his corpse into the water with the other two corpses.

Bolan's airboat thumped into a waist-high fence of brush, plowed right through it, then rocketed over the grass as the engine wound down and the boat bounced off stunted mangrove trees. Thin branches hung down like tendrils that snared the propeller cage.

It felt as if he were riding a car with no tires across a jagged security grate.

Bolan managed to keep the boat heading straight until its speed slowed. Then, without the high speed keeping it moving like an arrow, it went out of control. It took one last hop, came down hard, then spilled the crew out onto the swampland.

"Anyone hurt?" Bolan asked as he and the others staggered to their feet and picked up their weapons.

"Not from bullets," one agent replied. "But that boat ride was something else."

Sounds from the distant hammock proved that the battle wasn't totally over yet. There were still echoes of automatic gunfire drifting over the water.

A few grenade-launched rounds pounded the hammock, followed by a much louder explosion. Then a volcano of fire scorched the air above the forest, pluming up into the sky.

One of the planes had been hit.

Bolan and the customs crew headed back to the edge of the water. One of the agents fired a colored flare over the forest to signal their position to the dark helicopters circling the battle zone.

SLATER RAN through the tall grass, staring in shock at the plane that was rolling across the tattered landing strip.

Behind him was the wreckage of one plane, a smoldering piece of metal spread out over the field. The fuselage was nearly torn inside out, and the landing gear had flown through the air before coming down and sticking into the ground like a spear. That was about all that was left intact.

The second plane was out of reach now. Even if Slater wanted to board the plane, he couldn't catch up to it.

He didn't want to get on it, though. The wraith-thin man wanted Scofield to get off it. It was a death trap.

The raiding party that had reduced the Cracker Corps and the pilots to ruins wasn't the kind of force to let anything escape untouched.

Scofield had to know that, even if he'd denied it to Slater, even if he'd begged him to get on board. He'd told him the two of them would fly out of this one like they'd flown away from so many before.

Not this time, Slater thought.

He stopped running in midfield and held his 9 mm Spectre at his side.

Off to his right he saw a couple of dark shapes approaching. A halo of brush surrounded their heads and upper torsos, remnants of the camouflage they'd used to filter across the hammock in the mop-up operation, taking prisoners or taking life depending on the resistance they met.

In the distance he could see other men pushing captured men before them. They were rounding up the survivors.

"Drop your weapon!" one of them shouted to Slater.

For a moment he thought he wouldn't, and he thought of firing at the man. But he knew there were others around. Too many of them to make Slater's bullets accomplish anything. He might as well fire a few rounds into his own head for all the good it would do.

Slater dropped his weapon to the ground.

The drug-running air force was finally grounded, Slater realized...except for Scofield. Slater held his arms over his head and looked at the plane while the raiders approached him.

ARMAND CANE CROUCHED at the incline on the southern edge of the hammock and watched the nose of the Embraer aircraft heading straight for him.

The twin-engined cargo plane rattled over the ground, bumping, rocking and shuddering as it wound its way along the smoky landing strip.

For a moment he didn't think it was picking up enough speed to get airborne, that instead it would just keep rolling right off the slightly raised lip of ground and take his head off.

But then the wheels rose off of the bumpy ground. The Embraer angled upward, and the roar of the twin engines battered him from above as the plane sailed over his head.

It was going to make it.

For about fifty yards.

The launch tube of the LAW 80 antitank weapon was extended, and the striker spring was cocked.

The weapon was armed, and Cane was ready.

He held the disposable tank-buster steady as the plane headed toward the trees on the other edge of the water.

It just had to clear the forest and it was gone.

Cane followed it through the weapon's sight, locking on to the belly of the plane, exhaling evenly as he pulled the trigger.

The 94 mm projectile streaked toward the plane, catching the metal underside just as it cleared the forest.

The bottom of the plane exploded, then set off the fuel tanks as the aircraft hung suspended in the air for a fleeting second.

Fire rained onto the forest as the plane cracked in two with an ungodly wrenching sound. Then the two halves made a scattered and flaming landing in the upper reaches of the forest canopy.

Bits and pieces of metal disintegrated in the sky before dropping into the forest.

Eddy Scofield was among the remnants, surrounded by a husk of metal that engulfed him like a glowing metal shroud as he came down to earth for the last time.

CHAPTER NINE

Nicholas Vreeland looked out the cockpit window of the aging Beech King aircraft and saw World War III breaking out down below.

Explosions lit up the Everglades.

Small-arms fire, tracer bullets and grenade blasts painted bright yellow-and-red flashes across the dark terrain. Airboats raced through the myriad waterways that splintered around the hammock.

As he made his approach, he leaned closer to the windscreen and tipped the visor of his baseball cap to the right to get a better look. He tried to raise Scofield on the radio.

But there was no answer.

The radio was dead, and most likely so were the radio operators.

Vreeland was forty-five years old, trim and sober after a long bout with bottles and barbiturates. He'd spent fifteen years in the Air Force and ten years in the drug trade.

It was enough time to prepare him for the devastation he saw below. It was the ultimate landscape that awaited all of them in that line of work.

Vreeland had flown into and out of danger zones for years in varying stages of battle. By now he could tell when the situation was hopeless, when it was insane to push your luck any further.

Such a time had come.

From this elevation it was like looking down on a war game, only it wasn't a game.

Smoke billowed up from the forest where the remnants of one of the planes were scattered across the treetops. The second plane was smoldering near the north end of the hammock, where a litter of airboats had also been grounded. Several bodies were scattered around the metal debris.

If Vreeland kept to his original flight pattern, he would have flown his crew right over the combination graveyard and junkyard below. And he would have probably ended up down there with the rest of the hulks.

His copilot, Dan McCall, a man with a linebacker's build and a bushy head of graying hair, looked out the windscreen with equal measures of dread and fascination. McCall had his usual flight uniform on—a holstered side arm, an antique tie-dyed T-shirt, cutoff shorts and hiking boots.

McCall had made the leap from military to paramilitary, and from there he made the relatively short jump into the trafficking trade. He'd climbed up the pay scale with each career move and, until now, figured it was easy money.

There'd been plenty of skirmishes and close calls in the past few years, but nothing to compare with this wasteland.

"We're too late," McCall said.

"The hell we are," Vreeland replied. "We came at the right time, man. Any earlier and *we'd* be down in that death trap."

"You mean we're not going in?"

Vreeland looked at the other man, unable to read his face. McCall was always like that, a cautious man who carefully weighed all of his options. It was impossible to tell what he was really thinking until he actually made his move. It was a good habit in poker. A bad habit if your life depended on his next move.

"Go ahead and grab a chute," Vreeland said. "You can do what you want. Anyone else can do the same."

"You serious?" McCall asked.

"This is a democracy, isn't it?"

"No, it's not," McCall said. "Not the way you run things, man. You might say it is, but you always get your way."

"Right," Vreeland said. "So shut up and live a bit longer. We're not going to help anybody by killing ourselves."

Vreeland pushed the yoke to the right and veered off over the mangrove forests, flying low and unseen. The dual Pratt & Whitney turboprops droned with a familiar roar as they carried the thirty-five-foot-long aircraft away from the battle.

A skilled pilot could have made a landing on the airstrip under normal conditions, but from what he had seen, the airstrip was bombed out and burning. If anyone was left down there, he was on his own.

He continued accelerating away from the conflagration, thanking the stars that they'd been delayed.

The third plane in Scofield's drug fleet had run into some rough weather that buffeted it about and caused it to fall a lot farther behind the others. Originally they'd intended to make staggered landings so all three of them wouldn't be bottled up at the same time.

The lead planes would off-load the cargo, get their

money and make their escape. If they ran into trouble, the backup plane was supposed to be right behind them.

But a thunderstorm had forced the Beech King off course. At the time, Vreeland thought it was his bad luck to get caught up in the tail end of a tropical storm sweeping over southern Florida. But now the rough weather seemed like a gift from the gods.

If Vreeland *had* arrived on time, the Beech King would have been buffeted by a lot more than rough winds.

There was no dissent from the rest of the crew about turning back. One glance through the windows was enough to convince them the operation was a bust. And even if they couldn't see any heat flying around the air right now, soon the sky would be crowded with customs, DEA or whatever other law was in the area.

The crew wanted to be long gone by then.

About ten miles east of Big Cypress Swamp, while Vreeland was flying low and slow over the treetops, the men in the back of the Beech King slid open the cargo doors.

As the air streamed into the cabin, the men started to push ten bales of marijuana they were carrying toward the door.

One by one the burlap-and-plastic-wrapped packages tumbled out the door and crashed into the upper reaches of the mangrove-and-hardwood forest.

Smoke bombs, the crew called them, as they watched the jettisoned sacks crash through the forest to the ground below or rip apart on spear-shaped branches. Pound after pound of Colombian hemp burst into the dank, lush foliage, spilling twigs and seeds in the watery fields, creating new cannabis patches that would never be harvested.

It was like casting money into the wind, but the smugglers really had no choice. If the plane got forced down by the law or ran into customs wherever they landed, there would be no quarter given.

They were part of an outlaw air force, and it wouldn't take much to connect them to Scofield's downed crews. Any dope on board would have cemented that connection.

But the third plane really wasn't there for ferrying drugs. The bales were strictly small change, a few leftovers that hadn't made it on the first two planes.

The real mission of the heavily armed crew was to fight. For that they carried a much deadlier cargo—grenades and subguns and rockets and automatic pistols.

Every man was experienced in their use, but now there was no one left to fight for. Nowhere to land.

They were in limbo, and every man knew it.

Both Vreeland and McCall fell silent as they flew east, away from the men whom they'd flown with all these years.

But there was something else on their minds. Regardless of why they had to turn back, they would soon have to answer to somebody who wouldn't like their answers.

Thomas Quinn.

It was no secret to many of the pilots whom they were really working for. It just wasn't spoken about very much, the same way superstitious people didn't like to mention vampires or demons, thinking that to speak their name was to invite them into their souls.

It was a bit late for that, Vreeland thought. Quinn already had their souls bought and paid for.

That was the way of the world, he knew. There were no saints in this business, but an awful lot of martyrs.

In the past Scofield had always dealt with Quinn. He was the one who made the deals and gathered together the crews.

Now Vreeland would have to deal directly with Quinn. The prospect almost made flying back into the battle zone look attractive.

Vreeland never liked to be around the ISS executive. The few times he'd been in his company with Scofield, Quinn had looked at Vreeland and the other mercenaries as if they were little more than machines to be programmed, maintained and eventually disposed of.

Until then, they were dogs of war to be sicced upon whomever Quinn wished. To question his judgment or refuse an assignment was to write your own death sentence.

Vreeland wasn't alone in his opinion of the well-connected captain of war. The few others who spoke of Quinn all had the same reaction. They were pawns on Quinn's chessboard, and he thought nothing of sacrificing them if it would advance his position.

The best thing Vreeland could do was to get his ass off the board.

Glancing over at his partner, he guessed that McCall was probably thinking about the same thing.

Then again, maybe McCall was thinking about how *he* could improve his position on the board.

They rode in silence for a while before McCall came out with it. "So what are you going to tell Quinn?"

"The truth," Vreeland stated.

"The truth!" McCall echoed. He smacked one

hand against his forehead, then ran his tobacco-stained fingers through his unruly gray hair. "Are you crazy? You're better off making something up."

"Like what?" Vreeland exploded, gripping the yoke in a fit of rage that sent a shudder through the metal bird. "Tell him we landed in the middle of a holocaust, shot up as many of the bastards as we could, then took off again without getting a scratch? Is that what you want me to say?"

McCall looked blankly at him.

"That wouldn't even fool you," Vreeland said.

McCall puffed his cheeks and exhaled loudly as he sat back in his seat, then shook his head slowly from side to side.

"So what's your version of the truth?" McCall asked.

"I'm just going to be straight with him. Do some damage control up front and tell him Scofield was baked, bombed and burned to ashes by the time we got there."

"We don't know that for a fact," McCall said.

"You still want to go back there and check it out, McCall, be my guest. You know how to fly this thing."

McCall ignored him. He wasn't about to turn back. There were no heroes left on the ground and no heroes in the plane.

Realists, maybe, soldiers who were caught up in one of a dozen war fronts operated by Thomas Quinn.

An uneasy silence filled the cockpit as the Beech King flew through a tier of billowing white fog that hovered over the Everglades. Both men looked out at the suddenly murky night, trying to figure out the best course of action once the flight was over.

They flew through the tier of white clouds for several minutes before breaking through into clear skies again. By then, they were on the edge of the Everglades, and thousands of distant lights brightened up the horizon.

They were back in civilization.

But neither man felt completely out of danger.

McCall tapped his fingers nervously on the windscreen. He was full of energy and full of doubt. Most of that stemmed from being cooped up with a man who would soon have a shortened life expectancy.

"What about the coke?" McCall asked. "What are you going to tell him about that?"

"That it wasn't on the plane."

"Yeah. So after you tell him that Scofield's been killed or captured or might be running through the jungle dodging bullets, you tell him you have no idea what the hell happened to any of that powder."

"That about covers it," Vreeland said. "It's the truth."

"It doesn't matter if it's the truth. What matters is what Quinn's going to say."

Vreeland nodded in agreement. "That's why I don't plan on being around to listen to him. What about you?"

McCall shrugged. He was detached now, listening to inner voices that had kept him alive this long. Whatever he was thinking, he wasn't going to reveal it to Vreeland. "Maybe it's time I took another vacation."

"Take my advice," Vreeland said. "Take it far away from here."

"Where you going to go?" McCall asked.

Vreeland looked at him. He took in the wild T-shirt, the unruly hair and McCall's apparently neutral expression. "Why do you want to know?"

"Don't get so suspicious, man," McCall said. "Maybe I want to stick with you for a while."

"It's a thought," Vreeland said. But it wasn't a good one. From here on in, Nicholas Vreeland was not going to be a very trusting man. "Right now we got more important things to think about."

"Like what?"

Vreeland nodded at the fuel gauge. "Like how far we can make it," he said. "We'll be out over the water soon. Keep flying straight and we might make it to the Bahamas."

"And we might not," McCall said.

"That's right," Vreeland said. "Even without the storm throwing us off, we were cutting it pretty close. Maybe it's time to think about where we can refuel."

"We got any friends in the area?" McCall asked.

"Maybe," Vreeland said.

They were about a half hour away from Plantation and several other small towns on the outskirts of Fort Lauderdale.

There was always a lot of air traffic in the area, and that meant there were a lot of small airports and private runways that could service just about any kind of plane.

But Vreeland needed the kind that would accommodate a midnight airline. His passengers had long records and outstanding warrants that couldn't stand up to much scrutiny. What he wanted was a private airstrip where they could land and refuel without attracting much attention.

Preferably a strip owned by someone who owed them a favor.

"There's a skydiving school about ten miles away

from here," Vreeland said. "Right alongside a small back-country road."

"Friend of yours runs it?" McCall asked.

"Not exactly a friend. More like a customer. We moved some heavy quantities a while back."

McCall laughed. "He'll be happy to see *you*."

"I don't care if the man's happy," Vreeland said. "All I care about is the gas in his tanks."

THE BEECH KING MADE a smooth landing on the small runway, wheels spinning once again in a comfortable whining cadence as Vreeland taxied past the mostly dark terminal.

The one-story office building was compact, about the size of a two-bay garage or a small-town diner. Parked just outside was a chromed-up motorcycle and an off-road Jeep.

Across the runway from the building was a hangar with two small planes, and farther out on the field there were three more planes in a row.

Except for the planes, the small complex looked more like a highway rest stop than a private airport.

But it was home to a charter airline and skydiving school. Even though it didn't do all that much business, the planes were new and well maintained, and the jump gear was all top-drawer stuff.

Most of it had been purchased with the help of some clandestine cargo brought in by Vreeland and Scofield on some of their runs. Profits from one load were enough to keep the business in the black for years.

Vreeland brought the Beech King to a stop at the edge of the runway and parked it in the shadows near a tree-lined canal. In case they'd been followed, the crew would have plenty of time to run for the woods and maybe toss their weapons into the canal.

There'd been a lot of air traffic lately, and Vreeland had the feeling he was under a surveillance net. But Vreeland always felt like he was under surveillance on these operations.

It was probably only his conscience playing tricks on him, but Vreeland felt like he was the star of some spook show. He shrugged it off as psychic fallout from seeing the shoot-out back in the swamp. Maybe he *was* riding into some kind of trap, but the important thing was to see how long the ride would last.

"Let's take a walk," he said to McCall. "I might need some backup." He also didn't want to risk McCall flying off without him.

Both men pushed open the cabin doors, then climbed down onto the tarmac.

The air was hot and damp and carried the scent of oil and rubber wafting up from the runway. Vreeland was sweating, not just from the heat. Until now he'd practically been flying on autopilot, eager to get them out of the battle zone.

Now he realized just how close they'd come to dying. It was obviously a well-organized ambush that took down Scofield. And with professionals like that involved, death was never far away.

It was hard to tell where it would come from.

Quinn?

The DEA?

Maybe someone as close as McCall.

Vreeland wanted to get out of the country as quickly as possible. Once he was out of Quinn's backyard, he'd be able to think a lot clearer and figure out his best chance of survival.

First they needed the gas.

By the time they walked halfway to the office building, one of the doors banged open with hinge-rattling force.

A door-shaped corridor of light spilled out into the darkness, then a six-foot shadow hurled down the steps and started coming toward them.

Somebody was angry.

The man had a rifle and a temper and a well-earned reputation as a bar brawler. He wasn't used to unscheduled landings at his private playground.

A second man came out of the building, but he hung back and paced nervously at the bottom of the stairs.

The man with the rifle swore every step of the way as he raced toward Vreeland and McCall. His cursing was almost unintelligible except for the word "bastard," which followed every other word out of his mouth.

"Hey, listen," McCall said, savoring the string of curses as the man drew closer. "He must remember you. That's a good sign."

Vreeland laughed. He kept on laughing until the man came within three feet of them, then he leveled him with a stone-cold look.

It matched the same cold gaze from McCall. Both of them had faced down men with rifles before, men who were ready to use them and not just put on a show. They didn't have time to play any games.

"What the fuck are you doing here?" the man demanded. But a lot of his fire was gone now that he'd picked up on their attitude. "No one told me anything about a run. Shit, there's cops all over the place. Something heavy went down somewhere in the Everglades."

"Yeah," Vreeland said. "We heard something about that."

The man with the rifle nodded. "Damn right, man. It's all over the news. Some kind of shoot-out."

"Is that right?" McCall asked. "Come to think of it, we did hear a lot of noise when we passed over Big Cypress."

The realization finally struck home that these men and their craft were involved with whatever had gone down in the swamp. "Why stop here?" the man asked.

"Because we want to keep on flying," Vreeland said. "Put down the rifle, Hougan, and unlock the pumps."

Hougan shook his head, then looked around him as if he could see into the shadows. "Too risky," he said.

"Yeah it is," Vreeland agreed. "Maybe you should see just how risky it is." He nodded toward the Beech King. "Come on and take a look."

Hougan tried to hang back, but a tap from McCall got him moving. He followed behind Vreeland, glancing now and then at the armed man behind him. McCall just smiled.

When they reached the plane, Vreeland rapped his hand against the side door. The door slid open, revealing the somber faces of the men inside—and the heavy-caliber weapons pointing outside.

"They want to get out of here," Vreeland said. "They want you to help them. What do you say? Get your pal there to unlock the pumps and load us up?"

"Sure," Hougan said.

"Thought so." Vreeland unbuttoned his shirt pocket and took out a roll of bills. Then he handed the cash to Hougan. "Here, this ought to cover it. That includes a tip for you."

"Thanks."

"Don't mention it," Vreeland said.

Hougan nodded and pocketed the money.

"I mean it," Vreeland warned. "Don't mention it. To anybody. We weren't here. If anybody asks, you didn't see us."

THE REFUELING WENT OFF without incident, and the Beech King took to the skies again, carefully watched over by the electronic-surveillance net Hal Brognola's task force had cast over southern Florida.

Bronco OV-10s and high-altitude recon planes had picked up the Beech King as soon as it made its way into the Everglades.

It was tracked through the storm and through its pass over the battle-scarred hammock, then on to the private landing strip.

The recon network kept watch over the Beech King all the way back to the Bahamas, then down to Puerto Rico, where Vreeland dropped off the crew. By then, there was little camaraderie left among the crew, and they went their separate ways.

Nicholas Vreeland tried to lose himself in the back streets of San Juan before checking into a hotel where he spent most of the night looking out his window at the street below for signs of surveillance.

But the ground-surveillance teams that had been waiting for him ever since he landed in Puerto Rico were very discreet. They managed to keep tabs on him throughout the night and into the next morning when he booked the first flight out to Costa Rica.

The other crew members were also followed to see

where their trails led. But the prime target was Nicholas Vreeland.

He was considered a substantial asset in the trafficking hierarchy. That meant he could be even more substantial if they were able to turn him.

Vreeland was allowed to fly to Costa Rica unharmed but heavily watched. He finally seemed able to relax as soon as he reached the Central American haven. It had long been a refuge for wealthy fugitives, CIA troubleshooters and troublemakers, aging mercenaries, arms dealers and semilegitimate privateers.

Like many others in the trafficking trade, Vreeland was more at home out of his native country than when he was back home in the U.S.

Especially in a place like Costa Rica. At least here was a country where he knew the rules. You minded your own business, you paid the right people and you didn't attract any negative publicity.

It was a place where Vreeland had contacts in all levels of society, smugglers and government officials, who were often one and the same. They would be glad to see him—in time. As soon as the heat wore off.

Much better than contacts, Vreeland also had some real friends in Costa Rica who had weathered some rough times with him. Since he was a friend, he wouldn't bring his troubles to them. At least not until he knew whether they could help him.

Until then, he had several bank accounts he could tap into in case he had to buy some new friends.

All in all, he was almost a free man.

He just couldn't see the leash.

AT THREE O'CLOCK the following afternoon, Vreeland called Thomas Quinn's Boca Raton headquarters from a hotel phone in Limón, on the Caribbean coast of Costa Rica.

During the night it was a high-crime city, but during the day it was relatively safe.

"Where the hell are you calling from?" Quinn greeted him. Before Vreeland could respond, Quinn hit him with another question. "Do you realize you're the last one to call in?"

"Don't worry," Vreeland said. "I'm calling from a safe place."

"I'm not worried about you," Quinn said. "I'm worried about the harm you've done to the operation."

"I've done nothing to the operation, Mr. Quinn," he said. "I've done a lot for it. Because of that, I didn't feel like talking things over until you had a chance to calm down."

"That could be a while," Quinn replied.

"I don't doubt it," Vreeland said. Then he gave the ISS chief a straightforward account of his flight into the Everglades and his escape from it. He sanitized his language, using a verbal shorthand developed over the years. But he didn't bother trying to bolster his reasons for taking evasive action instead of landing in the firestorm.

By now Quinn had already made up his mind and wasn't going to let the facts get in the way. He needed a scapegoat.

Quinn paused as if he were mulling over Vreeland's account before he said, "McCall tells a slightly different story."

"I'm sure McCall told you lots of things."

"Enough to make me want to iron this out,"

Quinn said. "I think it's time we all had a sit-down. When can you get here?"

"The year 2000 looks good," Vreeland answered.

"Don't try my patience any more," Quinn grated. "We've got to meet. Where the hell are you?"

"I'm in a safe place."

"Don't count on it," Quinn said.

"I'll be in touch," Vreeland told him. "We'll talk again—when you can admit the security leak was on your end, not mine."

"There was no security lapse on this end," Quinn declared.

"Maybe, but I'm a pilot, Quinn. Not a private eye. That's supposed to be your speciality. You really want to find out what went wrong, take a good look at the people helping you plan these things."

"Vreeland—"

"The operation should have been aborted, Quinn," Vreeland argued. "We both know you sent us into that hellhole just to see what would happen, thinking maybe you'd get lucky."

Vreeland found himself enjoying the conversation, though the distance between Limón and Boca Raton helped it a bit. He'd been holding in a lot ever since Scofield filled him in on the possible hazards with the Everglades action. It felt good to get everything out in the open.

Quinn was to blame for it.

Maybe he should be the one who paid for it.

"I'm giving you one last chance," Quinn said.

"I'll take my own chances." Vreeland hung up the phone, then walked out of the hotel he'd checked into under a false name.

In Limón identification wasn't nearly as important as currency. He was registered in several different hotels under several different names. In case anyone came looking for him, he didn't want to make it too easy.

He had a reputation to live up to—or die protecting.

CHAPTER TEN

Florida

The modest two-story safehouse sat on the banks of the Intracoastal Waterway just north of Fort Lauderdale. It had a screened-in back porch that looked down on the houseboats and cabin cruisers drifting along the water, their chrome trim gleaming in the hot afternoon sun. Weathered white steps with sturdy railings led down to a private dock where a sky blue speedboat was tied.

The house was strategically located. From the waterway it was just a short run to the Atlantic, and on land it was an equally short run to Federal Highway.

But most important, it fit right in with the nearby waterfront properties, which were landscaped with lush foliage to provide privacy. On the side of the house there was a screened-in swimming pool and a whirlpool, a trellis fence covered with bougainvillea vines and a carport that was occupied by a late-model station wagon and a Ford Probe.

It looked like anything but the safehouse it had functioned as ever since the DEA confiscated it from a smuggling network operating in Broward County. For several years now, undercover tenants and their caretakers regularly worked out of the well-kept "rental" property.

At the moment the house was occupied by Mack Bolan, Armand Cane and a two-man security detachment from the U.S. Marshal Service. They were playing host to a reluctant guest—Robert Slater, who still had on the same sweat-soaked, swamp-stained clothes he wore when he'd been taken prisoner in the Everglades.

Brognola had dispatched several marshals to take care of Slater and any other notable prisoners.

So far the pilot's fate was undetermined. Robert Slater was about to become a prisoner or a confidential informant.

And the man who would decide his fate was Mack Bolan, who sat across from Slater at a rustic wooden table on the screened-in porch. Cigarette burns and coffee-cup rings were etched into the tabletop, relics from operatives who'd spent countless hours here waiting to go into action or keeping their eye on prisoners like Slater.

The Executioner wore his Beretta 93-R in a shoulder harness over his short-sleeved black shirt. He sat leafing through a pocket-sized reporter's notebook now and then jotting down something on one of the pages.

Occasionally he glanced over at the pilot as if Slater were a nagging detail that had to be taken care of.

Survivors from the flight crews had identified the slender-framed pilot as Scofield's right-hand man, but at the moment he didn't look too formidable.

Now and then the pilot tapped his fingers on the wooden surface, nail-bitten drumbeats that sounded like a rat trying to scratch his way out of a trap.

Slater spent most of his time looking down at the water and ignoring his present situation.

The Executioner had purposely selected the waterside porch for the interrogation, where the tinted screen kept out the sun and let in the warm breeze that swept in from the water.

It was also a reminder to Slater of how close he was to freedom and how much he had to lose if he didn't cooperate.

After giving Slater plenty of time to stew about his dark future, Bolan suddenly flipped shut the small wire-bound notebook and slapped it on the table. Then he made a half fist and rapped the plastic cover. "This is a list of people we've taken into custody here and in Puerto Rico," he said.

"Yeah?"

"It's an unofficial list," Bolan continued. "No one really knows who's alive or who was killed in the swamp. We haven't got an accurate body count yet."

Slater nodded, obviously agitated by the direction the conversation was taking. But he tried to put up a stoic front. "So?" he said. "You didn't bring me here to talk about bookkeeping problems."

Bolan shook his head. "Actually it's much more serious than that."

Slater shook his head, keenly aware of his hopeless circumstances. "How can it get any worse than this?"

The Executioner picked up the notebook and held it like a hatchet in his fingers as he gestured toward Slater. "The thing is, we're trying to decide whether we should even put you on the list."

Slater frowned, not yet getting the gist of the Executioner's conversation.

"Or take you off permanently," Armand Cane added, stepping out from the position he'd maintained behind Slater ever since he'd escorted him out to the porch.

The DEA agent leaned against the screen sill and folded his arms in front of him, which coincidentally placed his hand near the Colt automatic in his underarm holster.

The movement wasn't lost on Slater. "What are you talking about?" he said, looking first from Bolan to Cane. "It's too late for that. The marshals already know I'm here."

"They know what I tell them to know," Bolan said. "For now, I told them to stay inside until this is over."

Cane took a few steps closer, still angling himself so he was behind Slater. "This kind of thing works better without witnesses."

Slater looked paler than usual.

From his previous run-ins with the law, the pilot was familiar with the good-cop, bad-cop routine used in briefings. But this was a black-op routine. Off the books and out of sight. Neither one of his interrogators bothered with pretense.

It didn't help his peace of mind that he was facing the same men who just a short time ago had wiped out a substantial guerrilla force.

"Look," Slater said, "I'm here, I'm ready to talk—"

"That might not be enough," Bolan said.

"What do you mean?"

"Plenty of people have already talked. Your crew, the Crackers. Everybody. At this point we need something more than talk."

Slater hunched his shoulders, obviously ready to

deal. "Okay," he said in a reasonable tone. "So what's the problem?"

"You are," the Executioner replied. "We're not sure if you've got the right kind of chops anymore."

Slater's face reddened. Either his anger was getting to him or maybe Bolan's assessment was too close to the mark. The pilot had the appearance of a man at the end of his run. "Chops for what?" he asked.

"Maybe a sting operation," Bolan said. "We've got some other people lined up, but there's a chance we might need you. There's also a chance we'll have you float some stories in the media and with your underworld contacts. Or..."

"Or what?"

"Or maybe we can use you as bait. If someone wants to kill you bad enough, they might come out of hiding."

"That's a comforting thought," Slater said. "You don't waste any time, do you? We're talking five minutes, and already you're putting me on the hook."

"On the hook, behind bars or maybe in the ground," Bolan said. "What happens from now on is up to you. Cooperate with us, and you can consider me the best friend you ever had."

"And if I don't?"

"Consider me your executioner."

Armand Cane glanced at Bolan for a moment. Nothing had been said about his real identity during the briefing with Hal Brognola, but now it was obvious that the warrior in black was the Executioner.

Slater took just a few seconds to make his choice. "Under the circumstances," he said, "I guess I could use a friend."

"Good," Bolan stated. "Now that we're friends, let's start off with some names. First who bankrolled you for this operation?"

"Scofield," Slater said.

"That's convenient. Blame it on a dead man. Give me a name I can use. Someone living."

Slater leaned forward. "It's hard to say." He spread his hands in front of him as if he were an open book with nothing to hide. "Everything I worked on these past years has been with Scofield. He called the shots, and I backed him up every step of the way."

"But this time you backed out on him," Bolan said.

A fierce look colored his eyes. "Look, I didn't let him down. Scofield left me behind on this one."

"Maybe," Bolan said. "Way I heard it, you didn't try too hard to get on that plane—and you threw down your weapon pretty quick."

Bolan played the man by instinct, keeping him off balance so he'd stay rattled and ready to talk. A few pressure points now would have a lasting effect on him. The problem with a lot of people who turned was that once they talked, they thought their part of the bargain was over.

He wanted Slater desperate enough to prove himself and to take some risks. Let him do some thinking about how to take down ISS.

"A man who folds that easy on his friends will fold on us just like *that*," Bolan said as he snapped his fingers.

"We were sitting ducks," Slater protested. "It didn't make any sense to keep on fighting. There was no way out."

"Don't expect any apologies. That whole setup was originally designed as an ambush for us, right?"

Slater shrugged his shoulders. "I don't know all the details. We were just told to bring a lot of firepower."

The Executioner paused, thinking of the customs agents who fell during the encounter. "By whom? And don't tell me Scofield. Otherwise we'll stop being friends."

Slater sat back in his chair and exhaled slowly. He looked more relaxed now that he was ready to give up everything. "None of these deals are one-man operations. Different elements work together to carry it off. Each faction brings something different to the party."

Bolan nodded, figuring it was the prelude to some hard intel.

"You've got someone who brokers the deal in the first place and sets up the contacts," Slater continued. "Someone else handles the distribution route. Then there's the manpower, the transport, the payoff arrangements. And you've got your suppliers, sometimes several different ones putting together a load, where they all have a piece of the profits. Like a consortium."

"I know how it works," Bolan said. "I just want to know who controls it."

"There are lots of chiefs," Slater replied. "They stay in the background. I can't say for sure who was ultimately running it."

"Make a guess. Someone here in Florida who has enough pull to carry off this operation. Someone willing to go to war with us. You know someone like that?"

Slater hesitated.

"No games," Bolan warned. "You know what we want."

"There's Thomas Quinn," Slater said. "His ISS outfit."

"Did he hire you?"

"Like I say," he replied, "I don't know all the details—"

"But you worked with Quinn before, didn't you?"

"Worked for him during the, uh, Central American days. Sanctioned operations mostly. We ran weapons in, did some training."

"Is that when the drug runs started?"

Slater shrugged. "Hard to pinpoint when. Or how. But we used the same networks that Quinn's people set up for the weapons deliveries. I don't know if Quinn was directly involved in arranging the cargo for our return flights. People who used to work for him helped set it up."

"That's the way he operates," Bolan said. "Usually one step removed from the actual delivery and payoff."

A loud whine suddenly drowned out their conversation. Down on the waterway a cigarette boat plowed through the water with its bow rising out of the water, coming their way.

Bolan glanced toward the water to watch the boat's approach, for a moment wondering if maybe the safehouse was burned and a "rescue" operation was under way.

The house had been used by other DEA agents before, and some of them might have been noticed, or word could have slipped out.

Cane had the same thought. He picked up a set of binoculars and studied the boat's occupants, following them as they soared past on the high-speed craft and cut a churning white wake in the water.

"Anything?" Bolan asked.

"Nothing to worry about," Cane said. "Guy behind the wheel's middle-aged and with a gut, well past his prime. The girl with him is half his age."

Bolan nodded. It was a bit early for Quinn to zero in on them even if he had some contacts in the DEA. Besides, the ISS honcho didn't even know if Slater was alive. That was what made the captured pilot so valuable. If Bolan started floating inside information about Quinn's operation in the media, the ISS executive wouldn't know where it was coming from and might send a team of plumbers out to shut down the leaks. Slater would make good bait if the time came.

Brognola's surveillance network could shadow the plumbers and turn them against Quinn or shut them down the hard way. Either way, it would help unravel the threads of Quinn's operation.

But there was a chance Slater could have even more value. So far the pilot hadn't revealed much information that wasn't already coming in from other sources. Slater could implicate Quinn, but it would be the word of just one more drug runner against the "patriotic" head of ISS. With all of his pals in Congress and the Senate, that was hardly enough to topple Quinn.

Until they got some concrete proof of Quinn's guilt, Bolan had to maneuver him out into the open, maybe even tempt him to come out shooting. Then Brognola's team could move directly against him. Until then, Bolan had to outflank him on every war front.

"You're safe for now," Bolan said, noticing how

jittery Slater became when he saw their reaction to the boat. "No one's trying to rescue you yet."

"I don't want to be rescued."

"Good thinking. Quinn's people might rescue you out of this world and into the next."

They spent the next few minutes going over Slater's connection to Quinn in the old days, semilegitimate operations that Quinn had conducted supposedly for the good of the United States. But even back then, the operations were mostly conducted for the good of his private bank accounts.

Slater hesitated at first when it came to talking about every deal he'd been involved in. Not only did it implicate him in a litany of crimes, but it also painted in black and white what he had become.

Not a gun for hire but a ghoul for hire. Instead of the high-flying soldier-of-fortune image he'd painted for himself when he first got into the business, Slater had turned into a man who sold death and degradation to the people who ultimately bought the powder.

The pilot considered himself removed from the actual street-level buyer for the drug deliveries he made, deceiving himself that the act of flying made him literally above it all.

But there was no denying that Slater was a vital link in the cocaine chain. It just took someone like Bolan to point out to him what he'd allowed himself to become and what the next stage of his evolution was.

"Look," the Executioner explained, "this is how it works. You give us something we can use against Quinn, and it goes into an information pool. You screw with us, and *you* go into a shark pool."

Bolan leaned forward, sliding his clasped hands across the table like a judge about to give sentence.

"Until you give us something no one else can, you're still nine millimeters away from joining Scofield."

Though the soldier's voice was low, there was enough menace to jump-start Slater again. The pilot leaned away from the table and raised his hands in a reflex gesture of surrender to halt Bolan's threat.

And then Slater came out with something that had obviously been in the back of his mind ever since he was caught. The trump card he'd been holding all along and waited for the right time to play it. "All right," he said. "I can give you something. How about the Texas armory?"

Bolan nodded, acting as if he were aware of it. "What about it?"

"It was supposed to be shut down after the Central America thing got out of hand. When it was still legit—or as legit as these things ever get—Quinn had a temporary arms depot that funneled weapons down through Mexico to Colombia, Costa Rica, Nicaragua—the whole circuit. Mortars, small arms, rockets, mines. You name it, he stocked it. I was involved in those transfers. So was Scofield."

"Keep going," Bolan prodded.

"When the hammer came down, ISS apparently closed up shop. Abandoned the place entirely."

"So what's the problem?"

"Quinn did what his contacts across the border did. Even while he shut down one operation, he opened up another. He just moved it up north a bit, bought out a desert mining camp. Better location, bigger inventory, higher prices. His main clients were Mexican Mafia and their Colombian connections."

Bolan nodded and listened to Slater's account of

the arms operation. It fit in with what he knew about the situation south of the border.

The Mexican Mafia—an ever changing association of drug dealers, federal police, judges, generals and an attorney general or two—ran the drug-and-weapons concessions just like franchises.

Dealers paid off the officials to operate in certain territories, then gave them a percentage of profits from every deal they made. In turn the dealers were given protection. Now and then, the government raided a marijuana field and burned it, after having soldiers or cartel workers harvest it. Or they busted a cocaine warehouse after its contents were shipped out.

Periodically one of the dealers would fall out of favor with the officials or try to double-cross them. Then there would be a shoot-out. The dealers would die, any drugs or money they had on hand would vanish, then the franchise would be sold to someone else.

That way the government could keep getting money to fight the phony drug war and at the same time keep their cartel clients happy.

It wasn't just Mexican cartels that profited. The Colombian crime clans had been paying off their Mexican counterparts for years to store cocaine all along the border with the U.S., using Mexico as an alternative route when things got too hot in southern Florida.

Throughout all of the wheeling and dealing in whatever drugs were in demand, the cartels in Colombia and Mexico were steady customers for top-quality weapons in order to conduct the never ending wars against rival crime clans.

It looked as if Quinn's arms bazaar was doing a

steady business. He was just using a shell game, closing down one facility while opening up another one to carry on business as usual.

Bolan figured that if they looked into it, ISS would have some kind of cover story to justify the new arms operation, cloaking it in some clandestine U.S. program. But the Executioner had the means to remove those cloaks.

"This place still operating?" Bolan asked.

"Last I knew, it was doing a good business with the cartels," Slater said. "It's not a full-time thing, but it surfaces whenever there are customers around."

Bolan kept Slater talking for an hour about the armory and any other operations he knew about. Then he called the marshals out to the porch to take charge of Slater again.

The man had earned a reprieve.

When Slater was taken inside, Bolan stood and stretched. He looked out at the waterway. It seemed peaceful, almost idyllic as more boats drifted by, brilliantly colored crafts full of pleasure boaters on a perpetual holiday.

It was another world out there, far removed from the covert war waged from isolated bases like this one.

"What do you think?" Bolan asked. "This tally with your intel?"

"On the money," the DEA agent said. "We know it happens, but we don't know all the names involved. Sounds like Quinn's still playing both sides."

"All right," Bolan said. "I'll run it by Hal, see if he wants to put it on the hit list."

The soldier went inside, called the big Fed's D.C.

number, then helped him fill in the blanks on Quinn's operation.

Then he headed into one of the Spartan bedrooms facing the waterway. Sun splintered through vertical blinds into the room.

Bolan shut the blinds, dropped back onto the bed and shut his eyes. He'd been on the go for days, grabbing sleep wherever he could. Now he needed to shut out the world and rest for a while.

It wouldn't be long before he was called back into action.

Washington, D.C.

FOUR DAYS after the Everglades attack, Hal Brognola walked down Massachusetts Avenue in Washington, D.C., at ten in the morning.

He passed a series of row houses that looked as if they were poured from the same mold. Now and then, some of them had gold script on the door bearing the name of a law office or some harmless-sounding association.

They were all very anonymous looking but somehow had an official aura about them. These were houses where covert business was conducted, houses full of secrets and secret leaders.

With a glance over his shoulder Brognola noticed the sedate black Ford that was cruising down the street a short distance behind him. It had kept an easy pace ever since the big Fed got out at the corner.

The armored vehicle contained his driver and a bodyguard who'd been persuaded to give him some breathing room. After all, he was on his home turf here and didn't want to come off like he was a chieftain with an everyday entourage.

Brognola disliked the idea of using protection, but he was a realist in these matters. When you practically started a war with someone who killed for a living, you expected to be hit sooner or later.

And though he was close to Embassy Row, that didn't mean as much as it used to. In fact political assassinations had been carried out right on that strip of baronial mansions and well-fortified embassies. The terrorists came to where the targets were.

Brognola stopped in front of a redbrick town house with iron railings and a walk-down entrance. There was a plaque off to the side of the door that read Research Services Associates.

Unless you were a government insider, the deceptive name wouldn't give away the nature of the work conducted in the building. Even if you were an insider, you wouldn't find out much unless you had a genuine reason to do business with the Massachusetts Avenue outfit.

The research center was staffed by consultants who had originally worked for a special Justice Department internal-security task force set up in the seventies. Back then, it was formed to investigate links between the terrorist underworld and military or ex-military operatives.

But to keep up with the increasing sophistication of the terrorist network and their connections to organized-crime groups, the center had become a quasiofficial agency that provided hard intelligence to the people who needed it.

It was a Justice Department think tank, and at the moment Hal Brognola was the tank commander.

Brognola walked down the concrete steps to a sublevel alcove where a discreet camera observed him from just above the doorway.

Once he was inside the door, another camera watched him from a corner of the ceiling as he walked through a small anteroom. If he were a threat, there was plenty of time to study him and intercept him before he went through the final door.

Brognola wasn't exactly a stranger to the building, but it had been a while since he had any official business there, so he didn't recognize the receptionist who was on duty when he entered.

Her desk was off to the right. Directly opposite the door was a hidden and much more serious reception room where armed guards were looking down at him through one-way mirrors.

"Yes?" she said when he walked up to her desk, taking her eyes off of a computer screen that was full of e-mail messages.

Brognola gave her his name, the reason for his visit and flashed some ID. The ID didn't impress her as much as the entry on her screen when she pressed a couple of keys to summon an electronic scheduler. She smiled broadly. The computer had him listed and validated his reason for being here.

"I'll call him out," she said, picking up the phone.

"Don't bother him," Brognola replied. "I can find it."

"Of course," she said, first pressing a button on the phone bank to announce his presence, then pressing a security button that unlatched a door at the back of the room. A simple sign on the door read Staff.

Once through the door, Brognola went down a cream-colored hallway past several doors with opaque glass. Each office handled separate areas of interest to the Justice Department.

But it was the office at the end of the hall that most interested Brognola. The door read Archives.

Brognola knocked once, then tried the door, which was locked.

A moment later the door opened inward, and he was looking into the face of Timothy Williamson, a scholarly man who had spent nearly thirty years as an investigator in the military, the Agency and the State Department.

Williamson was one of the "gray men" who looked so unlike a spook that they made the best spooks. His deceptive college-professor appearance had helped him stay afloat in the treacherous waters of the intelligence world.

"Hal, it's been a while," Williamson said as he shook his hand and ushered him into his office. "Thank God," he added.

Brognola laughed and returned his grip. "I'll try not to make it a habit."

"Good. I'm looking forward to keeping regular hours again. You know, like maybe five hours' sleep a night instead of four. Ever since you called me, I've been seeing what I could dig up."

This was the first time Brognola had seen him face-to-face since he'd first tapped Williamson as his key man in the paperwork war against Thomas Quinn and ISS. The man was a contemporary of Brognola's, someone he could trust and someone who could follow the endless string of front companies and cutouts that covert operators used to cloak their activities.

So far they'd talked several times by phone, but until now Brognola hadn't had a chance to get away from the minute-to-minute management of a covert war.

Up close Brognola saw that Williamson wasn't exaggerating about the hours he was keeping. He had the sunken-eyed look of an accountant who'd been handed a set of cooked books to balance. His eyes were tired from scanning acres of hard copy and studying brightly lit computer screens full of data.

Williamson had been cooped up in these subterranean offices poring over the secrets of the clandestine community, trying to weave together a tapestry that made sense of the life Thomas Quinn led.

At the moment a good deal of that chronicle was gathered on top of a long metal table with a set of gray buckram binders. Each binder was packed full of official documents, reports, recommendations and condemnations relating to Thomas Quinn and the people he dealt with.

There were also several folders arranged in stacks on the table, and some computer diskettes.

The rest of the room was covered with floor-to-ceiling shelves that held other binders, other operations, other spooks who were trying to hide their misdeeds in the shadows. But all of them left some kind of tracks.

Williamson motioned Brognola to a chair at the long table, then pulled out a chair for himself and sat.

"You said you wanted a history of Thomas Quinn," Williamson began as he patted one of the thick binders. "Well, here's Quinn's secret history, cross-referenced and annotated with my comments. I've provided summaries at the beginning of each entry."

"Actually," Brognola said, "I was more interested in Quinn's current connections or maybe his future operations. Sorry if I didn't make it completely clear, Tim, but I was hoping you'd do some crystal-ball gazing and help us predict what he'll do next."

Williamson cocked his head, then slowly nodded. "I know what you needed, but to get that we had to start with the history lesson." He pushed the thick binder to one side. "Consider that a preview of coming attractions."

The researcher pulled another binder in front of him and laid it flat on the table. He opened it with a flourish and thumbed through the leaves. "These are some present-day operations I believe Thomas Quinn is connected to, mainly through some of his former people at ISS or major players he first did business with during the so-called good wars."

Brognola nodded. There had been some mistakes over the years. Inevitably there were occasions when U.S. forces should have acted but couldn't because of political pressure, just as there were moments when they were thrust into conflict as part of gamesmanship.

Inevitable, yes, Brognola thought, but unaccountable no. And Thomas Quinn had been involved in too many wrong wars by selling his services to dictators, cartel leaders and organized-crime figures to let him walk away unscathed.

And the proof of that was lying on the table in front of him, Brognola thought as he looked at the second binder. It was smaller than the other one but still held a lot of material to wade through.

Williamson noticed the temporary gloom on Brognola's face, almost savoring it for a moment. It was all part of his routine. He wasn't asking for brownie points by showing how hard he'd been working, but demonstrating the foundation he'd established for the conclusions he would make.

"I assembled everything I've been able to find on Quinn and his enterprises," Williamson said, "both pro and con. You can paint him as a saint or a sinner, depending on what reports you read and who you talk to.''

"That's why I came here. I figured if anyone could get it straight, it would be you. You're in the loop—you know what's going on.''

"One thing I do know," Williamson said, "is that Quinn's been getting a lot of press lately. Sometimes direct, sometimes indirect. I can safely predict his name's going to appear in a lot more columns.''

"We're doing what we can.''

Along with the relatively sanitized accounts of the Everglades operation that had appeared in the media, several newspapers had run comprehensive articles about the smuggling trade and its connection with former intelligence operatives.

The articles had been generated by "informed sources" from the intelligence community who'd proved their reliability to a select number of reporters in the past. Strictly speaking, the reporters weren't assets who blindly took what was handed to them. But they were reporters who'd proved to be sympathetic to the government's cause as long as they knew they weren't being handed a line.

In return for providing information when reporters questioned them on other matters, the informed sources generated their own items in the media. Despite the Hollywood myths about intrepid investigative reporters, the truth was that information was rarely uncovered by Watergate-style reporters. Instead, information was traded. Truth was hard currency in both the intelligence and private sector, and it had its own rate of exchange.

Brognola's people were using the subtle route with their media contacts, twinning articles whenever possible. An article about the dangers and excesses of private intelligence agencies would coincidentally appear next to a neutral or even slightly positive article about "respected" agencies like Quinn's ISS.

But the necessary connections would be made by those who knew how to read between the lines. It would serve notice that some serious people were looking into ISS.

In some cases a few carefully placed items in the media would be enough for Quinn's associates to desert him. Others would hang in until the campaign started in earnest and the eyewitnesses started to sing about Thomas Quinn.

There was plenty more to sing about, according to the material Williamson had assembled.

On the political front one of Quinn's most vulnerable points was his connection to Senator Ritenour. For years the senator had used his power and his reputation as a "patriot" to steer sanctioned covert arms deals to Quinn's outfit. Quinn would charge triple the cost and funnel payoffs to Ritenour in campaign contributions and good old slush funds.

Though there had been some complaints from his colleagues when details of the legal swindle started to surface, Ritenour was considered untouchable. But now a long-simmering investigation into a group of lobbyists who routinely bought votes from other politicians had implicated Ritenour. The indicted lobbyists were giving up everyone they'd ever paid off, and Ritenour was right up at the top of the list.

Williamson ran off a few other incidents that Ritenour had a hidden hand in. "He's on his way out," the investigator said. "The bad news is we don't know when. The senator's got his claws into a lot of influential people who can delay the inevitable.

They'll help him dodge bullets until the day his mom's ready to convict him.''

"Democracy in action," Brognola said. "So what's the good news?"

Williamson smiled. "Quinn won't be able to count on Senator Ritenour's protection much longer. Not while the senator is under attack. Which means we can pare down the list of Quinn's most likely operations. It'll have to be operations he's been involved in on his own and ones that can bring in substantial fees.''

"Such as?'' Brognola prodded.

"This," Williamson said. He slid a thin plastic folder across the table, one with no markings on it, no title, no situation report.

That meant it was off-the-books material, not some official report but raw data that Williamson had compiled for him. It was Williamson's best guesstimate based on intuition, experience and Quinn's personality.

As Williamson talked about the contents of the folder, Brognola flipped it open and found himself looking at black-and-white photos of "General" Derrick Fabreaux and his cabinet of thugs who had ruled the French Caribbean isles of Saint-Denis for nearly five years. These were the vice-jaded faces of men who plunged the island into a period of unprecedented brutality. During that time they looted the nation's coffers, executed dissidents and jailed most of the elected officials and turned the island into a refuge for cartel kingpins and fugitives from around the globe.

General Fabreaux had been a police captain before his magical transformation into an army officer. Considering that he'd never spent any time in the military, it was a powerful bit of voodoo. It was also contagious. Suddenly his supporters—some of whom had never served in any official capacity—underwent the same kind of transformations and began to wear uniforms for which there had been no positions.

The uniforms worn by the men in the photographs were strangely assembled, part fireman, part policeman, part soldier. It would have been a comical masquerade if it hadn't been so deadly.

Medals and ribbons from imaginary campaigns now hung on the uniforms of former crooked policemen and death-squad chieftains who took power and gave themselves fancy titles: ministers, commissioners, colonels and generals, titles used to distance themselves from the murderers they were.

The photos looked like mug shots, but unfortunately most of the members of Fabreaux's criminal cabinet escaped prison. Staying true to form until the very end, instead of turning himself in, Fabreaux took part in a brief mountaintop skirmish. He fled into exile moments ahead of the forces of the Caribbean coalition that finally invaded the former French possessions to restore the elected government to power.

As a result General Fabreaux and his associates were still alive and well and dangerous, especially since they had the services of Thomas Quinn to call upon. The general and Quinn had a long history together, stemming from the time when Quinn dealt with the Corsican Mafia, which was strongly entrenched in former French islands throughout the Caribbean. Fabreaux had worked with the Corsicans for years, running guns and drugs, and as a result had a natural kinship with Thomas Quinn.

It was Quinn who engineered their dead-of-night

evacuation from the island on the very hour they were supposed to turn themselves over to the authorities, and some people felt that Quinn had a hand in the original coup that brought Fabreaux to power. It was hard to prove, easy to imagine.

Since Fabreaux's regime was toppled, he'd been keeping a low profile in several Central American hideaways where he craved for the power that had been taken away from him. Though he had access to several bank accounts in Panama and other banking centers, rumor had it that Fabreaux had secreted much of the looted treasury on one of the Saint-Denis islands and intended to get it back.

Just as he hoped to get the seat of power back.

Thomas Quinn and several of his associates had been seen in Fabreaux's company a number of times during the two years since the invasion. But so far Quinn had been cautious.

"That can change real quick," Williamson said. "Especially if Quinn was hurt as much as you think. He's going to need some quick cash and a lot of it. That points him toward the cadre of Saint-Denis exiles."

Brognola quickly scanned through the thin folder again. Along with photographs of the people there were photos of guarded houses in the various countries the exiles lived in. There were also lists of banks and assets and phone numbers the exiles used.

It was a blueprint for surveillance drafted by someone who knew the kind of information Brognola needed and the kind of spycraft he could direct toward the general and his exiled partners. NSA and NRO could cover the electronic intelligence while Agency and Justice Department operatives could handle the human side of things.

"Saint-Denis is a good arena for us," Brognola said. "Provided we have enough time to get our people in place."

Ever since the regime of General Fabreaux had been expelled, the government of Saint-Denis had looked toward tourism to stabilize its economy and erase the island's image as a haven for cutthroats.

The island had sought closer ties with the U.S. in hopes they would never have to live through such a brutal time again. "I think we can work behind the scenes with the current government," Brognola said. "Especially when they find out it's their only chance to prevent another coup."

After Williamson finished his briefing on Saint-Denis, he and Brognola discussed other possible fronts where they could chip away at Quinn's empire or bring his activities out into the open.

Brognola passed on the intel he'd received from Bolan about the Texas arms depot. He also mentioned the trail they were following to Costa Rica in hopes of turning some of Quinn's former associates against him.

Then it was time for the big Fed to do some heavy-duty homework.

He opened the binders that Williamson had prepared for him and carefully leafed through them, memorizing names, code names and operations that appeared in the pages.

Now and then, he jotted down a few notes or asked Williamson for clarification. But most of it was black-and-white. The professorial spook had prepared the document well.

The binders weighed several pounds and would take several hours to read totally from start to finish, hours that Brognola couldn't afford. Instead he made photocopies of the summaries Williamson had prepared, folded them along with his notes and slipped them into his inside jacket pocket.

"Does this mean you're not going to take them with you?" Williamson asked, gesturing at the thick binders with mock disappointment.

Brognola laughed. "I kind of like this one," he said, picking up the slender plastic folder.

Besides, he agreed with Williamson's assessment. Saint-Denis was one of Quinn's most likely targets. By putting a watch list on Fabreaux and company's money transfers and monitoring their communications, it would be enough to tell when they were going into action.

Until then, Brognola could make his contacts with the Caribbean authorities and clear the way for Bolan.

"One more thing," Brognola said on his way out.

"There always is. What is it?"

"We need a hit list, people Quinn might try to silence and people we can try to reach."

"I'll work on it," Williamson said. "Who needs sleep, anyway?"

"Thanks." Brognola shook his hand and headed toward the door, then turned back. "Still one more thing."

"What's that?"

"We're probably on Quinn's hit list. He might not know us yet, but it's only a matter of time before he comes after us."

"Don't worry, Hal," Williamson said. "I'll know what he's doing before he does. It's all in the book, remember."

"Maybe," Brognola stated as he opened his suit jacket just enough to reveal the holstered automatic he carried with him. "Just remember, sometimes the sword is mightier than the pen."

Williamson nodded. "It's in the desk."

Brognola looked at him.

"All right, all right," Williamson said. "I'll start wearing it again. But then I have to wear a jacket."

"Or a vest. And make it a bulletproof one."

CHAPTER ELEVEN

Florida

The southern Florida sun beat down on Bolan's neck and shoulders the moment he walked out of the air-conditioned cocoon of the Sovereign Hotel and headed toward the pool area.

The temperature in Boca Raton was in the high nineties, and the humidity made it feel as if he were swimming through the air.

Even with the sleeveless T-shirt and khaki shorts that he was wearing to blend in with the real tourists who were booked at the hotel, he felt the clinging heat.

It was the kind of weather that made everyone slow down. But things were moving fast.

Hal Brognola had set up an operation down south that needed some attending to. According to the time frame Brognola had given him, there was just enough time for the Executioner to make a quick recon, liaise with the locals, then plan a counteroperation.

All on foreign soil.

A good thing he had Brognola paving the way for him. If not, the Executioner's presence on the islands might be as unwelcome as the other "guests" who were expected to visit Saint-Denis in the near future.

Bolan headed down the tiled walkway toward the main pool, heading for a tropical-looking thatched-roof "hut" that served as a breakfast bar in the morning and served as a liquor bar in the afternoon.

The pool was set off from the rest of the hotel by a string of palm trees that offered splintery shade and support for a few hammocks that were currently occupied and swinging back and forth in slow motion.

As Bolan walked towards the breakfast bar his attention was diverted by a woman with bronze skin and a shimmering two-piece white swimming suit that appeared to be painted on her.

Bolan grabbed a cup of black coffee and a morning paper from the breakfast bar, then walked to one of the umbrella-shaded tables near the pool.

He was on his second cup of coffee when Armand Cane appeared on the walkway.

His mane of blond hair was neatly combed and slicked back in a gangster tail tied with a thin leather thong, and his beard was trimmed. Cane was also in tourist garb, but he still looked like a Viking in disguise. His barrel chest, muscled and tattooed arms and his too observant eyes marked him as a man with other things on his mind than a dip in the pool.

Cane grabbed a cup of coffee and joined Bolan at the table, draining the coffee in a couple of gulps.

"What's up?" Cane asked.

"Our time's up. This little holiday is over."

After leaving Slater at the safehouse with the U.S. marshals and a couple of DEA handlers, Bolan and Cane were on downtime, waiting for wheels of justice too move.

"Good," Cane said. "I'm getting tired of this place. It's a bit too civilized."

"Then you should like where we're going," Bolan said.

"Where's that?"

"The Caribbean. You speak any French?"

"A bit," Cane said. "But I'm better with Spanish. Why?"

"French would be better," Bolan said. "But it doesn't really matter that much. The people we're going down there to deal with will probably be more interested in shooting at us than talking to us."

"Damn, you paint an attractive picture, wherever it is," Cane said. "You ever think of writing travel brochures?"

"I can't imagine many people wanting to be the places I've been," Bolan said. "Especially our next stop. Saint-Denis."

Cane whistled softly. A man with his background in the DEA would be familiar with the islands, one of several stepping-stones in the string of Caribbean nations that stretched up from the coast of Venezuela. For a while it had been a way station for many of the drug cartels, until the government became too much of an outlaw for even them to deal with.

"They've been hit hard," Cane said. "First General Fabreaux's regime, then the hurricanes. What next?"

"Quinn's next," Bolan said. "At least Hal seems to think so." He briefed Cane on some of the intel Brognola had shared with him about Quinn and his crooked clients in exile. "That's why we're going there."

Cane was reluctant at first. He was more interested in fighting the battle on his home ground than taking the war outside of the country.

Bolan understood the attitude.

Time and again Cane had put his life on the line in overseas DEA operations only to find that the host government was actively plotting against him. At least on your home territory you knew who the players were and whom you could count on.

"It's not what you think," Bolan told him. "We'll have carte blanche when we get down there, total cooperation from the government. According to Hal, the top people are looking for us to come in."

"That's what they say today," Cane replied. "Who knows what they'll say tomorrow?"

Bolan nodded. "Look, I know you've been burned before. We all have. But there may not be a tomorrow for the people of Saint-Denis unless we follow through on this."

"Take it easy," Cane said. "Your halo's showing. Besides, I didn't say I wasn't going. I just want to talk about it first."

"So talk."

"All right. What if this is all just a smoke screen to get us out of the way? Quinn's not sure who's hitting him, but he definitely knows some group is onto him and he wants to get them off his back. Maybe he's setting up another kind of deal, something that'll go off when we're not here. What happens then?"

Bolan nodded. "It's a risk. But two things point toward it as a good one. First Brognola's surveillance net has detected a transfer of money from General Fabreaux's accounts to one of Quinn's front companies."

The DEA agent shrugged. "Could be money for past favors. Or maybe Quinn really has something in the works with the general. But even so, we still don't know when it's going to happen."

"Taken alone, yeah," Bolan agreed. "There's no guarantee it's going to happen according to any timetable. But when you take a look at Quinn's psychological profile that Hal had some of his people put together—"

"The psych squad strikes again."

The Executioner shrugged. "It makes sense. Look at it from Quinn's point of view. Two of his operations have been blown out of the water. He's got to pull off a major operation to keep his reputation intact."

"It's not exactly something he can put in the company's annual report," Cane observed.

"You know how it works," the Executioner said. "Word'll get around that he's the man behind it."

"All right," Cane said, "I'll go. But what if nothing happens while we're down there?"

"Then we make a side trip to Costa Rica on our way home, and we pick up Vreeland and any other drug pilots we can run against Quinn when we get back."

Cane looked surprised. "Vreeland? That bird has flown, man. If he's got any sense, he's in hiding."

"He's hiding, all right," Bolan said. "But he's hiding in plain sight. Hal's got him under constant surveillance. If the time comes, we'll know where to pick him up."

"Good enough. When are we leaving?"

Bolan glanced at his watch. "One hour from now," he said. "There's a charter plane waiting for us at the Boca Raton airport. It's crewed by a team of pilots who shuffle State Department people around."

"Does it have any special platforms?"

"The works," Bolan said. "The plane's outfitted

with surveillance gear and customized weapons platforms that can't be detected. It can move in and out of airports and look just like any other passenger plane. It also has hidden compartments to carry whatever personal arms we decide to bring."

"Just what we need. A flying fortress to go on vacation. Make sure you put that in your next travel brochure."

THOMAS QUINN LOOKED DOWN at Boca Raton through the tinted glass of his rooftop aerie. His hands pressed against the cold panes, which were moist from the air piped through hidden vents.

For a moment the veins in his thick wrists pulsed as he tensed his muscles and pushed against the glass, almost like Samson pushing against the pillars.

But it was his pillar, his tower. Maybe someday it would be his last stand. But not now.

Quinn forced himself to relax and exhaled the tension with a long breath that helped him regain his balance.

If he felt like a prisoner at times, a man in a glass cage who was trapped by his possessions, it was his own doing.

Somewhere along the line he'd become a merchant instead of just a mercenary, a spymaster instead of spy.

In the old days when things got too hot, all he had to do was move on to the next assignment, the next stop on the underworld express.

But now that he'd become one of the leading players in the security industry, he needed high visibility to be taken seriously. That meant a base of operations where executives would feel comfortable in dealing with him and, more important, paying him his substantial fees. The Glades Road tower made him look like a genuine enterprise, a man of substance rather than a spook working in the shadows.

It was a question of balance.

When Quinn's covert activities were slow or he was feeling too much heat, he needed the above-ground business to bring in the money and keep the outfit going. And when his legitimate client list was slow, he had his underground work to bring in the money.

Now both sides of the enterprise were suffering. Thomas Quinn's picture was appearing in too many papers, and his name was being whispered in too many corridors of power.

A glint of sunlight drew Quinn's attention to a car turning off Glades Road and moving down the access road toward the ISS parking entrance.

It was a blue Jaguar—Gilberto Vicente.

A few moments later another vehicle turned off from Glades Road. It was a dark-windowed Ford Explorer—Claude LeBrun.

They were two men from the opposite ends of the spectrum, but both were indispensable to Quinn.

He'd summoned them both to a meeting at the same time. The tower was under siege, and they were the ones who could help him defend it.

The besiegers were nowhere in sight, but their presence was as concrete as the foundation of his building. The threat lurked on the edge of his empire and made itself visible only when it visited destruction upon him.

It was a perfect guerrilla-warfare campaign waged by skilled commandos who attacked Quinn's cash-flow operations and reduced his military ability at the same time.

They were too perfect, Quinn thought, mainly because they weren't *his* guerrilla force. He'd prided himself for years on the ability to put together teams that could carry off covert ops without leaving a trace.

Now there were plenty of traces, bloody traces left by the remnants of some of his most trusted operatives.

First he'd lost Monteras. His right-hand man had fallen in the Bahamas run. It should have been a flawless operation. The risks were low and the payoff was high. Everyone knew the part he had to play.

That could have been the problem, Quinn thought. Too many parts to play, too many parties involved: Cuban Intelligence, Bahamian middlemen, Colombians.

Looking back on it now, Quinn could see that he'd created the perfect atmosphere for disaster. Infiltrators could have come in from any of the separate groups involved.

Did the Cubans get too careless? Did they lose their protection from genuine Cuban Intelligence?

Or did the Bahamian middlemen do a bit too much talking to their confederates by hinting at the fortune about to fall into their hands?

Then there were the Colombians. It was hard to tell where you stood with them. You could do business with the cartels for years, then one day they might decide the world would be better off without you.

The Colombian cartels had been known to give up some of their own operations before. They were almost as treacherous as the politicians he'd had to work with.

Maybe the Colombians had given Quinn up.

Maybe some of them were working with the DEA or the CIA and needed some busts to justify being on the payroll. More times than he could count when he was working for the government, Quinn ran into cutthroats and mass murderers from inside the drug trade who happened to be government informants. They were protected and pampered because of their supposed knowledge of the drug world.

It was hard to tell where the threat came from.

Whatever its source, it was still close enough to Quinn to know about his Everglades operation. According to all of the reports that had come in, the Cracker Corps had been obliterated, and most of the underground veterans from Quinn's private air force were taken down with him.

Whoever was gunning for Quinn wouldn't stop there. Right now they were circling around his enterprise like sharks who smelled blood in the water. He was vulnerable, and they were closing in.

Sooner or later they would come to the tower itself, the gleaming headquarters that stood high above the Boca Raton landscape like a sculpted rook.

A rook in jeopardy.

Unless he countered with a frontal attack, he was in trouble.

The problem was, he didn't know whom to attack yet. His unseen enemy was outplaying him in the game of war.

Maybe it was time to become a traveling man again, he thought as he headed back to his desk. Maybe it was time to prepare the way for his own exile. Though his pride urged him to stay and fight it out, his more practical side urged him to retreat.

It couldn't hurt to have a safe haven to go to,

Quinn thought, a place where he would be indispensable to those in power.

Like the Saint-Denis islands.

But first he would have to get the right people back in power. And he would have to get his enemy force off his back. That would depend on Gilberto Vicente and Claude LeBrun.

Quinn dropped into the comfortable swivel seat and pressed a few soft-touch buttons on the smooth black onyx desktop, activating high-resolution flat television screens embedded into the surface beneath the glass, his electronic chessboard.

At the moment one of the monitors on the chessboard showed the images of Vicente and LeBrun.

Quinn eavesdropped on them as they spoke briefly with his assistant Lisa Kincaid, who greeted them like old friends.

Both men stood separate but equal in their own ways, acknowledging each other's presence with no warmth, just acceptance.

When Lisa buzzed him to announce their presence, he told her to keep them comfortable for a few more minutes.

Enough time to study them.

Quinn liked to read faces, especially when the subjects couldn't be sure if they were being watched or not. There were cameras all over the tower complex—in the stairways, in the doors, in the parking garage. Some were hidden in walls with lenses painted the same color as the walls. Some were disguised as lights or objets d'art throughout the complex. Statues in courtyards had real eyes.

And even the walls had ears.

Just about every bit of ISS was miked, bringing sight and sound to the man behind the controls.

As he watched Gilberto Vicente on the reception-room monitor, Quinn suspected that his longtime ally, the man he sometimes thought of as his European vassal, was having second thoughts about his involvement with ISS.

Vicente didn't like to be on the losing side, and right now the home office appeared to be taking heavy losses, while Vicente had prospered discreetly in Andorra by running profitable and untroubled operations. Though he hid it well, there was a slight look of resentment in his eyes that he'd been summoned here, almost as if he were thinking maybe it was time for Quinn to fall.

It was an understandable reaction, and Quinn would have felt the same way if the situation were reversed. But fortunately Vicente's destiny was tied forever with Quinn. If Quinn went, they both went. For now, the European's best bet was to shore up the covert kingdom of ISS.

Claude LeBrun sat calmly in the reception area, his face a neutral mask. The Ranger had let his Cracker image die back in the swamp. Now he looked perfectly at home in this new world. He was clean shaved, had a fresh haircut and an expensively tailored suit. He could pass for a businessman or at least someone accustomed to wealth.

In some ways it was a disguise. By nature LeBrun was a woodsman, but he was also capable of playing his role in regal surroundings. It was all a matter of training and attitude. LeBrun knew how to blend in with the natives, no matter what the surroundings were. He was one of those types who was always at home wherever he found himself. He made the world his own.

Both of them were formidable men.

Vicente was the more sophisticated of the two, a controller who could put together the right elements for an operation. He could take care of personnel, payoffs and logistics. LeBrun was more of a field agent. Someone who could go out and find the enemy.

With the two of them behind him, Quinn just might survive the attack on his empire.

But then again, with either of them against him, he'd go down in flames. They knew too much for *his* own good.

Quinn dismissed the paranoia—a constant companion for a man in his position—and then told his assistant to usher them into his office.

After a brief greeting and some small talk, Quinn said, "All right, let's get down to it." There was business to deal with and territory to defend.

Vicente reached into an inside pocket of his suitcoat and withdrew an unlabeled computer disk. "Here," he said as he passed it to Quinn. "This is from our friend."

"How is he?" Quinn asked.

"Scared."

"Wonderful," he said, leading them to a U-shaped white leather sectional couch in the middle of his office that was framed around a low, marble-topped stand. On the slanting front side of the marble base were slots for several video and disk drives that could accept domestic and foreign standards.

Quinn grabbed a hand-sized keypad from the stand and pressed a button that activated a projection screen recessed in the wall. It slid down into view with a soft whir.

"Okay, then," Quinn said as he leaned forward to

slip the disk into one of the slots, then pressed a couple of keys. "Let's see who we're dealing with."

A face appeared on the screen. The man looked like a biker type with a long mane of hair and a get-out-of-my-face look about him. He was bearded, mustached and had a stocky build.

Though the resolution was good, it was obviously a computer photo, a graphic downloaded from a DEA data bank.

"Who is he?" Quinn asked.

"His name is Armand Cane," Vicente said, "a DEA special agent from the Miami office. Bit of a troublemaker and a bit of a troubleshooter." He'd already reviewed the disk that his inside man in the DEA had handed over to him, and by now he knew the players by heart.

The disk was a treasure trove, the ultimate payoff from years of cultivating a well-positioned source inside the agency. Everything they could hope for was on that disk—faces, names, addresses, phone numbers, even some safehouses.

There were photographs of DEA agents, as well as informants, with their code names and real names. The disk also had lists and photos of physical assets like cars, boats, planes and homes that had been confiscated from DEA targets and were currently used by the agency.

Thanks to Vicente's insistence, their DEA contact provided whatever information could prove remotely useful to them.

"What's his specialty?" Quinn asked, studying the large-screen image of the blond-haired biker type.

"Us," LeBrun replied.

Both men looked at him.

"He was there."

"Where?" Quinn asked.

"Back in the swamp," LeBrun said.

Vicente looked skeptical.

But Quinn, who had dealt with LeBrun for years and knew his capabilities, entertained the notion. "Are you certain?"

"You don't forget the face of someone trying to kill you."

Vicente shook his head. "You were close enough to see his face?"

"Yeah," LeBrun said. "Almost close enough to count the slugs left in his clip."

"Are you trying to tell us that someone of his ability missed you?" Vicente asked, "at point-blank range?"

LeBrun shrugged. "Not exactly point-blank," he said. "But it could have been him. I saw someone like him moving with the other troops, giving orders to the ground team at the end of the swamp. I think he was the one who took down Scofield's plane."

"Then let me ask you another question," Vicente said in his calm and sophisticated voice. "If he was that close to you, why didn't you kill him?"

"Get real, man. I was going in the other direction, into the woods. It would have been the end of me if I stayed there. I figure I'm more valuable here."

Vicente looked at Quinn. "Is he?"

LeBrun laughed, as immune to the dig from the European chieftain as he was certain of the answer from the American boss.

"Worth his weight in lead," Quinn replied. "Claude gets rid of problems for me. Most of the time he doesn't miss."

"Very well," Vicente said, turning his attention once again to LeBrun. "Back to this Armand Cane.

How sure are you that he was one of the men in the swamp?"

"Not a hundred percent. But it's far enough from zero. That guy looks like the man I saw. The light wasn't all that great—except from the explosives bursting all around us—but I think it was him."

"It's still just a guess."

"Call it that," LeBrun replied. "But it's an educated guess. I mean, it fits, doesn't it? Having someone from the DEA leading a vendetta against us? Who else has the manpower?"

Quinn had been sitting back and letting the two of them argue their points. Now he joined in. "It could be an off-the-shelf group. Some kind of floating task force with no names or numbers assigned to it. But I'm leaning toward the DEA angle. What about it, Gilberto? What does our friend in the agency say?"

Vicente frowned at the mention of their informant. "He says a lot of things. Sometimes he seems too eager to please. Right now he says that this Armand Cane is the most likely candidate for the kind of trouble you've been experiencing. That's why his picture starts off the disk. Unfortunately Cane's current whereabouts are unknown. He's on some kind of special assignment."

"We're probably his current assignment," Quinn said.

He turned to LeBrun. "And that makes him yours. It's time he retired."

"Soon as I find him," LeBrun assured him. "But like the man says, his current whereabouts are unknown. It could take a while."

"Don't worry about that," Quinn said. "I'll put some of my best people on it. He'll turn up before long. In the meantime, I've got a few other people you can arrange retirement parties for. Starting in D.C. There's some people who know too much about me, and I don't think they'll be keeping it to themselves much longer.''

"It's your call," LeBrun said, totally unfazed by the prospect of plying his killer's trade in the nation's capital. "If they have to go, they'll go."

"They do," Quinn stated. Then he looked back at the screen and ran through the rest of the intelligence collected on the disk. Initially he spent a lot of time perusing downloaded photographs of alleged DEA safehouses spread across southern Florida. But there were so many properties on the disk that it was almost like looking through a realtor's tip sheet.

As the photos of seaside and suburban homes multiplied, Quinn spent less on each one until soon they were almost blurring by on the screen. "A lot of intelligence," Quinn said. "Maybe too much."

Gilberto Vicente clapped his hands quickly, then held them out in front of him to dismiss Quinn's complaint. "It is what is. Since our inside man is an expert sailor, I convinced him to troll up and down the Intracoastal Waterway and Biscayne Bay to photograph points of interest to us."

"Any chance you've been handed a fake bill of goods?" LeBrun asked, savoring the chance to chip away at the European.

"No. We've given him money, and we've given him a playmate who makes his life worth living. And I've personally given him fair warning. He won't cross us."

"That means we'll have to check all those places," Quinn said, gesturing toward the screen. "It might take around-the-clock surveillance before we find any worthwhile targets."

"That could be expensive," Vicente said.

"Very," Quinn agreed. "And that's another reason why we're all here. We need to bring in some big money, and we need to do it fast. It's time to do some serious planning."

"You have something on the horizon?" Vicente asked.

"It's already in the works," Quinn said. "The general's made his first down payment, enough to get things in motion."

Vicente looked surprised. "I thought you decided that such a contract was too high profile for us, that it could attract too much attention."

"Yeah, I did," Quinn said. "But that was before all this started. I can't get a higher profile than I've got now. And we need the money, Gilberto."

The European nodded. He wasn't happy, but he wasn't about to go against Quinn. At least not yet. "Understood. What is it you want me to do?"

"I want you to call in the Ravens," Quinn said as he stood and leveled the keypad toward the projection screen, clicking a button that killed the screen. He whirred it back into place, then placed the keypad on the marble base.

Then he looked down at the troubled face of Gilberto Vicente.

"You can't be serious," the European said. "We can get away with using Ravens in the Balkans. There are plenty enough devils over there already, so their tactics won't be noticed. But if we bring them over here, everyone will see the bloodbath."

"Perhaps," Quinn said. "But by then, it will be too late to do anything about it. We'll have what we want—money and grateful clients—should we ever need their patronage."

Vicente shook his head.

ISS had recruited mercenaries from around the globe for more than a decade now, seeking out over-the-top head cases and misfits who had grown too callous and bloodthirsty to ever serve in regular forces again. They were stone-cold killers who took to heart the practice of medieval crusaders who slaughtered everything in their path.

This legion of anonymous soldiers became known in the covert community as Ravens of War, a name also derived from ancient times when ravens were considered omens of war. Soon the Ravens would come to pick the bodies clean, looting, raping and ravaging the countryside.

Quinn and Vicente had fielded the Ravens across Africa and Europe and the Middle East, wherever hard-core mercenaries were in demand. The numbers of the Ravens varied depending upon the need. There was always a pool to draw from, and there was always a theater for them to perform in.

Vicente tried one more time to dissuade Quinn, but it was no use.

"What choice do we have?" Quinn said.

"You can always leave."

"And then what?" Quinn asked. "Be hunted wherever I go? Become a toothless old lion? No. It's time to make a stand."

"Very well," Vicente said. "I'll put a team of Ravens together."

"Good," Quinn said, nodding toward LeBrun like a priest giving his blessing. "In the meantime we'll do some hunting of our own."

CHAPTER TWELVE

Washington, D.C.

The man in the lightweight khaki trousers, hiking boots and forest green denim shirt moved slowly through the footpaths and roads that wound through the U.S. National Arboretum, the well-tended oasis on the northeastern boundary of D.C.

It was relatively deserted at that time of day and in that part of the preserve, a secluded capital haven with fountains, forests and delicate Japanese-style gardens.

Like some of the other midafternoon strollers who went there to lose themselves among the nearly 450 acres of government-approved wilderness, the man appeared to be an amateur photographer.

Straps from well-worn brushed-leather camera cases were draped across his chest like bandoliers. Slung over his right shoulder was a canvas pack large enough to carry additional equipment.

Now and then, he stopped to focus his camera on Edenlike strands of conifers and magnolias, and aquatic plants floating in landscaped ponds.

But the real object of his interest was the fauna, not the flora.

For the past half hour Claude LeBrun had been

following three men in corporate blues, the uniform of heavy-hitting D.C. deal makers.

After waiting a minute at a brick-lined path, apparently looking for another subject to photograph, LeBrun adjusted his telescopic lens and zoomed in on the three men in the distance.

The third man hung behind, a bodyguard of considerable girth who moved slowly as he guarded the rear. He was middle-aged muscle and carried more weight than was good for him.

The bodyguard was one of the old-guard gorillas who relied on his intimidating size to act as a shield against aggressors. He'd been with the target for several uneventful years now. During that time the target had become civilized and, to a certain extent, so had his bodyguard. Instead of inhabiting smoke-filled back rooms, now it was their custom to get away from the hustle of Washington to enjoy a daily sojourn into the arboretum.

It didn't hurt any that it was hard to be bugged in such a wilderness setting. Since there were so many arms merchants competing for a slice of war profits, they tended to be a suspicious lot who liked to conduct their deals out of earshot.

How unfortunate for them, but how nice for him, LeBrun thought as he scanned the trails all around him.

When he was certain that no one was watching him and no one was coming that way, LeBrun stepped back and slipped into the woods. He moved off trail and headed in a straight line through the forest toward a spot where he could intercept the trio.

LeBrun was careful not to disturb the natural rhythm of the forest as he glided through the brush.

He moved naturally, without making quick stops and starts, always keeping his steps fluid and balanced.

It took him a few minutes to reach the position he'd selected for the ambush, a patch of shadowed, moss-covered ground that would cover any of his movements. It was the type of soft and silent path he'd instinctively sought ever since his Ranger days.

He'd stopped halfway there to remove the special equipment that he'd been carrying in a lens-shaped case. It was a sound suppressor nearly ten inches long designed for the Heckler & Koch Phase II Special Forces Offensive Handgun made for U.S. troops.

He threaded the sound suppressor onto the .45 ACP handgun, which had fit comfortably into his pack.

The flat black metal felt solid in his hand, a five-pound piece of killing power designed for maximum punch and minimum sound. LeBrun had been provided with exactly the right kind of tool, courtesy of one of Quinn's associates.

It was a beautiful piece, a beautiful day and just the right atmosphere for a killing: unrushed, unworried, unalterable.

LeBrun waited quietly in the woods for the trio to approach his hidden vantage point to the side of the winding, narrow trail.

He didn't mind the wait. It was soothing here, as peaceful as a cemetery, which it was about to become.

The target and his latest client were the first to pass by his hiding place, their voices conversing in confident whispers. They were talking about creating a false pedigree for a stolen lot of weapons and bribing officials for doctored end-user certificates.

The usual details. These were men who enjoyed

playing their parts in the secret world. Both were middle-aged, immaculately groomed and royally fed.

They weren't quite grandfathers or sages, but gray eminences who still felt the need to keep their hands in the business. For them, making and spending huge amounts of money was too hard a habit to break.

They both looked off into the distance, eyes on the potential fortune coming their way after they cemented their latest deal. Neither of them even glanced in LeBrun's direction. Their sense of self-preservation had atrophied. The pleasant surroundings had created a false sense of security. And after all, a bodyguard was watching their back. What could possibly happen to them here so close to the city?

Claude LeBrun smiled. *He* was about to happen to them.

But first he had to take care of the bodyguard who was hanging back, pacing himself with the two men in front.

LeBrun forced himself to wait. It could be done now, but it would be messy. Besides, he had already figured out how he wanted to do it and from past experience he knew it was best not to change plans.

He peered through the screen of leaves as the target and his client continued on their way.

The target's name was Lee Jefferson, a semiretired arms dealer who used to work quite often with Thomas Quinn. But over the years Jefferson had moved into a higher realm, brokering surplus arms for overseas clients who were on Uncle Sam's good list.

He apparently forgot his underworld and underhanded days when he ran guns and drugs in Central

America for Quinn—until recent investigators had tapped him for information on the leader of ISS.

Jefferson had stalled them initially. But when he realized how many investigators were at work and how much information they were digging up, he knew it was only a matter of time before they closed in on him.

Since then, the arms dealer had made a few cautious approaches to people on the inside about the possibility of cutting a deal for himself. He made it clear he was willing to give up Quinn.

One of the insiders Jefferson had approached about a deal immediately passed the word on to Senator Ritenour, who in turn notified Quinn.

From that moment on Jefferson's fate had been sealed.

And now—as Jefferson and his client rounded a bend in the narrow path about thirty yards ahead of the bodyguard—the time had come.

LeBrun stepped out of hiding.

The bodyguard sensed the motion and started to turn his head.

The ambusher had expected it. He knew there was no way the man could see or hear LeBrun. The quiet assassin was too good for that.

It was a matter of instinct, the last-second awakening of a man who knew his neck was in the noose.

As the bodyguard finished turning, LeBrun's two-handed grip steadied the Heckler & Koch handgun as he anchored the sound suppressor into the man's chest and squeezed the trigger.

The first shot cored a hole through the man's breastbone. Since the man's heavy torso was pressed against the suppressor, it acted like a two-hundred-pound baffle to silence the round even more.

The second .45 round angled up a fraction, drilling a passage up through the man's neck and head.

The bodyguard crumpled then, a collapsing mass of muscle in a bloodstained suit.

Maybe it was overkill, LeBrun thought. One shot from the Heckler & Koch probably would have been enough.

But sometimes these old-timers didn't know how to die properly. For the life of them, they just couldn't check out when the time came and always had to make that last grab.

Now the man was grabbing air with his dead fingers splaying out as he toppled over to the ground.

LeBrun took the man's place on the footpath and began to walk with the same casual pace that the bodyguard had.

The sound of the bodyguard's fall had attracted the attention of Lee Jefferson and his client. Both were turning with a slight air of distraction about them when they saw Claude LeBrun rounding the bend instead of the bodyguard.

LeBrun continued his approach with a casual gait and a carefree expression on his face.

There was confusion and annoyance on their faces, but no sign of fear had registered yet.

LeBrun's calm face and the camera gear hanging all over him didn't seem to present any kind of threat.

But then he raised the Heckler & Koch pistol that had been hidden slightly at his side. The blunt sound suppressor was familiar to both men. In fact they'd traded in them several times in the past, making them available to just about anyone with the money and the need.

The client was the first to react. He took a side

step off the path, moving with a speed surprising for a man of his age.

A nova of red appeared on his chest as a .45ACP bullet drilled him. His hands flew out like a bird about to take wing. But he was grounded forever as the flaps of his suit were covered with the dark red.

That left Lee Jefferson standing alone with a heightened sense of his mortality. For a second his hand moved toward his jacket as if he were thinking of drawing his pistol.

But a part of him knew that would just hasten the end. LeBrun had superior firepower, and he had him in his sights.

The arms dealer raised his hands in surrender.

LeBrun shook his head.

"Why?" Jefferson asked, stepping forward, willing to negotiate. Right up to the end he wanted to cut a deal.

"You gave up the wrong man," LeBrun replied.

He gave Jefferson enough time to let it sink in and to go through his list of enemies and double-crossed friends. Unlike battlefield deaths, where there was seldom time to plan, these kind of killings had a rhythm of their own. Quinn liked to have his enemies know who was responsible for their deaths—if at all possible.

LeBrun waited until Jefferson's startled thought processes were functioning well enough to put things together again.

Enlightenment came suddenly, and with it came a quiet terror. Jefferson knew who had sent the messenger for him.

"Quinn!" Jefferson shouted. "Look, you can tell him I haven't testified yet. There's still enough time—"

LeBrun proved him wrong with four rounds that ripped him from stomach to sternum, giving him a .45ACP autopsy before he hit the ground.

Only about a minute had passed since LeBrun fired the first shot. There was still no one in sight.

It was time for some finishing touches.

LeBrun moved quickly. He lifted the wallets from both men and dragged their bodies into the woods, then he repeated the process with the bodyguard. He didn't haul any of them too deep into the forest. He wanted them to be found, but not right away.

Then the assassin drifted back into the shelter of the woods and stopped about thirty yards from the killzone. He was hidden well enough to escape notice if anyone happened to come along.

With practiced ease LeBrun rifled through the wallets and withdrew money and credit cards so the hit could look like a mugging that got out of hand, especially since he planned on dropping the credit cards in one of the seedier sections of D.C.

Whoever picked up the cards would probably sell them to one of the credit-card rings working in any big city, then lead the authorities on an endless chase through the underworld maze.

When he finished lifting enough bills and cards, LeBrun threw the wallets away just as casually as he'd thrown away the lives of their owners.

The point of the hit was to create some reasonable doubt about who carried out the killings—an assassin or an assailant.

Word of the killings would spread quickly to the people who mattered, people who understood the signal Quinn was sending them.

LeBrun kept to the woods for another ten minutes before emerging near the north entrance.

Then he glanced at his watch and picked up his pace. He had another appointment to keep.

FIVE HOURS LATER when Claude LeBrun settled into the first-class cabin of an Airbus A300 about to depart Washington International Airport, D.C.'s population had been reduced by one more soul.

A "suicide."

The sad news probably wouldn't be known until the following day, when the body of respected banker Leonard R. J. Parrington would be found in the study of his suburban Alexandria home. His friends would tell the press that he seemed to be happy, enjoying the kind of life a career in banking had brought him.

Those same friends would whisper to one another over drinks that the banker's two-tiered career had finally caught up to him. And at the funeral few tears would be shed by those who really knew him.

There might be an investigation, but most likely the banker's death would be ruled a suicide. It would be easier on the people he did business with, especially those in the government who'd made fortunes from some of his swindles.

But even if there was an investigation, LeBrun didn't have to worry. By then, he would be sitting poolside at a Florida hotel enjoying the fruits of his short but successful stay in the nation's capital.

As the plane taxied down the runway and he felt that familiar rumble as it picked up speed before takeoff, Claude closed his eyes. He could never quite get used to flying.

He told himself it wasn't a matter of air sickness or lack of faith in the behemoth plane—even if at times it seemed like nothing more than a skyscraper turned on its side with a pair of wheels stuck on it.

The main problem LeBrun had with flying was the fact that he had to yield control to someone else for the duration of the flight. On board a plane was one place where his fate was in hands other than his own. But it was a necessity, and like other necessities of his trade he accepted it.

LeBrun kept his eyes closed through takeoff, not opening them again until the plane had leveled off.

Far below he saw the sprawling and gleaming city lights of Washington, D.C. For a moment it made him feel quite patriotic. Compared to some of the desolate capitals he'd seen during his sojourns, it was almost like looking at the Pearly Gates.

And off to his right was Alexandria, Virginia, the home to so many of the defense contractors, high rollers and Agency spooks who greased the wheels of Washington.

There would be a vacancy in Alexandria soon.

It wouldn't take long to find a buyer for Parrington's sprawling Colonial estate. The late banker's property had plenty of acreage, and the house itself was quite comfortable. Especially the study where LeBrun had been waiting for him to return from the city.

Parrington had come in, dropped some material on his richly polished desktop, then found himself at the end of his own gun, which LeBrun had taken from the desk drawer.

The banker had taken it all in stride, almost as if he were used to having weapons drawn on him.

He proved to be a talkative sort, answering all of the questions that Quinn had provided to LeBrun.

Most of the questions concerned the bad old days, back when Parrington ran a cocaine bank in Fort

Lauderdale that specialized in laundering money for the cartels. He and Quinn had done a lot of business together, taking a considerable percentage of the cash given to them by cocaine dealers to launder.

Quinn and Parrington had also worked several savings-and-loans scams together, providing millions at a clip to politically connected insiders who never intended to pay anything back. The game was so rigged in their favor back then it was a wonder that it lasted as long as it had.

Men like Parrington got control of a bank and made loans to men of influence for bogus real-estate deals or front companies set up solely to siphon off cash. And when these men with sterling reputations defaulted on the loans or declared corporate bankruptcy, nothing happened to them.

The best part about this organized thievery was that no one ever had to pay anything back. The taxpayers were stuck with paying off the debts the government had insured.

Like most scams it had to end sooner or later. Fortunately in many cases the people in charge of investigating the savings-and-loan frauds were the same people who benefited from the shady deals to begin with.

The only downside of those ill-gotten gains was that Parrington had a lot of skeletons in his closet.

Among the skeletons was Thomas Quinn. And now that Parrington had come under investigation for one of his more current frauds, word had it that he was trying to bargain his way out of an indictment.

Since Quinn was his biggest bargaining chip, the leader of ISS decided it was time to make a preemptive strike against the banker.

LeBrun had listened carefully to everything Parrington said. Then, when the banker relaxed—after swearing that he hadn't mentioned Quinn to a soul—the assassin blew his brains out.

He made it look a suicide, a signature killing that could be taken as a murder or a suicide.

Parrington was right-handed, so Quinn held the gun against his left temple. It was a favorite technique used by spooks who wanted people to know when someone was "suicided."

Questions would be raised, but the truth would be buried. The banker's papers would be taken away, and all of his collaborators would breathe a sigh of relief.

All in all, LeBrun thought, he'd done a lot of people a favor by killing Parrington. Especially Thomas Quinn.

He settled in for the rest of the flight, satisfied that everything had gone well. He realized it was only a warm-up, though. Soon he'd be going after a higher caliber of killer, people as skilled and ruthless as himself.

Life would get interesting…or it would come to a stop.

CHAPTER THIRTEEN

Saint-Denis

Mack Bolan sat behind the wheel of a sand-colored Hummer parked along the edge of the coastal road that led from Port Saint-Denis to the ruins of an old stone fort that looked down on the island capital.

He was parked halfway up the hill, high enough for a cool mountain breeze to sift through the open window and chase away some of the late-afternoon heat. Bolan preferred the breeze to the air-conditioning that he'd been running intermittently to keep the high-tech equipment at a stable temperature.

The Hummer had been converted into a rolling command post. On top of the hood was a small satellite dish, and embedded into the dashboard were several computer screens and keyboards. It had satcom, phone, fax and video capability that flooded him with constant situation reports.

A light on the cockpit-shaped dash started blinking on and off, signaling that another satcom transmission had just been sent from Armand Cane and was being decoded on the Hummer's computer screen. The message appeared in digitallike letters.

KNOWN OPFOR STRENGTH IN CAPITAL NOW AT THIRTY-SEVEN. LATEST ARRIVALS INCLUDE TWO

MORE OPERATIVES CONNECTED WITH RAVEN GROUP/
BALKANS.

The news wasn't surprising. The rolls of the known opposing force had been rising since the first mercs began arriving two days earlier. And most of them had been part of ISS auxiliary forces who'd rented out their lethal skills across Europe.

From hidden observation posts at the airport, American and Saint-Denis customs officials had been able to tag them as members of the Ravens soon after they arrived at the airport. They'd arrived in ones and twos on separate flights, but the deception was short-lived, for most of them headed toward the same hotel and quickly settled into the bar.

Though most of the mercenaries had fake identification and passports, they were easily recognizable. At least half of them were wanted men and could have been picked up for various charges. Their rap sheets and photographs had been floating around several Interpol offices for years.

Bolan's attention returned to the screen as another message from Cane appeared.

SAU INTELLIGENCE INDICATES SECOND FORCE NOW GATHERING AT GRANVILLE MARINA.

The second force had made a much quieter approach. They'd come by boat, taking the island-to-island route followed by most genuine yachtsmen who crisscrossed the Caribbean. One by one they sailed into the marina five miles south of Saint-Denis.

But the second force had given themselves away by rendezvousing with sympathizers from the general's regime. Those same sympathizers were under constant surveillance by a crack team from the island's Special Action Unit.

The sympathizers had been biding their time while laying the groundwork for the old guard to return. And now it was obvious that the time was almost upon them.

ANTICIPATED SEA FORCE TARGET STILL GOVERNMENT HOUSE. YACHTSMEN SURVEILLING PRIME MINISTER.

Bolan acknowledged the message from Cane, then sent a transmission to the Hummer that was driven by the leader of the SAU, a soft-spoken man named Simon Tremaine who'd been the backbone of the counterrevolution that toppled General Fabreaux's thugs from power.

Tremaine reported that he was a few minutes away from the midpoint, where he and Bolan met on their patrols.

The SAU commander was patrolling the lower section of the coastal road while Bolan patrolled the section that led up to the old stone fort. They'd followed the routine ever since determining that the old fort and the rural police station next to it were the targets of the hotel-based mercs.

While he waited for the SAU commando, the Executioner picked up the binoculars and studied the seascape below, where the blue waters of the Caribbean sparkled in the sun. Sailboats, yachts, and Jet Skis jockeyed for position in the bay, the clearest sign yet that money and tourists were starting to come back to the isles.

Bolan heard the engine of the second Hummer as it came up the winding coastal road. A half minute later it pulled off the road and came to a stop facing him.

Simon Tremaine climbed down from the vehicle and stretched his trim, sun-bronzed frame. Like the rest of his handpicked SAU commandos, he wore sand-colored combat fatigues and brown boots with buckled tops.

Hanging from Tremaine's shoulder was a Colt M-633 submachine gun, which had become an extension of his arm in recent days. Ever since news of General Fabreaux's impending strike reached the island, Tremaine never went anywhere without an automatic weapon by his side.

It was a conditioned response to the last war he fought against Fabreaux.

Tremaine's hair was cut short and had a sharp widow's peak that came to a knifepoint on his broad temple. It gave the impression that his entire body was a weapon ready to strike at a moment's notice. But there was also a touch of gray in his hair that tempered this aggressive quality, making him look like a sage, as well as a soldier.

Bolan stepped out of the Hummer to meet him halfway.

"Well, Belasko," Tremaine said, "looks like Operation Cold Cache is about to heat up."

"Yeah," Bolan replied. "I got the messages from Cane."

"They're gathering in the hotel even now," Tremaine said, scorn in his voice as he gestured to the white-and-pastel-colored hotels that sat like toy castles in the sun. "One of my undercover people on the hotel staff is serving them, though he'd rather be cutting their throats. Right now they're sipping iced tea and lemonade, having a little picnic before they come out to do some killing."

"It's not too late to shut them down," Bolan said. "We can move in on them before it starts."

Tremaine was tempted, but he'd already made up

his mind. "It's best we stay the course. If we sweep them up now, another batch will take their place. Better we catch them in the act."

"It's up to you," Bolan said. "You know how I feel, but these are your people at risk. We're just here to help any way we can."

Tremaine nodded.

They'd talked over all the possible scenarios for dealing with the mercenaries, coming up with a separate plan for each one. Bolan could help Tremaine execute any of those plans, but it was Tremaine's homeland, Tremaine's decision.

The SAU commander was aware that the Executioner's main target was Thomas Quinn and ISS, and a battle on Saint-Denis would be one way of striking at him.

But they were still fighting the same enemy no matter what name it went by. The Ravens were an extension of General Fabreaux just as much as they were an extension of Quinn's ISS.

Tremaine reflexively tugged on the strap of the submachine gun hanging over his shoulder. He was ready for war, not for a round-up of mercs in the hotel.

"As I said before," Tremaine replied, "the people of Saint-Denis welcome your help and your assistance." He gestured toward one of the customized Hummers, which had enough armor and armament to conduct a small war. "Our mutual friend, Mr. Brognola, has been most generous."

"You needed them, we had them," Bolan replied. Three of the Hummers had arrived by ship a day before Bolan. Cane had one down in the city, parked behind the walls of a pastel-colored villa near the hotel strip.

"Yes," Tremaine said, "we do need them. Unfortunately we must let this little war take its course. At least out here we can keep it away from the city. Hopefully only the soldiers will fall."

"Theirs, not ours."

Tremaine nodded, then walked back to his Hummer. He drove down the hill, past the hidden SAU commandos who were scattered in the forest like human land mines waiting for the war to come to them.

ARMAND CANE SAT in a café across from the hotel on the main street of Saint-Denis, sipping from a mug of coffee that had gone cold long ago.

The café was close enough to the villa Tremaine had provided for him, so he could slip away to make his reports to Bolan.

The Ravens were in good spirits, acting like men about to take part in a sporting event. There was an aura of expectation about them, as if they knew their team was going to bring home a trophy.

Positioned around the front of the hotel and the parking lot were several motorbikes and rental Jeeps the Ravens had gathered. It wouldn't be hard to track them when they moved out. But stopping them could be another matter.

Cane focused his attention on a man he'd identified as one of the leaders of the group, Hugo Xavier. He had a solid look about him and was a head taller than most. His brush cut was long in the front and combed straight up.

Xavier was a professional killer who considered atrocities just another tactical matter, a way of doing business that guaranteed good results. For that reason he'd excelled in all of the backwater war fronts that Quinn had dispatched him to.

Many of the mercenaries with him had the same kind of reputation, and they had considerable training. Cane had recognized the faces of several mercenaries who'd served with well-known forces.

There were a number of Green Berets and regular Army vets who were no longer choosy about whom they worked for. The ranks also held several Royal Marine Commandos and ex-paratroopers from the Legion's Second Parachute Regiment. They'd all been heroes at one time or another. But those wars were history, as buried and forgotten as their consciences.

It wasn't going to be an easy fight.

Cane felt the way he always did before a battle. There was an air of disbelief about his surroundings. Here he was in a beautiful seaside city where by rights he should be having the time of his life. Instead he was watching almost forty well-mannered killers relaxing over a brief meal before they went out on the road eager to turn this island heaven into another hell.

Of course, if everything went well, it would be their last meal.

THE EXECUTIONER DROVE uphill at an unrushed speed, carefully negotiating the curves that he knew by heart. Sprawled on the seat next to him was a collection of gear he'd used for sight-seeing and surveillance these past few days: maps, night-vision devices, binoculars, surveillance cameras and state-of-the-art comm gear.

The back of the Hummer was loaded with a variety of special-purpose weapons Bolan could call upon depending on the type of opposition he encountered: rocket launchers, light machine guns, grenades and flamethrowers.

It had been impossible to guess what type of force they would encounter on the island, so Bolan and Cane had requested a small arsenal, which had been loaded on to the plane that brought them down here. The same type of weaponry had been parceled out to the vehicle that Tremaine was driving.

Bolan hadn't neglected small arms, however.

His Beretta 93-R was holstered in a quick-release shoulder rig, and a .45 pistol rested in his hip holster.

A short, fat-barreled Colt M-633 with a 32-round stick magazine was on the floor of the passenger seat. The compact 9 mm subgun was ideal for close-quarters combat. It could fire 800 rounds per minute and with a bit of practice it was easy to control.

The Colt had become the standard issue for the Special Action Unit. Tremaine had put together a solid group of men. The islander had received military training in both France and the U.S., where he first made behind-the-scenes contacts with his American counterparts. He'd served with several Caribbean Community task forces, working as the CAR-ACOM liaison with U.S. Intelligence during the Grenada invasion and the Trinidad coup. He was paid back in kind during *his* struggle to topple the corrupt Fabreaux regime.

Critical intelligence on Fabreaux's movements that had been gathered by U.S. agencies was forwarded to Tremaine along with matériel he requested. Once Fabreaux was ousted, Tremaine could have easily won office in the new government, but he preferred to work quietly in the background to make sure the new government could survive any threats from the old guard.

That required a man with absolutely no political ambitions. Simon Tremaine quickly began to build up the SAU commando unit. He had chosen his men carefully and shaped them into an effective force that could handle most threats to internal security.

It was a small force, but Bolan felt comfortable working with its members. They didn't need baby-sitting, and there was an added plus that came from working with the locals. They were on their home turf and fighting against an occupying force. They would give everything they had.

By themselves the SAU didn't have the numbers to deal with the Ravens who'd flocked to the island.

The Executioner's team helped balance the scales.

Along with Cane and some of the men from the Everglades operation, Bolan had access to a U.S. Special Forces strike team maintaining a discreet presence on board Coast Guard cutters sailing in the waters on the Atlantic side of the island. Additionally, a helicopter squadron led by Captain Jack Parsons was conducting "training" operations with the Coast Guard.

Tremaine had welcomed the offshore support just as Bolan and Brognola had figured. It had probably been a major factor in deciding to go with the combat scenario.

With Bolan and his people tasked with setting up military operations outside the capital city, Tremaine's men had been free to concentrate on identifying and shadowing the Ravens.

Soon Bolan would see them up close.

He crested the hilltop curve that led to the old stone fort. The upper section of the thick-walled redoubt had been turned into a Caribbean Stonehenge during the struggle to remove General Fabreaux, though some of the lower levels were intact.

The strategic site had been a fortress for hundreds of years, dating back to the days when pirates ruled the Caribbean. It had been refortified by General Fabreaux and his new breed of pirates after they took control of the island. After seeing how similar structures survived bombardment during the Grenada invasion, they'd tunneled into the hilltop and prepared an invulnerable bunker for themselves.

The only problem was that General Fabreaux was out of the bunker when Tremaine's forces moved against him. He'd negotiated a surrender with Quinn's help and then, instead of turning himself in, he and his cronies landed on the hilltop with three helicopters and tried to fight their way in.

It was a near suicidal attack. And at the time it seemed totally purposeless. With the surface of the fort already obliterated and the garrison overrun, there was nothing for the general to gain. At least nothing that appeared to make sense at the time.

But the general kept trying to fight his way in, until one of the helicopters was blown out of the air.

The wreckage from the trashed aircraft was strewed all along the hillside and much of it was visible to this day, a monument to the struggle for freedom.

A second helicopter was hit and had to land halfway down the city. But the third helicopter managed to get away with Fabreaux and his men.

The general had stayed away ever since.

But now he was trying to return by proxy.

SAU intelligence had long ago discovered why such a lonely outpost would attract the attention of the exiled general or any other treasure hunters. One of the lower levels in the fortress was the site of General Fabreaux's private cache. It contained U.S. currency, gold bullion and security notes he'd stolen from the Saint-Denis treasury.

The SAU had quietly restored the money to the treasury, then built up a small police garrison next to it to handle the rural community outside of the capital.

The stone fortress was a cold cache now—hence the operational name given to it by Bolan and his Saint-Denis counterpart.

General Fabreaux's mercenaries had no idea the vault was empty.

To them it was still a cause worth fighting for. Bolan wondered how much of a reward they'd been promised for retrieving the general's cache.

Now they'd be lucky enough to get funeral expenses.

A light flashed on the Hummer dash again, signaling another transmission from Armand Cane.

Bolan looked down at the screen and saw the message they'd been waiting for ever since they reached the island.

OPFOR EN ROUTE...LAUNCH OPERATION COLD CACHE.

CHAPTER FOURTEEN

The first three motorcycles cruised slowly along the coastal road until they were two miles outside the city.

Once they were past the first major bend in the road, they cut the throttles and pulled off the shoulder into a tree-shrouded clearing with a gravel bed.

The thin but heavy-treaded tires crunched over the gravel as the three riders moved in a half circle, ending up with the bikes facing the road again like steeds ready to lead a charge.

Still sitting on their bikes, the men waited for the other riders to catch up to them at the selected staging area. Every few minutes another group of motorcyclists joined them, wheeling their dirt bikes off the road and waiting for the Jeeps and cars carrying their ordnance to arrive.

The casual exodus from the city continued until there were about twenty dirt bikes. The dirt bikes, which could move well on the islands' undeveloped or washed-out roads, were in good condition with plenty of chrome trim. Their bright yellow-and-red fuel tanks gleamed in the sun that sliced down through the thick boughs overhead.

Some of the bikes looked like they'd come right off a showroom floor, thanks to a team of mercs who'd gone over the motorcycles the night before, tuning the engines and working the brakes until they were in fighting shape. Their lives could depend as much on the bikes as they could on their weapons.

About five minutes after the last bike reached the staging area, a pair of Jeeps came around the bend and stopped at the gravel. Right behind the vehicles was a 1985 black Cadillac convertible in perfect condition. The four men inside it were going off to war in fine style.

The last vehicle to pull into the staging area was a dilapidated van with rough patches of bodywork held together by several coats of pastel-colored house paint.

Hugo Xavier jumped out of the lead Jeep and hurried to the back, where he swung down the tailgate. Then he moved to the van and rolled open the side doors.

"Suit up," Xavier ordered as he stepped aside.

Inside the vehicle were enough bullet-resistant vests to outfit the entire team. The Jeeps held stacks of automatic weapons and explosives that had been brought in to Saint-Denis aboard one of their yachts that was now moored at Granville Marina.

The Ravens moved quickly from van to Jeep, first slipping the vests over their holiday gear, then equipping themselves for war.

When all of the mercenaries were outfitted, Xavier jumped onto the tail bumper of his Jeep and gestured for silence.

"You all know your targets," Xavier said, speaking in a loud and clear voice. "But don't forget the timetable. We hit the police station and the fortress at the same time. I don't want a single one of those Keystone Kops to walk away from this."

The Ravens didn't really need the first part of the instructions. Their standard operating procedure was to move in like a hurricane and leave nothing and no one standing.

But it was part of their ritual.

Orders from on high.

"After we blow the vault and load up the van, everyone moves full speed down to Granville Marina," Xavier said. "There we'll make the transfer to the boats. Everyone clear on that?"

Several of the mercs nodded. Others shrugged. They were used to hit-and-run operations.

"But remember one thing," Xavier said. "If the other team does their part, it'll be clear sailing and we won't have to make a run for it. We'll be sleeping in Government House tonight. Hell, we might even be heroes!"

Some of the Ravens laughed, others swore, others silently checked out their weapons. It didn't really matter to them if they stayed in-country or moved on after the battle. What mattered was that they won it.

They'd been in similar situations before. At the start of the action they were considered outside invaders, hired guns who just had to be pointed in the right direction. But by the time the action ended, they might be considered the new government-approved troops.

Xavier jumped down from the Jeep. He slammed the tailgate shut, climbed back behind the wheel and revved the engine. "Good hunting!" he shouted as he signaled the Ravens to move out.

The motorcycles roared to life one after the other as the mercs kick started the bikes, producing a rumbling sound that echoed up and down the coastal road.

Then the wave of riders rocketed forward like angry hornets about to strike.

Xavier stomped the pedal of the Jeep, kicked up a spray of gravel, then shrieked up the hill. The other Jeep and the Cadillac followed right behind him, then came the van they'd brought along to retrieve the general's cache.

The vehicles quickly caught up to the lead motorcyclists, followed closely by the rear-guard riders.

The mercenaries had weapons draped around their shoulders like necklaces. Some of them rode two to a bike, the first for navigating, the second for killing.

THE EXECUTIONER STOOD on the remnants of the stone fortress and watched the progress of the motorbike brigade through a pair of field glasses.

There were several stretches of road that couldn't be covered by the binoculars, but the crucial areas of the road were easy to see.

So were the riders who were now coming their way. The mercenaries were moving en masse—no recon team, no reserves.

It was going to be a blitzkrieg.

Bolan handed the binoculars to Semple, one of the four SAU commandos standing beside him.

"Take a good look," Bolan said. "See what we're up against."

Semple focused the binoculars and zeroed in on the rapidly moving line of mercenaries.

"You still up for it?" Bolan asked, carefully studying the young commando's reaction.

Semple was highly recommended as a marksman and had seen some combat with CARACOM troops. But that had been in pitched battles where he was part of a much larger force. Now he was part of a handful against a horde.

The commando's hands were steady and his breathing was calm as he took their enemy's measure. He looked at Bolan with the hint of a smile on his face. He knew he was being judged. He also knew he could make the grade. "I'll do my thing, man. You do yours and we'll be all right."

Bolan grinned and took back the binoculars. He scanned the road below one more time, then handed the glasses to one of the remaining commandos who'd been stationed at the fortress in case any of the mercenaries made it that far.

Another SAU squad was spread out in the woods along with some of the DEA and customs operatives who'd come down to Saint-Denis with Bolan.

"Keep watching the killzone," Bolan said to the man he'd given the glasses to. "If things get out of hand, come down to help. If too many get by us, we'll come up here to reinforce you."

"They won't be getting by," Semple replied, smacking his hand on the stock of the Colt M-633.

"Then let's go meet them," the Executioner said, heading back to the Hummer.

Semple climbed in the passenger side of the combat field car and dropped his light pack onto the seat. The commando rolled down the window and rested the thick barrel of the Colt subgun on top of the door frame. He was ready for a strafing run.

Aside from the 32-round magazine that was already in the Colt, there were a half-dozen more stick magazines protruding from the open flaps of his pack.

Bolan's Colt was by his side with a couple of spare

magazines. His Beretta 93-R was nestled in the stretch-canvas utility pouch built into the door panel.

The Executioner switched on the ignition, hit the gas, then wheeled out onto the road.

He drove the Hummer downhill at a high rate of speed, not looking at the speedometer, but using his innate sense of the road to adjust his speed to the terrain.

He knew how long it took to get down to any section of the coastal road from the stone fortress. Both he and Tremaine had conducted exhaustive recons of the strip to determine the best possible spot for the moving ambush they were about to spring.

The Executioner had laid out the snap roadblock technique to Tremaine and his men. It was a fluid trap that, if conducted properly, would eliminate at least half of the force coming against them.

If it wasn't done right, then they'd be delivering themselves right into the hands of a well-armed and extremely mobile enemy.

The main advantage to a snap roadblock was the high probability of catching the mercenaries off guard. There was no chance of the Ravens studying the roadblock ahead of time. It wouldn't exist until the Ravens were caught in the middle of it.

It was up to Bolan to catch them.

The Executioner barreled down the hill, estimating where the lead riders of the Ravens would be. He took one of the turns fast enough to produce a gasp from Semple, which was quite an accomplishment considering the breakneck driving skills the islanders were notorious for.

And then the Hummer was on the straight stretch of road leading to the midpoint curve.

There was no one in sight.

"We're too early," Semple said.

Bolan shook his head. He felt that everything was moving according to schedule. The landmarks were right, the speed was right...but most of all, the cause was right. The Executioner was in combat mode, and he was totally in sync with his senses.

With his foot steady on the gas pedal and the steering wheel held in a fixed position, Bolan kept the Hummer in the middle of the road, following the white line that blurred beneath the wheels.

To his left was the forested hill with trees speeding by like jagged green fence posts. To his right was a ridge with a sheer drop to the sea below.

Bolan was running out of road. The sharp bend at the midpoint was coming up soon. His hands gripped the steering wheel tightly as he neared the end of the straightaway.

Three bright yellow motorcycles came around the bend.

The Executioner spun the wheel hard to his left and slammed his foot onto the brake at the same time.

Semple swore.

The tires screeched as the front end of the heavy field vehicle angled toward the left lane and the back end skidded across the right lane.

The lead motorcyclist had one hand on the handlebars and one hand on his Heckler & Koch submachine gun. He'd been startled by the tons of machinery bearing down on him out of the blue, but his split-second reflexes prevailed and he managed to squeeze off a short burst.

His aim was wild, and the slugs burned nothing but sky.

Bolan cut the wheel to the right, straightening the

Hummer just enough so the reinforced ramming bumper clipped the back of the gunner's bike. The impact spun the light dirt bike like a top, causing the rider to drop his weapon and hang on to the handlebars.

For a moment he looked like a rodeo rider, eyes wide, mouth open in shock. Then he was thrown from his mount. As the motorcycle dropped out from under him, he flew sideways through the air and smashed his back into the trunk of a tree several feet off the ground.

It happened in an instant, but Bolan's senses were so heightened that he felt almost as if everything around him were moving in slow motion. Every action and reaction was clear to him as the visual input flooded his brain.

As the first rider went spinning off the road, Semple chopped a short burst out the window. The first slugs from the Colt M-633 whapped into the rider's bulletproof vest and tilted him back like a knight hit with a joust lance.

The next few 9 mm rounds climbed up from his neck to his forehead and practically turned him into a headless horseman.

The rider flipped off the bike and landed on the road in a bloody smear. The unpiloted motorcycle skidded sideways onto the road in a shower of sparks and ripped up shards of sun-weakened tar that followed it over the ridge.

The third rider had instinctively wheeled toward the edge of the road at first sight of the Hummer, which sent him soaring in the air.

He managed to escape getting hit by the Hummer and avoided the Colt gunfire at the same time, a temporary triumph that he was about to carry with him on the long flight down.

The realization that he was going to die anyway caused a panic reaction in the rider, making him grip the handlebars in a death lock, as if somehow the bike could drive him out of here.

His scream echoed on the way down the cliffside, cut short as the bike glanced off an outcropping and jarred him loose. The impact launched him into free fall toward the rock-strewed seashore below.

Semple strafed the Colt M-633 from left to right and back again, hosing the killzone with 9 mm bursts as the next pack of riders slammed on their brakes or tried to avoid the Hummer blocking the road.

Two of them were dead before they hit the ground, entangled in the bikes that dragged them across the road in flesh-ripping skids.

Another rider fell off his bike and tumbled onto the side of the road, still clutching his Heckler & Koch submachine gun.

He stood up in a groggy haze and swept the subgun toward the Hummer, but Semple beat him to the punch. He triggered a burst that stitched the merc's arms and tore the weapon from his hands. Almost as an afterthought the next rounds from the Colt ripped into his throat.

By now, the front ranks of the mercenaries were bottled up. Some of them drove off the forest side of the road into a ditch. Others skidded onto the loose gravel shoulder that perilously bordered the dropoff.

A few riders rammed into the unyielding tonnage of the Hummer, then sailed on top of the hood, their bodies temporarily blocking the view as they tried to regain their balance.

The Executioner freed his Beretta from the side

pocket, then snaked his arm through the window. As soon as the nose of the Beretta was clear, he began to fire at the riders.

Three rounds caught the first gunner as he was trying to push himself up off the glass.

Bolan fired another burst that ripped into a dazed mercenary who was almost sitting up, one hand massaging his bruised temple where he'd crashed into the glass while he wondered where he was. The Beretta's burst put him right were he belonged, with his dead body slumped over the Hummer like a hood ornament.

Semple took care of the other dismounted mercenary who'd managed to slide off the hood and make a run for it.

The panicked Raven tripped over the broken forks of a trashed motorcycle, causing him to fall face first toward the shoulder. Semple's 9 mm burst followed him to the ground and made sure he wouldn't get up again.

While the first wave of Ravens was disoriented by the Hummer blocking the road, the second wave crashed into the machines and men that littered the ground.

There was no room to move, nowhere to go.

And still the mercenaries kept on coming, crashing into one another, shouting, swearing and dying. The ambush site was chosen to create total confusion and allow little room for escape. As soon as the mercenaries rounded the curve, they saw nothing but a heavy metal barricade with their cohorts bleeding on the ground in front of it.

Their choices were to run right into the deadly hail of fire, hurtle off the cliff or try to turn.

Each choice led to certain death.

By now, Bolan was outside the Hummer, shielding himself with the reinforced armor of the driver's-side door as he trained the Beretta 93-R on the men in the ditch and the roadway.

With controlled bursts, Bolan carefully rationed his fire as he sought out moving targets in the ditch, catching the mercenaries before they had time to return accurate fire.

Several rounds thunked into the Hummer's body and windshield, pocking the chassis and bullet-resistant glass with 9 mm lead. But the mercenaries were still firing blindly, attempting to fight their way out of the area with saturation fire.

It was a full-auto maelstrom with the mercenaries caught in the middle of it. Some of their bullets hit their own men. Most of the slugs pounded into the dirt or singed the air.

Several of the now unseated mercs performed a grisly dance as they staggered across the road with blood pouring from their wounds. They squeezed off dead-man bursts, their fingers desperately clutching the triggers as Bolan and Semple chopped them down.

The SAU commando had followed Bolan's lead and barreled out of the passenger-side door, covering his exit by triggering a full-auto burst from a fresh magazine at the shocked mercenaries.

He was moving toward the back of the Hummer, where the heavy firepower was.

The surprise roadblock wouldn't hold the mercenaries for too long. They still had the numbers on their side, and most of them had the kind of battlefield experience that would let them recover and launch a counterattack.

Unless they received another shock.

"Now, now, now!" Bolan shouted. Even as he spoke, the ambushers opened fire from their positions in the forest. Some of them had already been taking single shots at any of the mercs who posed immediate danger to Bolan or Semple.

But most of the ambushers had held their fire, waiting until as many men as possible were trapped on the road.

Then they fired for maximum effect.

Bright bursts of flame seared through the woods as Colt M-633 subguns poured lead down into the trapped mercs.

The rattle of gunfire and the screams of the Ravens filled the air as they tried to avoid the volleys.

The SAU commandos and the DEA operatives maintained a steady fire into the killzone. One group fired full-auto blasts while the other group slapped fresh magazines into their weapons.

By the time the Jeeps, Cadillac and van piled into the gauntlet, most of the first-wave mercenaries were dead. And more corpses were joining the ranks with every passing second.

There was no room for the vehicles to turn even if they had wanted to, for behind them was a second Hummer that angled sharply across the road to cut off any avenue of escape. Phase Two of the roadblock locked them into place.

Simon Tremaine was out of the vehicle and firing his short-barreled subgun into the crowd of thunderstruck mercenaries.

The Ravens had been anticipating some resistance at the old fortress, but before that happened, all they expected was a quick ride up the coastal road and a quick hit on the islanders.

Instead they found themselves on an expressway to oblivion.

Thinking almost as one, the ambushers fired into the convertible, wiping out the exposed gunmen with full-auto bursts that painted the car seats red.

Realizing a second too late that the Cadillac was a magnet for the ambushers' fire, the driver flung open his door and tried to leap out onto the road. He managed to touch the ground with one foot before a 9 mm triburst drilled through his skull.

The dying driver fell back into the Cadillac and with his last breath reached for the steering wheel to catch his balance. His fingers curled around the wheel in a rictus grip. Anchored by the wheel, the bullet-ridden husk fell back to the seat, a grisly chauffeur driving the dead mercs into the afterlife.

A few mercs sought cover from the 9 mm broadside streaming from the forest. Seeing a brief chance to get out of the lead rain, they crouched behind the Cadillac.

But that movement placed them in the line of fire of the SAU commandos positioned near Simon Tremaine.

The mercs fired several bursts into the woods before the heavy fire from Tremaine's team drove them back toward the front of the car, where they were once again exposed to fire from the woods.

One of the mercs dropped with several bullets in his upper body, but the two other mercs had had enough.

They stood and charged toward Tremaine's Hummer. The lead Raven held an M-3 submachine gun out in front of him like a bayonet and triggered half of the 30-round magazine as he ran forward. Most of the slugs punched into the hood of the Hummer, tracking toward Tremaine and the SAU sharpshooter beside him.

Three rounds from the woods hit the man with the Browning, two of them in his bulletproof vest, one in the shoulder. He ignored the spray of blood from his wound and let his momentum carry him toward the Hummer. The last burst from the Browning subgun hit the commando standing beside Tremaine and dropped him into the ditch.

The suicidal attack had produced some effect, but the Browning was empty now.

Tremaine stepped away from the Hummer and unloaded the rest of his magazine into the merc as he tried to reload the Browning. The subgun fell from his hand as he crumpled onto the dusty road, dead.

The second merc had changed direction and was charging right for the woods, leaping over the ditch as he triggered a burst from his Armalite assault rifle.

The weapon's wild volley ripped through the edge of the forest and into the chest of another SAU commando who'd been close to the road. The commando tumbled forward into the ditch, almost crashing into the merc who'd downed him.

The mercenary managed to land on the far side of the ditch, momentarily tottering as he tried to catch his balance.

Several snipers from the woods unloaded their weapons, the multiple bursts sledgehammering the hardman back down into the ditch.

Hugo Xavier's voice bellowed above the gunfire.

Seeing his men cut to pieces all around him, the leader of the Ravens raced up and down their tattered ranks and marshaled them into a firing line behind the Jeeps.

There was nowhere to go, so they stood their ground to pour concentrated fire into the forest.

A variety of Uzis, Ingrams and Heckler & Koch MP-5 submachine guns pointed toward the middle of the woods where most of the fire had come from.

Then all of the Ravens fired at once.

The combined firepower had a shock effect on the ambushers, who fell back from the onslaught.

The mercenaries had found a killzone of their own, and that realization urged them on. From the middle of what seemed like a certain massacre, they'd found a possible exit—right through the ambushers.

Smoke and flame burst from their gun barrels over and over as they slapped fresh magazines into their weapons to keep up the sustained fire.

Some of the mercs strafed the woods from left to right while others poured fire in a figure-eight pattern that climbed up and down the wooded hill.

Branches dropped to the ground, and chunks of bark flew into the air as the bullets burned through the forest.

The Ravens advanced, now and then picking out targets in the woods, but mostly firing by instinct. They'd found their mark and were saturating it with everything they had.

The desperate stand paid off.

Some of the Ravens fell where they stood, but their steady fire was producing gaps in the ambushers' ranks.

The SAU commandos on the left and right flanks kept up their fire, but the ones in the center were overwhelmed. Return fire still erupted from some pockets in the center line, but bursts from the commandos were rapidly dwindling, either from increased casualties or forced retreat.

Gauging the withering effect of their fusillade, Xavier signaled the Ravens to move forward yet again. Acting as one, they followed his lead and charged straight for the ditch.

Xavier was the first one across. He paused at the edge of the woods and triggered a full-auto burst from his L-34 A-1 Sterling Patchett submachine gun to clear the way in front of him. The silenced version of the Sterling was a lot longer than the regular subgun, but even with the unfolded stock, the ten-pound British subgun looked small in Xavier's hands.

He was obviously accustomed to the length and weight of the weapon, which moved easily like an extension of his hand. It had seen him through several campaigns before and from the look of determination on his face, it appeared that it might see him through this one.

As he stepped into the shadows, Xavier burned off another ten rounds from the side-mounted magazine, the *phyyt-phyyt-phyyt* sounds of the silenced burst marking his progress.

All around him the Ravens were using the same technique, recon by fire, to make sure their path was clear.

Their minds were clear now, uncluttered by any long-range plans.

They'd given up any hope of reaching their objective at the stone fortress. The cache was forgotten.

All that mattered to the Ravens was survival.

THE EXECUTIONER STOOD in a rock-strewed waist-high ditch. At his feet were the bodies of two dead Ravens who'd made a break for it in his direction.

The Executioner had retrieved an Ameli Squad Automatic Weapon from the back of the Hummer as soon as the mercenaries started piling up in the road-block.

He'd fired one hundred rounds already and still had another hundred rounds to go before he had to change magazines. The 200-round box magazine hung like an anchor just below the machine gun's lightweight metal frame.

All told, the box of NATO assault cartridges and the Ameli itself weighed less than twenty pounds, giving him a highly maneuverable weapon with accurate range up to one thousand yards. At this close range it was taking a definite toll on the mercenaries caught in the middle of the road.

Bolan had jumped into the ditch near the front of the Hummer and kept up a steady rate of controlled fire, left hand holding the bar on the barrel, right hand on the pistol grip.

At a rate of 850 rounds per minute, each trigger pull of the Ameli sent a blizzard of metal cartridges into the killzone.

By slightly angling the barrel of the machine gun, Bolan could cover most of the blockade area. His deadly accuracy chased away a small group of mercs who'd been running toward the ditch only to find that he was more of a blockade than the Hummer that crossed the road.

Nothing got by him.

Semple was covering the other side of the blockade with the heavy-duty road sweeper he'd pulled from the back of the Hummer. It looked giant in his hands, but the Armsel Striker semiautomatic shotgun was easy to control with an extra grip in front of the magazine to cut out recoil and muzzle rise.

The spring-driven coil magazine could fire twelve shotgun loads in seconds.

Semple triggered the shotgun, punching holes through the van that some of the mercs sought shelter in.

Instead they found themselves showered by metal fragments and 12-gauge slugs. Two mercs were killed instantly inside the van, but two more jumped back into the open and ran right into several more shotgun loads.

Between the Executioner's Ameli machine gun and Semple's shotgun, there was hardly any refuge to be found.

But when Xavier regrouped his men and led them into the woods, the heavy weapons were of little use. Too many SAU commandos were in the zone now. Bolan set the machine gun in the ditch, slapped a fresh magazine into the Beretta 93-R and moved into the woods.

Semple stayed behind to cover the almost deserted roadway where several wounded or dazed mercenaries were still moving around. But they were still dangerous. Even if they were dying, they didn't plan on going alone. The SAU sharpshooter fell back against the Hummer, looking over his shoulder every few seconds as he reloaded the Armsel.

HUGO XAVIER MADE IT about thirty yards into the woods before he saw a shape moving off to his left. It was an SAU commando with an automatic weapon. The soldier spotted Xavier at the same time and pivoted toward him with the Colt subgun.

But the Sterling M-34 A-1 was already bearing down on the man, its stout black barrel homing in on the target as if it had a mind of its own.

The first burst of the silenced Sterling caught the commando in the gut, doubling him over from the impact. His finger clutched the trigger of the Colt subgun and unleashed a burst that sliced through the trees around Xavier.

Xavier wasn't about to be killed by a dead man.

He'd already triggered a second burst that drilled into the dying gunner's chest and kicked him backward into the trees.

Sensing motion behind the slain islander, Xavier triggered a sustained burst through the trees, then darted forward.

Behind him the trees disintegrated as gunfire from several directions homed in on him.

SAU commandos and DEA operatives closed in from both sides and clashed with the Ravens.

Xavier was past the battle line, free and clear to escape the trap. But he couldn't leave his men behind. He stopped and turned slowly, taking in the sand-colored uniforms and the familiar shapes of the mercenaries he'd fought alongside for so long. Then he headed back toward the area where the fighting was thickest.

BOLAN SAW THE BODIES falling near the broad-backed mercenary leader fighting his way through the thicket.

By the time the Executioner reached the area where he'd last seen Xavier, two more SAU commandos were lying dead and another Raven was dead.

The firing was dying down on both sides, though there were still sporadic bursts.

Some of the mercenaries were surrendering, recognizing that it was only a matter of time before they were hunted down.

But Xavier would never surrender willingly, Bolan

thought as he scanned the woods for the mercenary until he caught a brief glimpse of him on the move again.

The Raven leader was about ten yards away, and he was bringing his Sterling to bear on a commando who was holding an automatic pistol.

Before Bolan could snap off a shot, the mercenary dropped out of sight again, marking his position with a fiery burst from the Sterling, and marking his target with a spray of blood.

The commando lost the shoot-out.

Bolan used the time to close in on Xavier, finding himself face-to-face with the mercenary leader just as he stepped back from cover. It was like running into a bear in the middle of the woods.

The mercenary's immense shape moved almost too fast for Bolan to follow. They were both too close to fire, too close to rely on anything but instinct.

Bolan caught a quick glimpse of the Sterling swinging toward him, and the Executioner barely had time to deflect the barrel with his Beretta. The 93-R came down like an ax on top of the Sterling, metal clanging against metal as the snout of the Beretta pushed the long barrel toward the ground.

"No!"

The mercenary's bellowing war cry thundered in Bolan's ear. The shout was loud enough to stun a man not used to such tactics, but the Executioner had used the martial-arts tactic himself several times before and knew how to control his reaction.

Instead of flinching from the war cry, Bolan relied on his instinct and swung the Beretta in a short arc that brought the barrel against Xavier's forehead. It gouged a chunk of flesh and bounced off his skull a split second before Bolan could pull the trigger. The burst fired harmlessly overhead.

Though he was dazed by the blow from the barrel, Xavier struck back at the same time. His left fist crashed into Bolan's shoulder with the weight of his body behind the blow.

Bolan moved with the punch and let the impact spread through his shoulder. There was no time to acknowledge the pain, just time to kill. He dropped toward the ground and used his momentum to try to tug the Sterling's barrel free from Xavier's grip, but the bigger man held on tight.

From his peripheral vision Bolan saw several SAU commandos in the distance. The reinforcements were too far away to distinguish the combatants and besides, the Executioner and Xavier were too close for anyone to risk a shot.

Bolan whipped his right elbow back into Xavier's face, feeling the cartilage crack as an explosion of blood cascaded from his broken nose. The pain and shock gave the Executioner enough leverage to rip the Sterling free and dive forward.

For that he paid a heavy price.

Xavier charged behind him and unleashed a snap kick just as Bolan turned toward him. The massive foot caught Bolan in the side of the face and almost took his head off.

He'd managed to angle a few inches out of the way but not far enough to avoid damage.

The pain exploded inside Bolan's head, a huge nova of whiteness that threatened to black him out. He felt the Beretta fall from his fingertips, felt his body crying out for him to fall unconscious. But if he gave in now, it was all over.

Instead Bolan willed himself to keep moving.

Somehow he leaped out of the way of a second kick and landed on his back. Without stopping to think, he cocked his right leg and struck out as the heavy footsteps bore down on him.

Xavier went down with a shattered kneecap.

He landed hard on top of Bolan and clawed one huge hand at this throat. The Executioner swept it away with a circle block that brought his palm in striking position under Xavier's chin, pushing hard enough to clack the merc's teeth together.

Xavier's thick neck hardly moved.

The Executioner tumbled forward then, his right hand scooping up the Beretta as he came up in a half crouch and swung the barrel toward his adversary's face.

The merc's long legs were stretched out in an awkward position. One of them was shattered, the other anchored in a position that helped him sit up. His eyes were glassy from the pain, but he was still focusing on the Beretta and calculating the best way to knock it out of Bolan's hand.

Then he studied Bolan's face and saw that there was no way he could disarm him. The Executioner was anticipating his every move.

"It's over," Bolan said, gasping to regain his breath as he moved out of range of Xavier's hand or foot. "Give up."

The leader of the Ravens shook his head.

"There's nothing left to fight for," Bolan told him, gesturing uphill toward the fortress. "The vault's empty. There's nothing left up there for you or the general."

Xavier's eyes flashed at the mention of the general.

"You knew everything."

"Just about. You've all been cashed out. All you can do now is cooperate."

Xavier laughed. "No chance of that."

"No choice," Bolan said, lowering the Beretta and studying the merc's eyes. There was no fear, nor any anger. In his eyes was acceptance of his lot.

The Raven reached behind him as if he were spreading his fingers on the ground to steady himself and find a more comfortable position to ease the pain. "Like you said...it's over."

There was a familiar sound of a knife sliding from a leather sheath, then Xavier's hand came back into view. He held a dull black blade in the hand that was now cocked behind his head, ready to throw it, aware he wouldn't make it.

Bolan pulled the trigger. Three rounds thumped into the Raven chieftain, giving him the death he desired.

The Executioner stepped away from the slain man and looked around the forest. He saw several commandos leading a handful of Ravens who had no qualms about surrendering.

Bolan jogged over to the prisoners. "Xavier's dead," he shouted. "Who's next in command?"

A man with a bandaged bloody arm hanging limp by his side turned toward Bolan. "That would be me," he said as he took a few steps away from the others. His voice was as dull as his eyes.

"What's your name?" Bolan asked.

"Mike Gibbons. I'm second-in-command to the late Hugo Xavier." He spoke as if he was having trouble convincing himself that Xavier was indeed dead. "What do you want?"

"I want you to talk some sense into the other

strike team,'' Bolan said, pulling a satcom transceiver from his combat vest.

''You know about them?'' Gibbons asked.

''Right down to their birthdays. And if it comes to that, right down to the day of death.''

''I can see that.''

''See that it doesn't happen.''

Bolan gave a few terse instructions to the captured mercenary, then waited for Tremaine to arrive with the rest of the commandos.

While they waited, the seven mercenaries who were left alive dropped down into the grass. They looked smaller now, humbler, blood lust taken out of them.

The omens had proved to be true. The Ravens had come to the island as portents of death and destruction.

Their own.

CHAPTER FIFTEEN

The clapboard-and-stone buildings facing the marina belonged to prosperous islanders who had weathered the storms that battered the coast for years. They were mostly merchants or civil servants who had enough money to rebuild the traditional red-roofed island cottages trashed by the hurricanes or by the cronies of General Fabreaux who'd occupied them during his reign.

Standing proudly in their midst was Government House with its high white walls, gatehouse and garden-flanked driveway tended by a six-man landscaping crew.

Today Government House was an armed camp, though an outsider wouldn't know the difference. The level of activity behind the wrought-iron gates remained the same, but the people behind the gates were different types of government servants.

SAU commandos and undercover police officers had quietly taken the places of most of the ministers and workers at Government House. The landscaping crew was made up of sharpshooters, and the chauffeurs who stood by armored government cars were counterinsurgency specialists.

Despite the threat from the mercenaries, Prime Minister William Lorraine and a handful of his advisers had refused to leave Government House. If the seat of government came under attack once again, Lorraine would meet it at the gates. The prime minister believed in Simon Tremaine, and in the high-tech help provided by the U.S. government.

A team of DEA agents with SEAL backgrounds had made an underwater approach to the marina-based mercenary force and attached miniature limpet microphones to the hulls of their yachts and power-boats. The main target of the underwater microphone boxes was David Puckett, the leader of the seaborne Raven force.

Just about every word Puckett uttered—the bragging, the swearing, the planning—was broadcast to the temporary listening station set up inside Government House. From there the conversations were immediately transmitted to the island commandos and U.S. operatives positioned around the marina.

Some of the operatives were in boats, others were in taxis or Jeeps, patrolling the area in a lazy pattern that kept them close enough to the marina. All of them were plugged in to the surveillance operation, ready to strike at a moment's notice.

While Bolan and Tremaine dealt with the motor-cycle brigade, Armand Cane handled the marina-side scenarios with Roger Hagen, Tremaine's right-hand man. Together they had devised several possible action plans, ranging from a preemptive strike to a pitched battle outside Government House. But hopefully, if they planned well enough, the seafront assault wouldn't happen at all.

THE DISTANT SOUND of gunfire had floated down to the marina for several minutes. As soon as the mountaintop battle began, several of the mercenaries came up on the decks to listen.

They responded like Pavlovian dogs of war attracted to the music of destruction. The sound of grenade blasts and rapid bursts of automatic fire queued them up for their own performance, as soon as David Puckett gave the word.

The motorcycle brigade had made contact with the enemy much earlier than any of the mercenaries on board the docked flotilla had expected, and then the firefight ended as suddenly as it started.

The silence that followed was deafening.

Hugo Xavier was supposed to contact David Puckett the moment they'd taken the fortress, but no calls came in.

Puckett tried raising Xavier several times, then he tried to contact his backup man.

Still nothing.

Finally Puckett went down into the main cabin of his forty-eight-foot yacht and tried to raise the motorcycle team on the more powerful comm gear.

The results were the same as before.

No one answered; no one called.

That put Puckett's plan in jeopardy. As soon as Xavier notified him of success on the mountain, Puckett's group was supposed to storm Government House. If necessary, they could call upon reinforcements from Xavier's men.

The skeletal island force would be overwhelmed—outfought and outthought—then Puckett would be calling the shots from inside Government House.

But now someone else was calling the shots.

As Puckett tried to raise Xavier yet again, one of his men stepped into the cabin.

"Mr. Puckett," he said, "you're wanted on deck."

"What for?"

"Someone's got a message for you."

Puckett followed him onto the deck just in time to witness a horde of men in sand-colored combat fatigues boarding the yacht with their submachine guns trained on his men.

The docks all around them were full of similarly clad islanders, and the main road was suddenly full of vehicles. Armed men stepped smartly out of the taxis and rental cars and took up positions facing the yachts and powerboats. Their weapons were at the ready, but no one had fired yet.

They didn't have to.

The seagoing mercenary team was in a U-shaped trap with men standing on the docks and the main road. And there were probably boats out at sea ready to cut them off.

A moment later, when he heard the unmistakable sound of helicopters coming in from the sea, Puckett knew there would be no exit from the marina. He glanced briefly toward the sea and saw a half dozen helicopters zooming toward them like hornets.

Now Puckett could see why there'd been no call from Xavier. These people knew what they were doing, and what they were doing was shutting him down.

Puckett's right hand had been edging closer to his side arm by instinct at first sight of the boarders, but another kind of instinct took over when he noticed the snouts of several subguns following his every move. He moved his hand safely away from the holster.

Then he noticed two men stepping forward from

the rest of the group who'd boarded the yacht. One of them, a heavyset islander in fatigues, was obviously the leader of the commandos. His eyes bored into Puckett as if he were vermin in need of an exterminator and they just happened to have one available.

The commando chief spoke briefly to the man beside him, a blond-haired and bearded man with a Colt M-633 submachine gun slung over his shoulder and a satcom device in his hand.

The bearded man stepped forward and held the satcom unit toward Puckett like a weapon.

"Who are you?" Puckett demanded, looking down at the stocky man who was a head shorter and forty pounds heavier than himself.

"I'm just a messenger," the bearded man said as he handed him the unit. "And here's the message."

Puckett glanced around at his men scattered on the other boats. They were all looking to him for a signal.

If he fought, they would fight. He would die, then they would die.

The merc leader took the satcom unit, telescoped the antenna and listened to a brief burst of static before a familiar voice came from the small speaker. It was Mike Gibbons, one of the long-time mercs who signed on with the outfit the same time as Hugo Xavier.

"Puckett?" the voice said. "That you?"

"Yeah, it is," Puckett replied, speaking into the transceiver. "Where the hell is Xavier?"

"Xavier's dead."

"What? Are you sure—?"

"Dead sure," came the reply. "I saw him. Xavier's dead. Morgan's dead. Robertson the same."

The man from the mountain listed several more names before saying, "Just about everyone left alive—five of us, as far as I know—have been hit. We're finished, Puckett. Hold on. There's a guy here who wants to talk to you."

"Wait!" Puckett said. "Who is it?"

"One of the guys who set this up. Here he is—"

A soft-spoken but firm voice came through the transceiver. "This is Simon Tremaine. You know the name?"

"Yeah. I heard of you."

"Didn't hear enough, though," Tremaine said. "Otherwise you would have stayed away."

"I guess."

"So make sure you listen now, Puckett. Like your man said, just about every last Raven has flown on to the beyond. You and your men can join them or you can take our offer and leave the island—in time, that is. You want to listen?"

Puckett looked around him. He saw the weapons the commandos handled with easy familiarity. He saw the organization in their ranks and the trap they'd sprung. And he also saw the future if he tried to resist. The Ravens might be able to give a good account of themselves in battle, but in the end they'd be obliterated.

He wasn't ready to retire from the mercenary game. He had too many paydays ahead of him. "I'm ready to listen," Puckett said into the transceiver.

"Then listen up to the man who's with you on the boat right now," Tremaine said. "His name's Roger Hagen, my second-in-command. He has authority to make a deal, or to make certain you don't ever leave here. If you're smart, you'll still be alive by the time we get down there."

Puckett collapsed the antenna back into the transceiver and handed it to the bearded man. Then he stepped up to the islander he'd earlier guessed was in command. "You're Hagen?"

"I'm Hagen."

"Tremaine said you've got a deal for us."

"You talk, you walk. We don't need any more bodies here to make our point." The commando nodded toward the mountains.

"There was nothing up there for your men to find in that fortress. The money was taken out long ago." Then he turned toward Government House. "As far as taking out the prime minister, between us and the Black Hawks you wouldn't have made it ten feet off the boats. And if you did, you'd find an army waiting for you inside those walls."

Puckett nodded.

"I just wanted you to know what you're up against," Hagen said. Then he laid down his conditions. Puckett and the remnants of the mercenary force would be free to go—once they revealed everything they knew about General Fabreaux and the man who hired them.

"We came down here to work for the general," Puckett said.

"Yes, but someone paid you," Hagen replied. "You're Quinn's people. That makes him the paymaster."

Puckett hesitated, looking ready to stonewall after all.

Armand Cane stepped forward. "Look, we know who's behind it. We've been tracking you people every step of the way. We just want to hear it from you."

"We're no one's people, particularly," Puckett replied. "We work for Quinn sometimes. We work for other people other times. This time around we were just working for the general—far as I know."

"That's not far enough," Hagen said. He nodded to a few other commandos standing by. They spread out, spacing themselves far enough apart to set up a skirmish line.

The motion produced a ripple effect throughout the ranks of the commandos, who also spread out to avoid making easy targets. The men on the docks and on the shore were ready for a battle.

Hagen's voice grew cold. "This is the way it is. We don't want to put you away in the jails. If we do, it'll prompt some other Raven fanatics to come down here and free you, and we'll have to fight this battle all over again. So jail's out. The only other place with room for you guys is the cemetery."

Puckett realized it wasn't just talk. He was on the brink of battle...and execution.

"Or you can talk," Hagen said, "and talk loudly. We want the names of the general's contacts on the island and off. We want everything you can give us about your dealings with Quinn. After we're convinced you're telling the truth, you can go."

Puckett glanced over his shoulder again. The closest powerboat was rocking up and down in the water. Four of his hard-eyed men stood there watching him.

It was the same from all of the other boats. All eyes were on the leader of the Ravens. He was used to giving tactical commands in the past. Usually it was fight or flight. It had been a long time since he'd had other signals to give.

Puckett crossed his arms in front of him long enough to form an *X*, then threw his hands down in front of him.

The sign was unmistakable. The Ravens laid down their arms instantly. They'd trusted him in war and now they had to trust him in peace.

Puckett carefully unhooked his holster and handed it over to the island commando. "Let's do some talking," he said. He followed Hagen off the dock, stepping down from the boat just in time to see a drove of commandos streaming down the road.

The column of commandos had come back down from the mountain in Hummer vehicles, a van and battered motorcycles, motorcycles once driven by Raven mercenaries.

Simon Tremaine stepped out of one of the Hummers, and a man in black stepped out of the other. They were the engineers of the Ravens' destruction on the mountain.

And almost his.

He'd made the right decision.

By selling out his employers, he was buying back his life.

CHAPTER SIXTEEN

Panama

The villa south of Nargana on Panama's Atlantic coast was close enough to Colombia that the reclusive occupant could slip across the border in case the federal authorities ever came looking for him.

Fortunately General Fabreaux had more than enough money to make sure the authorities would never find him—except for those times when they needed a bit more than the usual payoff.

Then the troubled officials would show up at his villa to discuss the pressure being put upon them to apprehend such a dangerous fugitive as himself. Perhaps if a little more money came their way, they could reach the right people and make the pressure go away....

General Fabreaux understood.

When he'd ruled Saint-Denis, he had offered safe haven to fugitives and no matter how profitable an arrangement it was, there were always sudden unforeseen expenses. At those times Fabreaux or one of his subordinates would approach the fugitives he'd welcomed to the island and explain the situation. They always understood that freedom had its price.

So now General Fabreaux paid whatever he was

asked whenever he was asked. In return he was allowed to conduct his business, which mainly involved bankrolling deals with the Colombian cartels who'd made substantial down payments on the government of Panama even before Noriega came to power.

Panama had changed considerably since the American invasion that ousted the dictator—the cocaine was purer, the banks had become even more efficient in their money laundering and the ministers and military men were much more sophisticated in covering up the day-to-day corruption that was the real economic backbone of the country.

It was a profitable arrangement for Fabreaux, enabling him to live the life of the landed gentry while paving the way for his triumphant return to Saint-Denis.

That time was almost upon him.

It had been almost upon him for several hours. By now he should have heard word from Quinn that Government House was ready for his return and that the cache in the fortress was uncovered. But Fabreaux had heard nothing of substance from the man he'd entrusted the operation to. Quinn had spoken with him only once, and then he'd offered the general nothing but vague assurances that the operation was under way.

That had been hours ago.

Maybe the Ravens did find the cache, Fabreaux thought. His next thought was that maybe the Ravens took it off the island for themselves and were even now dividing the spoils.

And what about the prime minister? Was he still alive? Or had Quinn finally rid him of that democratic fool?

Fabreaux resumed pacing back and forth in the richly furnished top-floor room of the main house that looked out onto the Atlantic. He'd tried to stop pacing and force himself to relax, but he was too much on edge.

Too much was at stake.

Fabreaux opened his gold-lined cigarette case and lit yet another unfiltered cigarette. That made it nearly twenty he'd smoked within the space of a few hours. He'd also sipped much too frequently from a freshly opened bottle of American whiskey, which was now almost empty, sitting on top of the table like a glass tombstone. The whiskey was supposed to soothe his smoke-scorched throat and steady his nerves, but it had made him unsteady in the process.

He walked over to the open French windows and leaned forward with both hands on the sill, letting the fresh night air clear his head. The sea breeze felt cool on his forehead and temporarily brightened his mood.

He would hear from him soon, Fabreaux thought. Quinn would ring him up to say the cache was secure and so was the government. Saint-Denis would be his for the taking.

He could almost picture his triumphant return—addressing the people once again in his gold-braided uniform, dispensing justice to the traitors who'd taken his place, importing a private army of mercenaries to make sure such a thing never happened again.

The brief air of optimism ended suddenly when Fabreaux's bleary eyes focused on the moonlit court-yard below where one of his men was supposed to be standing guard.

Instead, the man was lying down with his weapon

at his side, his body sprawled out beneath the shadows of a palm tree. At first it was hard to see clearly, but then the ocean breeze shifted the shadows above the guard's prone form. A pool of blood was forming around his head, darkly staining the imported tiles.

Quinn! he thought. The war merchant had betrayed him, sold him out to his enemies....

But no, it didn't make sense. Quinn had more to gain by getting Fabreaux back into power. Together they would prosper just like before. A man like Quinn knew how to make profitable deals. He knew the people to pay off and the people to pay back the hard way.

Quinn had nothing to gain from making the general an enemy.

But if not Quinn, then who could it be?

MACK BOLAN DUCKED beneath the palms that slashed against the side of Fabreaux's villa. The clicking and clacking of the razor-sharp fronds sounded like the rattling of bones.

The eerie sound was appropriate. Though the general's guards were not yet skeletons, they were all candidates for the graveyard. Silenced rounds had taken most of them out, blades the others.

The guards had been unprepared for a real military assault. Their past combat experience consisted mainly of shooting unarmed men or torturing captured women and children.

The past finally caught up to them in the form of the Executioner.

The black-clad warrior had been the first one to breach the villa walls, using a grappling hook with rubber-coated tines to rappel down the inside of the wall. Armand Cane had landed right beside him.

They'd taken care of the two guards by the gates, then opened the gates for the rest of the special team that had come ashore on black Zodiac inflatables from the Coast Guard cutters.

Once inside the gates, it took only a few moments for the black-clad commandos to secure the area.

Now there was only one man left to secure—General Fabreaux. Bolan nosed the air in front of him with the barrel of the Beretta 93-R as he stepped up the stone staircase that led to the second floor of the villa. He paused at the landing before advancing to the next level.

He was almost at the double glass doors when one of the panes exploded from inside. The heavy-caliber slug that broke the glass ricocheted off the stone wall and bit into the concrete at his feet. Two more shots sounded from inside the villa, and more glass crashed to the ground.

The shots were wild, just like the man who fired them. Bolan could hear Fabreaux swearing and screaming in rage as he staggered around the room, crashing into furniture, firing his weapon, shouting at the intruder to come and get him.

Bolan obliged.

Estimating the general's position from his last wild shot, Bolan angled close to the shattered doors and triggered a waist-high 3-round burst into the room. He fired a second burst at the same level.

Six shots. No reply.

Then he dived forward, holding the Beretta about a foot off the floor as he fired into the room.

The barrel of the Beretta followed the motion he detected. He had only a brief glimpse of Fabreaux moving toward the center of the room, but it gave him a clear target. Bolan fired another burst.

The general crashed into a table in the middle of the room and sprawled on top of it. His heavy revolver thudded onto the table and then, almost as if it had a mind of its own, swiveled back toward the doorway filled by the Executioner.

Bolan pulled hard on the trigger, stitching the general's gun hand with a 3-round burst that knocked the weapon free.

Bolan slapped a fresh magazine into the Beretta, turning just as someone appeared in the doorway.

When he recognized Armand Cane, the Executioner lowered the Beretta.

"That's him?" Cane asked.

"Yeah," Bolan said. "Our work's done here."

"What about the rest of his crew? There's got to be a slew of colonels and majors and whatever the hell else these phony soldiers have been calling themselves hanging around."

The Executioner shook his head. They had the locations of most of Fabreaux's so-called cabinet: Panama, El Salvador, Argentina, Colombia. Wherever they could purchase a safe haven, they had settled down. They deserved to be hunted down sometime, but right now their main objective was Quinn.

"Maybe we can enlist them in the cause," Bolan said.

"How?"

"Spread the word that Quinn took out the general. Maybe they'll put a bounty on his head."

Cane nodded his approval. "Works for me. Anything that turns the heat up on that bastard works for me."

"Then you'll like our next two stops," Bolan told him.

"Where?"

Bolan nodded south. "First stop is just across the border to pay a visit to Melitta Caporra. It's time we collected our investment from her—get her to set up a deal with Quinn."

"Then what?" Cane asked, not bothering to hide his disappointment. He was eager to get back to Florida.

"Then we stop in Costa Rica to pick up a pilot who's going to help Quinn carry out the deal," Bolan said. "Nicholas Vreeland is about to become a patriot again."

Colombia

MELITTA CAPORRA HEARD someone calling her name. It was just loud enough for her to hear above the soft music playing from hidden speakers in Vitorio's, one of the leading department stores in Cartagena's upscale shopping district.

She turned her head from the jewelry counter, where she'd been looking at an emerald bracelet under glass—and saw an elegantly dressed man with a clean-shaved face and dark blue eyes.

He was in his forties with a touch of gray streaking his black hair. He looked like a politician or a successful businessman whose business could have been anything from banking to cocaine.

"Yes?" she said, raising her eyebrows at him and wondering where she knew him from. "Do I know you?"

The man stepped closer, smiling as if they were old friends. "We have mutual friends," he said. He spoke Spanish well, but with a slight American accent that caused her smile to fade.

"Do these people have names?" she asked.

"Most of them have names best left unsaid," he replied. "But the name Belasko should be familiar to you. His friends are the ones who've been keeping in touch with you."

"I know the name," she said. "But he's a distant friend actually—"

"Actually he's not that distant anymore," the man said. "He's in the country right now and he wants to see you."

"Where?"

"I'll take you to him. My car's outside."

"Very well," she said. "Whatever you say."

"For starters I say you should accompany me to the car with a smile upon your face, as if you are looking forward to the ride—not as if you are about to be kidnapped."

"But I am."

"Only for a short while," the man replied. "And you can relax. No one is watching you now except our people. Otherwise I wouldn't have approached you."

Caporra swept her long dark hair back over her shoulder and managed a smile she didn't feel. Then she took his hand and lightly fell in step beside him. Her fingers tightly clutched his all the way to the front of the store.

The moment she'd been dreading had arrived. There had been several reminders from other anonymous contacts about her obligations to the man named Belasko, enough to let her know she hadn't been forgotten.

Ever since he'd let her escape from the Bahamas fiasco, she had been owned by the man in black. Now he was here to add her to his collection.

A white Mercedes with tinted windows pulled up

to the curb as soon as Caporra and her unwanted escort stepped out of the entrance. Her exposure on the street was limited to a few seconds, but she was frightened just the same.

She kept holding his hand tightly all the way to the car and tried to maintain an air of casualness about her, just another Cartagena beauty out for a drive with one of her suitors.

She kept up her pose until she climbed into the back seat of the car, then her smile broke. She leaned back into the soft cushion, pale and scared, not from the man who climbed in beside her, but from the knowledge of the irreversible course she was about to take.

The man nodded to the driver, and the white Mercedes blended in with the traffic flow.

Within minutes they drove out of the ancient walls of the Colombian port city and drove along the sun-struck Caribbean on the road toward Baranquilla. It was studded with the homes and hideaways of those who had made the Caribbean coastline the premier playground of Colombians and American expatriates.

After twenty minutes of driving, the Mercedes turned off the main road and followed a winding access road down to a seaside retreat where an American greeted them at the gated entrance.

He was tanned, smiling and armed. Another American spook, she thought. Their presence in Colombia was much greater than she'd imagined possible.

He waved them through the gates, and the Mercedes parked at the peak of a circular gravel driveway.

The man who'd politely kidnapped her in Cartagena opened the door for her, then led her to an open-air alcove on the side of the house. From there she could see down to the water and the stone steps that led to a sandy beach and a dock where a sleek cabin cruiser was waiting.

It was so easy to enter and leave the country unnoticed, she thought, wondering if she was about to go on a trip.

The man who had so far refused to give Caporra his name gripped her by the shoulders and looked coldly into her eyes. "It will be better for you if you forget this place," he said. "It's only a temporary stop, and we're moving out very soon. But if word reaches us that your people show any interest in this location, we'll know you can't be trusted and all deals are off. Full penalties will be exacted. Do you understand?"

"I understand you just threatened to kill me if I don't go along."

The man shrugged. "I'm here to facilitate whatever decision is made. The decision is up to your friend. He's waiting for you down there." He pointed toward the cabin cruiser. "I'll be here to take you back to Cartagena…if all goes well."

"It will," she said, turning her back to him and heading toward the dock.

The man she knew as Belasko was waiting for her in the cool and shadowed salon. He was sitting behind a table bolted to the floor, and gestured for her to sit across from him.

One side of his face was bruised, making her think of that night in the Bahamas when he had single-handedly destroyed her people. He'd obviously been involved in similar action since then.

"I'm glad to see you kept your side of the bargain," the man in black said.

She shrugged. "There wasn't much choice. You're a persuasive man."

"Let me persuade you some more."

"What do you want?"

"I want you to get the Mescone cartel involved in another deal with Thomas Quinn," Bolan said.

"That's not possible. There's still too much fallout from the Bahamas venture."

"Not only is it possible. It's inevitable. The Mescone cartel will be looking for Quinn to make good on his screwup. They'll also be looking for you to make amends because of the role you played in it. Correct?"

"There has been some talk. The Mescone brothers want me to recoup the losses—in time—but it has to be a logical deal, something my people will believe is genuine. Especially after the way the last one turned out."

"We've taken care of the logic," Bolan told her. "Quinn owes you a considerable amount. He has in his possession certain advanced weapons that can repay the Mescone cartel and still make a profit for everyone."

"What are they?"

"Phase Two Heckler & Koch sound-suppressed weapons designed for Special Forces use. And smart rifles, automatic weapons that will hit anything even a cartel soldier fires at."

Without getting too technical, Bolan explained the concept of the Individual Combat Weapon, which had been developed for the U.S. Army. A futuristic and streamlined version of a grenade launcher-automatic rifle, the ICW fired air-burst munitions with miniature electronic guidance systems built into the bullets, which exploded like grenades when they reached their target.

"These rifles can shoot behind rocks if you want," Bolan said. "The rifle comes with all the candy— tube to fire the shells, a barrel to fire regular bullets. The rifle determines the range, the soldier pulls the trigger…and goodbye target. The bullets are like computer-guided artillery shells."

Caporra steepled her hands together, then slowly peered through her fingers at Bolan. "Where are they located?" she said. "The Mescone brothers will not deal in Florida anymore. At least with Quinn."

Bolan nodded. "No problem. You meet with Quinn in Florida to set up the deal, but it goes down in Texas. The weapons have been diverted from standard military channels and are very hot, so he'll be eager to move them. He's got a spot close to the Mexican border—"

"Why Mexico?"

"We know all about the arrangements your people have with Mexico. The Colombian cartels rent storage facilities near the border, just like they rent the officials owned by the Mexican Mafia. The good thing about Mexico is that your people won't expect to run into the same kind of trouble as they did in the Bahamas."

"What kind of trouble *will* they run into?" she asked.

"First thing you should know," Bolan said, "is that they won't be walking away with any of these weapons. And Quinn probably won't deal unless there's something in it for him. These are restricted weapons, and they're worth millions to him. He'll probably agree to pay back what he owes but you've got to sweeten the pot with whatever the Mescone cartel has available near the border.''

"Brown heroin," she said. "Cocaine. Smoke."

"Sounds like a regular supermarket."

"Whatever the market demands," she replied.

"Whatever it is, it won't be coming back. The guns will be confiscated, and the drugs will be destroyed. None of the people who come with you are to know about the deal until the minute it goes down. Then you and your people are free to leave, providing you don't cross me."

Caporra looked at the bruised face of the man in black. His hard eyes were judging her in turn, wondering if she could be trusted. He would let her walk or he would bury her. The choice was hers.

"I want to get in and I want to get out," she said. "Nothing else. But there is one problem before we set this up. How am I supposed to have put these deals together?"

"There's a pilot in Costa Rica by the name of Nicholas Vreeland," Bolan said. "He used to work for Quinn, and he's kind of in the same position you are. Quinn thinks Vreeland owes him, so Vreeland's looking over his shoulder. It's natural for him to want to buy some peace of mind—make things nice with this deal. Plus Quinn will feel better working with someone he knows."

"How are we supposed to have met?" Caporra asked.

"Costa Rica," Bolan said. "Or in Cartagena. We'll work that out as soon as I talk to Vreeland."

She pulled her head back. "You mean he doesn't know about the deal yet?"

"No, but he'll go along with it. Either that or he'll be going through a sudden change of life."

CHAPTER SEVENTEEN

Costa Rica

Nicholas Vreeland looked perfectly at home in the waterfront tavern in one of the worst—or best—sections of the port city of Limón, depending upon your point of view. Worst if the ambience or food mattered, best if you wanted to remain unseen and unknown.

The windows were painted a dark green to keep out the sun, and the lights were comfortably dim. The music was low and so were the conversations. Most patrons came here to drink alone or to escape for a while from their work on the docks. It was a quiet bar with a constantly changing clientele.

With his trim looks and his pleasant manner, Vreeland found it easy to fade into the background, just another American who ended up in Costa Rica for one reason or another.

Vreeland believed that he was relatively unknown in Limón. Ever since he abandoned Quinn's Everglades operation, with the wreckage of the grounded planes still fresh in his mind, he had kept to himself in the cafés, bars and inexpensive boardinghouses.

He had enough money put aside to live comfortably, but for now it was better to keep moving and keep hidden. Eventually he would contact some of his old network, the people who'd originally hired him to fly weapons in and drugs out of Costa Rica long before he met Quinn. First it had been for the Sandinistas when the Costa Rican government supported their camps on the northern border with Nicaragua. Then, when they fell out of favor, he flew guns in and drugs out for the Contras who'd moved into the same camps. It wouldn't be too hard to renew some of those old friendships, at least when he could stop looking over his shoulder.

Vreeland had friends in all realms of government who might offer their protection, but it was still too early to seek out their patronage. And too expensive.

When the time was right and the heat died down, Vreeland would surface and contact his friends in officialdom. If the time ever came, he thought when he saw the man in black stand up from the corner table where he'd been sitting.

The man had been watching Vreeland without appearing to watch him. It was a common habit for the kind of people who frequented bars like this, only natural to take the measure of the people around you.

But now the man's interest in Vreeland was obvious.

And there were other men who were interested in Vreeland's presence. One of them was standing at the bar, a bearded man with his long hair tied in a ponytail. The bearded man had turned to watch Vreeland just as the man in black got up from the table, almost as if it had been choreographed.

Two more men had also turned their attention to Vreeland. They'd hardly seemed to notice him when they'd first arrived and taken a table off to the side. They'd been engrossed in conversation then, hard

men making a hard deal. But now they were studying
him intently, looking ready to turn the bar room into
a battlefield. Mercenary types. Or spooks. It was hard
to tell.

What he could tell was that his number was up.

BOLAN PULLED A CHAIR from Vreeland's table and
sat down quickly, thudding the long-necked beer bottle on the surface.

Vreeland looked up at the Executioner. He wasn't
frightened or foolish enough to try to run. Instead the
pilot had a speculative look about him as if he were
debating whether he could kill Bolan before the others moved in on him.

The threat of violence was there. But as long as
people weren't shooting at him, Vreeland wasn't
about to bring it on.

"Drink?" Bolan asked.

"No," Vreeland replied. "I'm sticking with coffee these days."

"Yeah, I know."

"What?"

"It's in your file. You're a reformed drunk, though
you obviously can't stay out of these kind of places."
Bolan looked around the run-down establishment.
"Must be nostalgia."

Vreeland laughed. "Quinn's been doing his homework."

"I'm not with Quinn," Bolan said. "As a matter
of fact I'm very much against him."

"Aren't we all?"

"Not everyone." Bolan reached inside his shirt
pocket and took out a photograph, which he dropped
on the table.

It was a surveillance photograph of Dan McCall,

the bushy-haired pilot who'd accompanied Vreeland on the Everglades run. It showed him getting out of a car in a narrow, crowded street. A pair of local gunmen was with him.

Vreeland picked up the surveillance photograph and shook his head. "McCall," he said. "Last time I saw him was in Puerto Rico when I dropped him off."

"That picture was taken of him right here in Limón," Bolan said. "Your ex-pilot's closing in on you. Apparently there's a bounty on your head."

"That's Quinn's style." Vreeland tossed the photograph on the table. "How close is McCall now?"

"Real close," Bolan replied. "But he's under observation."

"By who?"

"By some friends of mine. Embassy personnel. Contacts in the Civil Guard. Agency operatives…the same people who've been tailing you ever since you bailed out of the Big Cypress gig."

Vreeland looked stunned. "You were there?"

Bolan nodded. "We let you fly out. Followed you to Lauderdale, Puerto Rico, then down here. Every step of the way we've had enough people to keep McCall from getting to you."

"Why go to such trouble for me?" Vreeland asked.

"We're about to become partners."

"In what?"

"In a deal to bring Quinn down," Bolan told him.

Vreeland mulled it over like a man who had plenty of alternatives to consider. "How can I trust you?"

"Simple," Bolan said. "If we wanted you dead, you'd be dead already. But we need you to get Quinn, and you need us to stay alive. Help us set it up, and you get a free pass back into the country. Good until the next time you screw up.''

Vreeland was stunned yet again. For years he'd been a stranger to the U.S. His record and his common sense kept him away. He missed his native land, but he knew he would miss his freedom even more.

Now here was a chance to start over.

It was also a chance to get killed.

''What do I have to do?''

''Convince Quinn to work with you again,'' Bolan said.

''That might be hard to do. It's going to be dangerous to show my face around.''

''I'll be with you.''

''As what?''

''As your right-hand man,'' Bolan said. ''Since you're a hunted man, it's only natural for you to have some protection. Especially when you're back in business on your own again.''

''Makes sense.''

''It also makes sense that someone finds you. The Mescone cartel has been hunting down Quinn's associates ever since one of their deals went bad in the Bahamas. They're trying to find out what really happened. Quinn's been telling the Mescones he wants to deal with them again to make amends, but he's been putting them off.''

''Was this thing in the Bahamas as bad as the one in the Glades?''

''Worse,'' Bolan said. ''There was only one survivor from the Mescone cartel—Melitta Caporra, one of the deal makers. Since she's got a personal stake in evening things out, we'll say she's the one who caught up to you first. And now she's forcing the issue. She wants to make a deal with Quinn, and she wants you involved because she trusts you.''

"Why's that?'' Vreeland said.

"Because you're one of the most honest men on the planet,'' Bolan said. "For us anyway. We'll work out the details soon enough and coordinate them with Melitta. She'll go to Florida to talk things over with Quinn. Then you and I will pay him a visit. And then the deal goes down…in flames.''

Vreeland nodded his agreement. "Sounds real enough. A deal could happen like that. But Quinn's a suspicious man. I'm going to need the protection. Maybe you and some others.''

Bolan shook his head. "I'm enough.''

"I'm starting to believe that,'' Vreeland said, realizing that the man across from him had already carried out two successful operations against Quinn, a startling average considering Quinn's background.

The pilot was ready to come on board with Bolan, and he was clearly relieved that he wasn't facing a hit squad. But the relief was relative. Vreeland knew he wasn't getting out of this easy. "So what's involved in this deal I'm supposed to be setting up?''

"Weapons,'' Bolan said, "from Quinn's Texas armory. It's active again, and he's been stocking up some restricted pieces that are extremely hot. He'll want to move them quick, so the deal should go down quick. You'll be the go-between for both parties, and you'll be flying in some contraband from Mexico.''

Vreeland whistled. "How'd you tumble onto the weapons thing?''

"Slater told us,'' Bolan said. "Our intelligence confirmed it.''

"Slater's still alive?'' he said.

"One of the few who walked out of there. He chose to cooperate."

The pilot looked at the Executioner, then at the heavyset man who was standing at the bar. The man with the ponytail raised a drink in a mock cheer to him. Finally Vreeland glanced toward the other two mercenary types who'd been watching him throughout his conversation with Bolan. "I imagine that's one way of staying alive."

"The only way."

"I'll take it," Vreeland said.

Colombia

THE SAME DAY that she received word from the man named Belasko, Melitta Caporra invited Bernardo and Federico Mescone to a dinner in her private suite at the Cartagena Hilton.

That meant she also hosted their two bodyguards and a private secretary who accompanied the brothers anywhere they went. Outside the hotel room were several other Mescone associates who had checked the suite beforehand and were now standing quietly on guard.

Ever since their days as up-and-comers in the cocaine trade, the brothers realized the importance of having a private army on hand wherever they went. They'd climbed over the backs of competitors who hadn't realized the importance of protecting themselves at all times—especially from the Mescone family.

Over the years the brothers had become more refined. Bernardo's intimidating bulk was hidden behind well-tailored suits, and Federico's street fighter's face had been altered by cosmetic surgeons to make him look more approachable, though there was still a feral glint in his eye.

Accustomed to wealth and its accompanying privileges, the brothers were far removed from the day-to-day violence of their trade. Instead they preferred to stay in the background, devising ways of generating wealth from their cocaine fortunes.

The fact that the brothers accepted Caporra's invitation spoke volumes of their regard for her. It also spoke of their interest in the money she would be able to repay them.

She had hinted that there was a profitable deal in the works.

The deal wasn't mentioned until dinner was over, coffee and cake were served on silver settings and the hotel staff had departed from the suite. Then Caporra addressed the brothers. "I have a proposition I would like you to consider."

Bernardo, the older of the two and the nominal head of the Mescone clan, feigned surprise. While holding his cup at eye level, he raised an eyebrow at Federico, then turned his smile upon the woman.

"So soon?" Bernardo asked. "I thought you would hide your pretty little head for at least a year—"

"I want to reestablish my position."

"You have no position," Federico said, leaning forward to savor her discomfort. "Not anymore."

"How can you say that," she protested, "after all of the things I've done for you?"

"That is why you are still alive," Federico said. "But after the loss you caused us...now it is an even slate."

Caporra turned toward Bernardo.

"My brother thinks you are a liability to us," he

said. "I tend to agree with him. While it's true you have done these certain favors for us, you also cost us dearly. That means you start from zero with us."

"Then let me start with something only a fool would refuse," she said, her voice rising as her old demeanor came back. The way to deal with the brothers was from a position of strength. Or at least implied strength. "What I have in mind will not only recoup our losses, it will make the Mescones the strongest family in all of Colombia."

"A most worthy goal," Bernardo said, amused at her fiery offer.

"An achievable one," the woman replied, "if you listen to me. This deal involves weapons that are easily concealed and totally devastating, and none of our enemies have access to them—yet. It will be at least a decade before these weapons make it to the arms market. By then, no one will dare move against you. Cartels, government, no one."

"You have our fullest attention," Bernardo said.

Caporra laid out the deal for them, stressing the futuristic qualities of the weapons and the fact that they came from Thomas Quinn. Not only would his debt be settled, but they would be in a stronger position than before. And the final transaction would take place far from Florida, where they no longer trusted his influence.

Bernardo Mescone made his decision instantly. "Contact him. Tell him we wish to be friends again and you will negotiate a deal that is acceptable to both sides."

Federico wasn't as enthusiastic, but he went along with the older Mescone's decision. "However," he said, "there is one thing we must get straight. From our inquiries after your...regrettable encounter in the

Bahamas, we have learned that Quinn makes two plans for every deal. The first plan calls for the successful completion of the deal. The second plan calls for the elimination of everyone in the other party.''

''Yes?'' she said.

''I think it is only fair that we make the same kind of plans.''

Florida

JULIAN MATTHEWS ARRIVED at the Miami marina at dusk, a gray time of day when there wouldn't be so many people about. Even if anyone took a close look at him, all they would see was a man with a fishing pole and a tackle box, someone who was looking for a bit of relaxation after work.

But Julian Matthews's work had just begun.

If they looked inside the tackle box, they would see a Heckler & Koch MP-5 submachine gun along with two full magazines and a sound suppressor.

The weapon had been provided by Thomas Quinn himself as a tool to carry out the first of several contracts. Matthews had performed similar services for Quinn before. Sometimes it had been in the States. Other times he'd worked overseas for Gilberto Vicente. He knew both men well, and they knew his abilities just as well, for which they paid him top dollar.

It had been a while, however, since Matthews had been pressed into service, what with Quinn's legitimate ISS enterprise taking up so much of his time these past few years.

But apparently Quinn was reverting to his old ways. The ISS leader found himself in the middle of several turf wars at once, and it looked like he was short of manpower these days. Matthews had the impression that he was not the only one from the old days who was being put on Quinn's payroll once again.

He tilted the brim of his baseball cap over his eyes as he neared the water. No, he thought, he wouldn't be noticed by anyone—especially the man he came here to see—until it was too late.

The contract was specific. First he was supposed to pump the target for information, then pump him with several rounds.

Matthews headed right for the slip where Special Agent Lawrence Savidge docked his cabin cruiser and wasn't surprised to see the sleek brown craft floating in the water.

Just as Matthews had been told, the DEA informant was a stickler about his schedule. He always went out into the bay about the same time every evening to catch the night falling on Miami.

Lately Savidge had been going alone out into the bay. The woman who'd been assigned to keep him company had been sent packing by the DEA turncoat. And right after Savidge gave her the boot, he broke off all contact with Quinn's people.

Apparently it was an annoying habit of Savidge's, annoying enough for Quinn to call for his removal.

Matthews knew just enough about the situation to carry out his part of it. From Quinn's briefing he knew that the DEA informant hadn't been keeping up his end of the bargain. Initially the information that Savidge provided to Gilberto Vicente seemed to be a treasure trove, but it hadn't paid off as much as expected.

Savidge supposedly provided names and addresses of DEA agents for some of Quinn's other operatives to take out. But when Quinn's people tried to hunt down those same operatives, they proved to be a very elusive prey...almost as if Savidge had warned the people he'd given up that they were in danger.

About forty yards from Savidge's cabin cruiser, Matthews sat down on a white wooden bench and put the tackle box beside him.

He looked around to make sure no one was in sight, opened the box slowly, then threaded the suppressor onto the barrel of the Heckler & Koch. It was time to go fishing for informants.

Matthews closed the tackle box, then slipped off his light windbreaker and draped it over the submachine gun. He picked up the fishing pole in one hand, the covered weapon with the other and walked toward Savidge's boat.

He stepped soundlessly onto the immaculately kept boat and moved quietly to the open door of the cabin, dropping the windbreaker to the deck.

The barrel of the MP-5 announced his presence as he stepped into the dimly lit cabin.

The man sitting behind the wheel didn't seem surprised to see him. In fact Savidge looked almost glad to see him step out of the shadows into the room. He, too, held a weapon in his hand. It was an automatic, and it was pointed in the assassin's direction.

But Savidge seemed casual, keeping his left hand on the wheel while his right hand held the automatic.

"I've been expecting you," Savidge said. "Or someone like you. I rather hoped it would be Gilberto."

Matthews maintained his composure. It wasn't the first time he'd been in a situation like this. He kept his subgun trained on the man behind the wheel.

Even though Savidge was armed, Matthews still

had the advantage. The DEA agent was holding his own weapon awkwardly, as if it were a last resort instead of an intimate friend.

It had been too long since Savidge had been in any kind of firefight, he thought, a lifetime ago. If Matthews fired first, and moved as he did so, he would probably walk out of this without a scratch.

But it was important to keep the man calm.

"Gilberto has more-pressing engagements. He sent me in his place."

"A shame. But I guess you'll do."

Matthews nodded. "I've come about the information you provided to Gilberto. It seems that it's not very helpful. There is some question about whether you're trying to deceive us."

"No deception," Savidge said. "Not anymore. I've decided that both sides deserve to know what's going on."

"I don't understand—"

"Gilberto didn't understand, either. When you push a man so hard he has nowhere to go, after a while he doesn't care where he goes."

"You were paid well for the information," Matthews said, keeping his voice calm and friendly, as if it were a reasonable thing for two men to discuss career choices while holding weapons on each other.

"I was paid very well," Savidge agreed. "Too well to say no. That's why it took me a long time to realize that I was the one who was really paying...with my life."

Matthews nodded. "So you betrayed Gilberto's trust in you."

Savidge laughed. "Call it that if you want. But yeah, that's what happened. Any agent whose name I gave to Gilberto was in danger. So I sent an anonymous e-mail to the DEA about threats on their lives. It wasn't hard to do, especially for someone who knows their computer system as well as I do. I also tipped them off that their safehouses were known. The DEA paid attention, neutralizing whatever information I gave to Gilberto.''

"But you made a deal," Matthews protested. "That's madness!"

"No," Savidge said, "not madness. For the first time in a very long time, I was able to see clearly. It's quite a sane way to end this thing."

The assassin studied the man behind the wheel. He saw a calmness in Savidge's eyes, an acceptance. It was the same kind of look he'd seen in the faces of men who knew they were about to die.

And that death didn't have to come from Matthews's gun. The agent was prepared to end this thing all by himself.

"We've created a lot of ghosts, you and I," Savidge said. "So have other men like you. Like Gilberto."

Matthews took one step back. He felt the fresh air of freedom behind him but knew there was a chance he wouldn't be breathing it for very long.

"Maybe it's time we join those ghosts," Savidge suggested, "tell them we're sorry."

As Savidge's hand moved to the center of the wheel, Matthews knew he wouldn't get off the boat.

He pulled the trigger of the subgun and caught the DEA agent with a 3-round burst. Even in the confined space of the cabin, the sound of the volley was low. But the sound of their impact was considerably higher, ripping a shriek of surprised agony from Savidge's lips.

The bullets nearly knocked Savidge off his seat.

Spouts of blood erupted from his chest, but he was still able to hold on long enough to finish his task.

Savidge pressed down hard on the wheel, sounding the horn once, demanding right of way into the afterlife.

At the same time, the pressure of his hand upon the wheel triggered the strips of C-4 plastique that lined the cabin. The horn blast was immediately followed by a much more final blast that thundered down the marina.

The force of the blast was aimed at the doorway right where Matthews stood for one second before the front of his face disintegrated and the rest of his body went airborne.

The explosion shot up through the roof and down through the hull, which took on enough water to carry the cabin cruiser to the bottom.

ECHOES OF THE BLAST still resounded through the halls of DEA headquarters in Miami the following day when Special Agent Savidge made one last, posthumous communication.

It came by e-mail from his computer, which had been programmed to transmit it every morning unless he canceled it. Now that Savidge was gone, the e-mail package was transmitted to his immediate superiors.

After identifying himself as the previously anonymous informant who'd told the DEA about the agents and locations at risk, Savidge's message included a brief confession of his guilt.

It was a confession that would probably never be made public. For with his confession were several files that detailed all of the people he dealt with inside the DEA and out during the time he was a turned agent.

Such information was potentially damaging to the agency's reputation if it ever got out. But even more important, if the agency kept the information to themselves, it could be used as a weapon against their enemies. The message would be doled out on a need-to-know basis.

Only the insiders would know that after years of betrayal, Special Agent Savidge had done the right thing and served his country the best way possible—by dying.

CHAPTER EIGHTEEN

The Arcadia was a restaurant and inn that rose like a Spanish castle guarding the Boca Raton shoreline. Manning the parapets behind the high pastel-colored walls was an army of waiters that drifted easily through the tables on the terrace. Landscaped palms, plants and canopies provided shade from the sun.

For those who wished to escape the elements, a large area in the courtyard was sealed off from the sun by lightly tinted windows that gave it the look of an aquarium.

At two in the afternoon it was almost full.

Lately the Arcadia had become *the* place to be seen for Boca Raton's media and corporate crowd.

Executives from film and publishing companies and ad agencies went there for working lunches with clients, models and actresses. Scattered among the tabletop bottles of wine were portfolios, storyboards and test shots from photo shoots, items that could be easily carried in slim leather attachés and displayed when the right moment came.

The Arcadia had also become the place where Thomas Quinn was accustomed to doing business. Usually Quinn dined there with celebrity clients in need of security services from the perfectly legitimate division of his ISS corporation. But this day he was there conducting business for the underworld branch of ISS.

For that reason there were at least a half-dozen well-armed men in the room, weapons hidden neatly beneath their well-tailored suits. They were sitting at nearby tables discreetly watching other customers for signs of Quinn's enemies.

And Mack Bolan was watching them with equal discretion from his table near the corner.

The Executioner had chosen the table for its ambience and for its strategic view. Esthetically arranged tropical fronds screened him from direct sight of Quinn. With the floor-to-ceiling windows all around him, he could see anyone coming. In case he had to move fast, a few rounds from the Beretta 93-R beneath his jacket could make a suitable exit through the air-cooled glass.

Though Bolan was the only one at his table, he wasn't alone at the Arcadia. A half-dozen members of the DEA strike team were enjoying their lunches courtesy of the federal government while they kept an eye on Quinn. The customs flying squad also had their people in place throughout the restaurant.

It was practically a catered lunch for the covert community. But it was all business.

Like Bolan, the other agents were watching the group of people who were sitting at Thomas Quinn's table.

Melitta Caporra sat next to Quinn. With her raven black hair, low-cut sundress and copper-hued complexion, she hardly looked capable of causing harm to anyone, except for a broken heart or two. But if not for the undying efforts of the man sitting beside her, Federico Mescone, she would have racked up the highest body count in the Mescone cartel.

The woman looked as fetching as usual, quite capable of luring Quinn into another off-the-books enterprise. It was a good thing she was working for Bolan this time, he thought. The threat of catching a bullet or spending fifty years or so in jail for trafficking, treason and terrorism had made her most agreeable. Not that he trusted her completely. She would probably turn on him in the long run, but not before she turned on Quinn.

Federico Mescone sat listening to the conversation at the table like a reasonable man, an exceptional performance for the uncontrollable enforcer. Bolan had seen earlier surveillance photos of the man, but they stemmed from the days before the knife of a plastic surgeon repaired the face that had been marked by much unfriendlier knives.

The other two people at Quinn's table were ISS operatives. Bolan was familiar with their names and backgrounds, but this was the first chance he had to see them in person.

Gilberto Vicente, the branch chief from Andorra, appeared to be paying special attention to Caporra, but he was really most concerned with Federico. There was some kind of feral radar occurring between the two men. They'd recognized each other as killers—from different castes but with equal abilities—and they were wondering if they would have to demonstrate those abilities on each other.

Claude LeBrun was the most familiar of the group. The last time Bolan saw him, the former Ranger was standing in a cypress thicket firing his Ilarco automatic weapon at the flak-clad customs agents gunning a customs airboat past him.

It would be nice to take them down now, Bolan thought.

But it would be even nicer to take down ISS forever, and that wouldn't happen if they jumped the gun. No, the deal had to go down the way he and Hal Brognola had worked it out. The big Fed needed incontestable proof of Quinn's guilt before he made his final move against someone of Quinn's standing in the covert community.

Once the deal went down, and Quinn was right in the thick of it, then the ex-spook would find himself on his last war front.

The Executioner scanned the room again, trying to pick out the rest of Quinn's people so he wouldn't be taken by surprise if something did happen. He knew the faces of some of Quinn's hardmen from file photos, but Quinn had brought in a lot of new soldiers to replace the ones who fell.

Everyone in the place deserved a second look.

Bolan had been eavesdropping on all of the conversations around him, picking up names and accents by habit. Sometimes paying attention to those small details kept him alive.

He continued to look slowly around the restaurant before returning his attention to Quinn's table.

He'd thought of having some of the DEA people wire the place, but Quinn was in the business. His countermeasures people would probably detect any bugging, and there was no sense in taking chances.

Better to wait until they got outside where the DEA phone phreaks and gadget men could listen in on conversations with directional mikes and laser mikes. The streets and the parking lot around the Arcadia were covered by fully equipped surveillance vans and Jeeps that could follow the ISS retinue.

Besides, Bolan thought, he knew the deal that was

being made. He was the one who put Melitta Caporra up to it.

The Mescone cartel wanted Quinn to pay off his debt for the botched Bahamas operation by providing Phase Two H&K sound-suppressed handguns and ICW electronic smart rifles for their private army. In turn the Mescones would fly in smoke and coke and some brown heroin to make the transaction worthwhile for all parties.

And Bolan would be there to bring the party to an end.

Until then, it would almost be like the old days for Quinn and his "freedom fighters." Guns for drugs. The difference this time around was that one of the pilots flying into Quinn's private armory would be another of Bolan's recent converts to the cause—Nicholas Vreeland.

Quinn would put up some resistance when Caporra insisted on using the pilot. After all, Quinn and Vreeland were still on the outs. But Quinn and the Mescones had used Vreeland on several previous successful operations, so it was almost natural to include him on this one.

Besides, it was a deal breaker. If Caporra's handpicked pilot wasn't included, the deal was off.

Quinn and the Mescone cartel would be at war.

But it wasn't going to come to that. Not yet. From what Bolan could see, the deal appeared to be developing smoothly.

It looked like a friendly dinner. Not too many drinks were on the table, and everyone's temper was under control. For the moment all of them were comfortably ensconced in the illusion of trust.

Caporra was putting on a good show, laughing brightly and touching Quinn on the arm, going through all the motions of a woman who wasn't about to hand his head on a platter.

And Quinn was probably doing the same thing, Bolan realized, bestowing his all-American smile upon her at every chance, putting her at ease while calculating whether he should make a preemptive strike against the Mescone cartel. Perhaps after they made the delivery...

They made a perfect couple, Bolan thought, and he was the matchmaker.

He waited a few more minutes before calling for his check, then walked past Quinn's cohorts without looking at the head of ISS. But he made sure that he was seen. It would come in handy when he paid a visit to ISS headquarters.

FEDERICO MESCONE accompanied Gilberto Vicente and Claude LeBrun to a metallic blue van parked in the back lot of the Arcadia. It had tinted windows, air-conditioning and two sample crates of weapons.

Federico and Vicente sat in the front seat, looking back at Claude LeBrun, who was doing his showroom-salesman bit.

"This is the smart rifle," LeBrun said. The Individual Combat Weapon he held was an over-under model with the laser sight mounted on top of the rifle barrel. The tube that fired electronically guided miniature artillery shells was located just under the rifle barrel.

LeBrun held up one of the four-inch bullets between his thumb and forefinger. "Miniature guidance system is built right into the shell. It's got a fuse and it's got air-burst explosives that take out everything in its area. The rifle does everything for you—calculates the range, guides the air-burst munition to your target, then sets it off right over his head if you want. In case that isn't enough for you, the top barrel still fires your regulation prehistoric ammo.''

Federico tried to hide his interest as he hefted the sleek high-tech weapon. ''Looks okay,'' he said.

LeBrun laughed. ''Okay? Man, one of these weapons can turn a single soldier into a rifle team. It's prototype. It's restricted. No one's got them but us. And with the quantities we're talking, no one will be able to come near you when you outfit your people with these.''

LeBrun recrated the ICW, then displayed a weapon from the other crate, the Heckler & Koch snout-nosed sound-suppressed .45ACP handgun. ''Heavy metal, low sound,'' LeBrun said. ''It'll knock anything down. Special Forces are just getting theirs now. You'll be ahead of the game when you get these.''

When the sales pitch was over, LeBrun threw a cloth over the crates, then stepped out of the van.

Vicente and Federico stayed behind to do some haggling. So far the ICWs were still classified and restricted. The price tag to the military was going to be close to twenty thousand dollars apiece. On the black market that price was doubled.

''At forty grand per, ten rifles is almost half a million,'' Vicente said. ''Twenty-five rifles is a million. Since Quinn feels responsible for your earlier loss, we'll knock the price down to thirty thousand each. We've got one hundred rifles already at our Texas location and plan on bringing in more.''

''Thirty thousand per weapon is too steep,'' Federico said. ''Especially for stolen rifles *you* get free.''

''The people who provided them must be paid,''

Vicente reasoned. "Everyone in the chain must get a fair price for their efforts."

"Understood," Federico replied. "We'll do you a favor by accepting enough rifles to cancel out your debt to us at thirty thousand per. Whatever quantity is left after that, we'll pay twenty-five thousand each."

"Done."

They moved on to the price for the Heckler & Koch weapons. The price tag was lower, but it still added up to a considerable sum. The Mescone cartel would take all that was available. In turn they would pay coke and cash, Mexican smoke and brown heroin.

When the exchange rates were figured out and quantities agreed to by both sides, Federico Mescone moved on to the arrangements for delivery.

"We'll send two planes to Quinn's Texas armory," Federico said. "They'll come in from Mexico. One will be piloted by Nicholas Vreeland, who we both trust. The other will be piloted by one of our regular pilots."

"Those arrangements are up to you. You come in, off-load and reload, then haul out of there. Whatever happens after that is your concern."

"Understood," Federico said. "But there is one more concern."

"Name it."

"Thomas Quinn must be there."

"Impossible," Vicente said.

"Necessary. The last time, when we trusted Quinn's subordinate, nearly all of our people were killed. We believe that if Quinn is there this time, nothing will go wrong."

"I'll ask him," Vicente said.

"No. You will tell him."

THE MORNING after the Arcadia meeting, two men appeared unannounced at the main-floor offices of ISS.

Mack Bolan and Nicholas Vreeland walked through the ground-floor entrance at ten minutes after eleven and ruined the receptionist's otherwise fine day.

New Age music played softly in the background, contemplative harp and woodwind. And at the moment the silver-haired woman behind the desk was contemplating how to deal with the men who stood before her.

During her stay at ISS she had obviously seen all kinds walk through the front door, and she probably greeted most of them warmly: executives, celebrities, bodyguards.

But every now and then, she'd also seen the kind of hard-faced men like these two, the kind that meant trouble for her and her employer.

Bolan was dressed in black jeans, T-shirt and windbreaker, looking lean, mean and alert. He wanted to give the impression that he was a dangerous hired gun who didn't care much about the usual niceties. That image was helped considerably by the bruise on the side of his face.

Vreeland also looked a bit weathered. Coming into the headquarters of the man who recently placed a bounty on his head was taking its toll on the pilot. He looked manic and slightly demented, like he was ready to explode if anything went wrong. Not a bad attitude for what was coming up.

"Yes?" the receptionist asked after she finished studying them. "Can I help you?" Though she managed to generate a pleasant tone, it was obvious the only help she wanted to give them were directions out of the building.

"We're here to see Mr. Quinn," Bolan said.

She smiled regrettably as if that were impossible. "I'm sorry, but Mr. Quinn is a busy man."

"Not too busy for us."

"Does he know you're coming?"

"Oh, yeah," Bolan said. "He knows we're coming. He just doesn't know when."

"Can I tell him what this is about?"

"It's about Mr. Vreeland here, a former business partner of Quinn's," Bolan replied. "Quinn's been looking all over for him, so we decided to drop in and get everything out in the open."

"I see," the woman said. "And you are…?"

"I'm his executive assistant."

"Of course." She shrugged, then picked up the phone and called Quinn's office.

Bolan glanced around the office to spot the surveillance cameras that had been carefully placed in the room, then he rifled through some ISS brochures on a table near the receptionist's desk. According to the brochures, ISS could solve just about any security problem that came along. Unfortunately it could also cause them.

"Mr. Quinn isn't sure he'll be able to see you right away," she said, holding one hand over the phone.

"We're here for thirty more seconds, then we're gone for good. Make sure you tell Quinn that—just in case he's not watching us on Candid Camera."

The woman listened to the phone for a moment, then said, "Mr. Quinn is waiting for you now. You can take that elevator over there. Top floor." She pointed to a bank of elevators.

Bolan led the way toward the elevator, but then walked past it toward a stairway. "Come on. We'll take the stairs."

Vreeland looked at him in surprise. "You crazy?" he asked in hushed tones. "She said top floor."

"Look," Bolan said, keeping his voice low, "I don't think he'd try anything, but accidents are easy to arrange in elevators. Besides, we want to rattle his cage a bit, keep him off balance. If Thomas Quinn wants us to use the elevator, then I want us to use the stairs. Make *him* wait."

As he pushed through the door, Bolan looked back over his shoulder and said, "And look sharp. You're on camera."

Vreeland did his best, but it was hard to disguise the fact that he was winded. By the time they were halfway up, Vreeland was clutching at the railing for support. But Vreeland was a pilot, not a commando. Bolan was supposed to be the enforcement arm. He took the stairs in easy, unhurried strides. Compared to the battlefield treks he'd been on, this was a walk in the park.

When they reached the top floor, the stairwell opened up into a long and wide lobby with wall-length windows that looked down on Boca Raton's cityscape. Plush sofas and gleaming black onyx tables were positioned by the windows, providing a pleasant waiting area for those waiting to see Quinn. But the lobby was deserted. Bolan and Vreeland were the chief business of the day.

Facing the long sofas was a tinted-glass wall that looked as though it could withstand several hits of autofire before the glass imploded. Through the dark glass they could make out only vague shapes of the office within.

Raised platinum lettering on the single glass door read Thomas Quinn, President. Just below was the ISS logo, whose *S*'s were intertwined like serpents.

When Bolan pulled on the recessed handle, there was a buzz and the door unlocked. As soon as they stepped through the door into the inner sanctum of ISS he heard several clicks, the unmistakable whir of motion-activated video cameras.

A harshly beautiful woman sat at a desk large enough for a landing strip, smiling as soon as she saw them. There was a sign on her desk that simply read Lisa Kincaid.

No title needed. She looked unperturbed at the sight of the two hard-faced men, unimpressed. She was the keeper of the gates. You only got past her if Quinn wanted you to.

"Mr. Quinn's waiting for you in his office," she said, escorting them down a corridor with wide walls and high ceilings. On one of the walls were four clocks for international time zones, so Quinn could coordinate his underworld dealings around the world.

Quinn's right-hand woman ushered them inside his office, stepped back, then closed the doors quickly behind them.

It was as quiet as a tomb and just about as friendly.

Four men waited for them.

Quinn stood behind his desk. He was almost smiling, but his lips were curled in a painful grin, as if the thought of Nicholas Vreeland dealing with him as an equal was too much to bear.

On Quinn's left was Gilberto Vicente.

Claude LeBrun stood at his right.

The three men looked like a pinstriped gang getting ready to protect their turf.

And standing in front of the desk, closest to Bolan,

was the man who would do the dirty work. He was a lean, almost thin man with a once broken nose. He looked like a kick boxer who'd stayed in the ring one too many bouts. His notched short-sleeve shirt was tight around the biceps, and his forearms were chiseled muscle.

Bolan knew the type—light, fast and lethal, one of the stone killers Quinn had recently signed on. His gaze swept back and forth from Bolan to Vreeland, like a guard dog waiting to be given his target.

LeBrun and Vicente were also studying Bolan carefully, recognition slowly dawning in their eyes.

"We saw you at the restaurant," Vicente said. "You were sitting at the corner table. You were much better dressed at the time."

"That's right. Mr. Vreeland wanted me to keep an eye on things. As far as the clothes, it's what's inside that counts. I mean, look around," Bolan said, affecting a streetwise manner as he studied the swank surroundings. "This place looks legit, but we all know it's a con from top to bottom."

Quinn ignored the dig. He was still busy studying Vreeland. "I'm surprised to see *you* here," he said to the pilot. "We've got a lot to talk about."

"Yeah, we do," Vreeland replied. His voice was steady, and there was a detached look in his eyes, as if he were enjoying the part he was playing. At last he would have a chance to take Quinn down. "It's time we straightened out that mess you made in the swamp."

"Oh, we will," Quinn said. "But first things first." He nodded to the lean man, who pushed himself away from the desk and came to a stop in front of Bolan.

Quinn nodded his head at the Executioner and

said, "You don't mind if he pats you down for weapons, do you?"

"Not at all."

The man reached forward and started to search Bolan for weapons. He smiled when his hand traced the outline of the Beretta 93-R holstered beneath Bolan's windbreaker.

"He's carrying," the man stated, then started to reach inside the jacket for the Beretta.

That's when he appeared to go into convulsions, immediately after Bolan cupped his right hand and smacked the man's left ear, popping the eardrum and jarring his head hard enough to crackle the cartilage in his neck. The motion tilted his head into the path of Bolan's left hand, which concussed the other ear.

The Executioner's hands moved in a blur that was impossible for the others in the room to follow. All they saw was a windmill motion from Bolan's hands, and then their man started to crumple.

Bolan kneed him in the groin hard enough to lift him in the air. He followed the motion by grabbing the man's shoulders while he was still airborne and throwing him flat across the surface of Quinn's desk.

The former spook leaped out of the way as the man slid across the desk and sailed headfirst onto the floor.

Bolan calmly resumed his position near Vreeland and folded his hands in front of him.

LeBrun looked amused, glancing down at the now unconscious man on the floor, then back at the Executioner.

Vicente was also impressed at Bolan's instantaneous reaction. It had been as natural as breathing.

But Quinn was furious. His man was damaged and so was his pride.

"What the hell is wrong with you?" Quinn shouted. "You said he could pat you down."

"Sure," Bolan said matter-of-factly. "I said he could pat me down. But I didn't say he could take whatever he found. I mean, the only way someone takes my weapon is when I'm dead. I don't think anyone here is capable of arranging that, but you're welcome to try."

The challenge was directed at LeBrun. The other two men had instinctively stepped back. LeBrun held his ground, carefully watching Bolan.

"No thanks," the former Ranger said, making himself busy by picking up the unconscious man and hauling him into a side room.

"Good," Bolan said. "Then let's get down to business. Mr. Vreeland here has been selected as the go-between for our transaction with the Mescone family. In turn, Mr. Vreeland has selected me as his military adviser. Is there any problem with that?"

There was no problem at all, even with Quinn.

Though the head of ISS was still upset at the trashing of one of his hired guns, he was a realist. He had to do business with Vreeland if he wanted to do business with Melitta Caporra. Since he needed to bring in some much needed cash, along with the profitable powders, he would do whatever it took.

It was a relatively small deal in the scheme of things, but it was enough to keep ISS floating until Quinn pulled off a bigger deal.

And it wouldn't be that bad dealing with Vreeland. Quinn's estimation of the pilot had gone up a notch, mainly because of the quality of his hired help. Quinn was a good judge of military talent. The one who was looking after Vreeland was one of the best he'd seen.

Regaining his composure and acting as if this were a perfectly normal business meeting, Quinn walked to the front of the desk and leaned against the edge of it.

"I guess you landed on your feet after all," Quinn said to Vreeland, folding his arms in front of him as he spoke. "When you took a powder on me, I figured it was the last we'd hear of you. That was why it was such a surprise when you called a few days ago to tell me about the upcoming deal with Melitta. And that's why I may have sounded a bit skeptical."

Vreeland laughed. "You were surprised because you expected Dan McCall to cash me out in Costa Rica. As far as sounding skeptical—if I remember correctly, you said that if I set one foot in Florida again you'd have it cut off. Is that still your position?"

"Things change. That was before Melitta contacted me and we became...partners in this thing."

"Glad to hear it," Bolan said. "For your sake."

Quinn gave a sidelong glance at Bolan, then turned back to Vreeland. "Does he do all your talking for you?"

"He says what he wants, when he wants. But he *does* what I tell him to."

"Then tell him to relax," Quinn said. "We've got a lot to talk about."

He gestured toward the U-shaped couch arranged around a heavy onyx table.

Vreeland played his role to the hilt and waved Bolan away as if the Executioner truly was a subordinate. Then the pilot followed Quinn to the sitting area.

The Executioner stepped back and leaned against

one of the windows where he could keep everyone in his sight.

Especially Claude LeBrun.

When the former Ranger had come back into the room he'd taken up a position in the doorway, hands folded in front of him while he watched Bolan. The Executioner maintained a similar pose as he returned the stare. His windbreaker was now open, giving him easy access to the holstered Beretta if he needed it.

And LeBrun was also visibly armed now. He'd taken off his jacket to reveal an automatic in an underarm holster.

The two of them stood there like bookends while Gilberto Vicente and Thomas Quinn began to discuss the logistics of the Texas deal.

"One thing before we go any further," Quinn said. "I'm a bit curious about Dan McCall. Is he still alive and well?"

"He's alive," Vreeland replied, "but not doing well at all."

"Where is he?"

Vreeland nodded toward the Executioner. "He put him away for a while. Kind of like your other man there."

Quinn shrugged. "These things happen. By the way, what's your man's name?"

Vreeland shook his head. "He's kind of superstitious about that. Figures if you know his name you have some power over him."

"He's right about that," Quinn said, pleased that even if he didn't know the Executioner's name, he thought he'd picked up some more information about him. Like most of the other people in the trafficking game, Vreeland's adviser appeared to be a man in trouble with the law.

A man he could do business with.

"Let's get down to it," Quinn said, "and start figuring out how we're all going to make some money."

CHAPTER NINETEEN

Two hours after the sit-down with Thomas Quinn, Mack Bolan and Nicholas Vreeland stepped into Hal Brognola's makeshift war room in room 402 of the Sovereign Hotel.

The hospitality suite was crowded with marshals, DEA agents and customs officers. Weapons and comm gear were carefully stacked all along the desks and daybeds. It looked like an army had come to town.

Vreeland's eyes went wide at all of the activity. Until now he'd seen only Bolan and Cane and a couple of marshals. This was the first time he'd seen one of the covert strike teams up close. It was also the first time he realized just how big the operation was, big enough to convince him he'd chosen the right side this time around.

Most of the covert specialists were gathered around a table in the center of the room where Armand Cane was guiding them through a map of the west Texas border with Mexico.

"This is where Quinn's old airstrip and armory were located back when he was handling legit ops," Cane was saying as Bolan and Vreeland neared the table. "Those days are gone forever. He sold out to the highest bidder long ago."

Bolan glanced at the map to where Cane's index finger was tracing a path west of the El Paso and Ciudad Juárez border towns.

"There's plenty of wilderness to get lost in out there," Cane said. "Got the Chisos Mountains and the Guadalupe Range on the south and west. Rio Grande and Big Bend forest to the south. Desert, hills and desolate wilderness all around. It's the kind of place people don't just happen to stumble into."

Cane jogged his index finger a speck, covering a distance of about ten miles. "When the word came to shut down the cross-border flights, Quinn obliged—until he thought no one was looking at him anymore. Then he set up another airfield in the same general area, disguising it as part of a desert mining operation. It's an occasional armory. Now and then, he uses the place to put together an operation."

Bolan listened to Cane's briefing as the DEA agent went over the package—the storage areas the Colombian cartels leased from the Mexican Mafia in small, dusty towns along the border, the approach the planes made over the mountains, the heavy weaponry that Quinn and his people would have at their disposal.

"That's the bad news," Cane said. "Here's the good news. There's a customs station at Big Bend. Helicopters can refuel there without being noticed. Another resource we can tap is Biggs Army Airfield at Fort Bliss. It's an advanced-combat-training area. Whatever we could possibly need is available there, and Hal Brognola's made sure we have access to it."

Cane spoke for a couple more minutes, then said, "That's the bird's-eye view, assembled from several different sources. Now here's a guy who's actually been there before, a former pilot for Quinn's guns-and-drugs airline.''

All eyes turned to Vreeland.

''He'll be flying one of the planes for the Mescone cartel,'' Cane continued, ''with a copilot we're sending along to keep him company.'' The DEA agent nodded toward Vreeland. ''It's all yours.'' The pilot stood there self-consciously for a few moments. It was sheerly out of habit. He'd spent half of his adult life on the same side as these guys, the other half running from them.

He forced himself to remember that these men were no longer the opposition. Now that he was co-operating, they held their animosity in check. It was a chance to redeem himself. He had nothing to hide anymore and everything to share. That was the bargain he made with the man called Belasko. ''What do you want to know?'' he asked.

They fired a dozen questions at once. Just as the pilot started to sort through them, Bolan felt a tap on his shoulder.

It was Hal Brognola, looking tired and determined. ''I need a few words, Bolasko.'' The head Fed led Bolan into the adjoining windowless room and closed the door behind him.

Once they were sitting down, Brognola leaned forward. ''How'd Vreeland do?''

''Good enough,'' Bolan said. ''Quinn bought it. Another time he might have looked a bit closer at the deal, but he's under a lot of pressure and I kept him off balance.''

''So he's in?''

''To the end. It's going to happen, Hal, but it's going to be loud. You anticipate any fallout?''

Brognola's face brightened. ''Not much. Matter of

fact, any day now the honorable Senator Ritenour will be resigning. Soon after that, he'll be indicted. Several other pending indictments will keep the rest of Quinn's D.C. gang quiet. Catch him red-handed, and there's nothing to worry about.''

"There's so much surveillance involved in this thing," Bolan said, "you can have it for the eleven-o'clock news if you want."

"Then we're in business."

"Almost," Bolan replied. "Figure on Quinn covering all the bases. If things go wrong, he'll have a way to get out. I've got to be ready to close the door on him, Hal."

"What do you need?"

"There's some special equipment you can release to me," the Executioner said. "It's kind of restricted and you might take some flak for it, but I want it. I also want some dirty tricksters from technical services to give me a crash course in using it."

"Whatever it is, it's yours."

Texas

THE DUST STORM SENT a cloud of mesquite branches and dry topsoil whirling down the dirt runway. It left patches of sand behind as it moved on, shaking the corrugated-metal doors and rattling the windows of the west Texas warehouses.

The desert complex looked like several other abandoned mining operations that studded the stretches of dry land flanking the mountain range west of El Paso. During the boom years, there'd been enough ore in the region to support several mining camps.

But the operations folded one by one. The general stores and taverns that provided supplies went down with them, turning into crumbling ghost towns that were blown across the desert.

Quinn's complex was the last for several miles around that showed any signs of occupation.

There was enough heavy equipment to provide sufficient cover for the operation in case someone looked closely at the complex. Drilling machines, power-shovel excavators and open-pit blasting agents were stored in one of the high-ceilinged warehouses where they mostly gathered rust and dust from disuse. A front was a front. Quinn wasn't about to go into the mining business for real.

Whenever Quinn's corporate Windstar turbojet flew into the mining camp, it was to tap into a different kind of mother lode, mining profits from high-tech armament with high-price tags.

The gleaming Windstar and a Cessna Titan were sitting on the end of the runway that ran parallel to the warehouse docks, and a small collection of Jeeps and pickups was lined up in front of the office building. Most of them were desert-worthy vehicles, judging from the number of tire tracks that had come straight overland from the main access road a few miles south.

A gravel road that led to the complex still maintained some of its shape, but desert winds and rain storms had eroded and washed out considerable portions of it, making it almost as rough as the rugged desert terrain surrounding it.

It was the kind of desolate, abandoned place that no one in his right mind would ever visit.

Right now there were at least thirty men moving in and out of the shadows.

Mack Bolan watched them from one of the distant escarpments that looked down onto the valley floor.

Through the H3T-1 pistol-grip imager the Executioner could see the opposition clearly, and he could watch them for a relatively long time without his hand or his elbow tiring. About the size of a lightweight automatic pistol with a miniature telescope for a barrel, the device's IR-focusing laser zoomed in on the face of the target and brought it into close-up view.

The third-generation imager was designed for all lighting conditions, from bright sunlight to total darkness. It was one of the former East Bloc gadgets used by the advanced-combat-training teams at Fort Bliss. The imagers had been handed out to several other two-man teams that were spread around the hilltops to keep watch on Quinn's people.

So far the Executioner had seen several mercenaries and veteran traffickers through the scope, including some remnants from one of Quinn's Raven teams. The ISS chieftain had put together a small but efficient fighting force.

Soon that force would be tested.

Bolan and Armand Cane had taken turns watching the armory ever since they dug in like desert rats after reaching the escarpment the previous night.

They'd trekked across the hills after helicopters dropped them off in a far-off canyon that masked the sight and sound of the aircraft.

The choppers stayed in the area just long enough to drop off enough men and matériel to cover the armory until the deal went down. Then they'd flown back to their staging area to wait.

It had been cold, then, and the ground was hard and damp. After morning approached, there'd been a few hours of comfort when the ground was the right temperature.

But now the sun was baking down on them.

The gray-and-sand-colored netting that covered their observation post gave scant relief from the heat. The only real relief came from an occasional sip of warm water from a canteen.

Bolan looked southward for any sign of Vreeland's Beech King, but the skies were clear.

It was too early anyway. He could tell by his watch that the planes were at least an hour away. It was just the long hours of waiting that was getting to him, the mind's normal reaction to spending hours lying beneath a hot sun.

Besides, if there were any changes in Vreeland's course or expected time of arrival, the ground teams would have heard about it from the airborne war room in the EC-130E aircraft tasked to the operation. It was flying in a pattern that took it far enough away from the target zone to avoid detection. It was in constant communication with the OV-10 Bronco observation planes and recon satellites tracking the progress of the drug planes.

Vreeland's Beech King had flown from Puerto Rico through Mexican airspace and landed at a ranch just west of the Conchos River where the Mescone cartel stored their narcotics in well-guarded storerooms. It was like an unofficial bank for the cartel. Whenever they needed fast money, all they had to do was move some product across the border.

The second plane from the Mescones' private air fleet flew directly to the ranch from Cartagena.

Neither plane had been challenged on the flight to the Mexican drug depot. The Colombians had paid off the right people and now had a license to smuggle all the way to the U.S. border.

Automated-digital-switching relays in the EC-

130E kept the ground teams and helicopter squadron instantly informed of the status of both planes. They'd both been loaded and were about seventy miles south of the border. Once they reached the border, they'd fly a northwestern route along the Rio Grande for a while before cutting across the mountains for a twenty-mile-run through American airspace.

Armand Cane stirred a few feet away from Bolan, noticing the Executioner's gaze to the south. Then he, too, looked at his watch. "Don't sweat it," Cane said. "He'll be on time. The weather's with him today."

"Yeah," Bolan said, training the imager on Quinn's warehouses again. "That's too bad."

They'd originally set the date for the weapons exchange on a day when the weather service called for bad weather. That followed the smugglers' tradition of carrying off a deal when it was least expected—in storm-tossed skies. It had also created a breed of pilots who thrived on the adverse conditions, like Nicholas Vreeland.

The expected bad weather would also provide the strike team with plenty of cover to carry out their assault on the armory.

But the weather was holding out.

Dark blue clouds had been gathering over some of the mountaintops throughout the day, but the sunlight still burned through.

Except for sudden gusts of wind that occasionally shrieked down from the mountain passes and crawled out over the desert, it was almost perfect weather.

"See many new faces down there?" Cane asked.

"Not too many. Estimate's still about the same. Not counting Quinn or Vicente, there are about thirty soldiers down there. Give or take a few. What concerns me, though, is a face I haven't seen for a while."

"Who?"

"LeBrun," Bolan replied, as he continued scanning the faces of the hardmen down below. "It's been a while since I've seen him." He remembered the brief glimpse he had of Quinn's gunman back in the swamp. The man had been in the middle of a firefight that was closing in on all sides, yet he'd managed to escape untouched and find his way back to Quinn.

Claude LeBrun was a capable man in close-quarters combat. The Executioner also remembered the way LeBrun studied him in the ISS office after Bolan took out the man who tried to pat him down, almost as if he were trying to place Bolan from an earlier encounter.

Bolan felt confident his own face had been unrecognizable in the swamp. He'd been painted with camouflage, and most of the time he'd been moving fast. But LeBrun was wary just the same. And now that the deal was going down, he'd be even more suspicious. "I think our ex-Ranger might be doing some ranging on his own."

Cane nodded. "If he comes out far enough, he's good enough to find some of our positions."

Bolan handed the imager to Cane, who took up his position at the edge of the escarpment.

"I'll take a look around on foot," Bolan told him, "just in case." He slid a few feet back from the escarpment until he was out of the camouflage netting.

Then he moved in a half crouch across the sandy ridge. Even if LeBrun wasn't out there somewhere scouting the rolling hills, it gave Bolan some time to kill.

Before the real killing started.

THE BEECH KING AIRCRAFT flew as close to the mountaintops as the weather allowed. Rain clouds had settled upon the eastern side of the mountain range, and the wind gusts that looped around the peaks were buffeting the wings of the plane.

The weather posed no real problem to Vreeland. It was clear up ahead, and if he wanted to right now, he could fly above the clouds until he got past the turbulent weather.

But Vreeland stayed on course, welcoming the sound of the desert downpour drumming on the metal cocoon of the Beech King. Any smuggler worth his salt would ride into a storm instead of away from one.

Beside him was an undercover FBI pilot on long-term loan to customs. His name was Gavin, and his long hair was slicked back over his ears, giving him a wild-eyed Rasputin look. His beard had a salt-and-pepper tint and looked as though it had been combed once or twice in the past year.

The undercover pilot had cultivated an outlaw aura about him that said if you asked too many questions you might end up dead. The Colombians and their Mexican counterparts had kept their distance throughout the loading.

Gavin was capable of flying the plane if he had to, and he was just as capable of putting a bullet into Vreeland or Melitta Caporra if either of them tried to move against him.

But Caporra was playing her part well. She'd sat in the back of the Beech King with the six-man team of traffickers she'd selected from the cartel, men she could trust to do whatever she told them.

Vreeland's real worry was the cartel plane that followed closely behind the Beech King.

The Rockwell Sabreliner, originally a small troop transport plane, was piloted by Colonel Oswaldo Navarre, one of the cartel's genuine soldiers, a former Colombian air-force pilot who still wore his military flight jacket and side arm.

Navarre was a highly trained man with a short temper, which he'd displayed back at the ranch when he thought the farm workers were taking too long loading the plane with bricks, bales and sacks of tightly packed brown heroin. He'd shouted out one curse-laden order, then waved his pistol like a magic wand—and the exhausted farm workers suddenly got their second wind.

The man was trouble, Vreeland thought, almost as much trouble as the man riding with him, Federico Mescone.

Mescone had come along to oversee the deal and get a piece of the glory for himself. The weapons could mean the difference in one cartel triumphing over another and maybe even triumphing over the Colombian government the next time it launched one of its so-called drug wars.

"We're home free," Vreeland said when the Beech King broke out into clear blue sky. He pointed toward a strip of acacia-covered mountains to the right. "Just over that rise."

Gavin nodded. He stared out the windscreen at the rolling hills, then the mountains dropped from view. There was nothing but valley below, and far up ahead was the cluster of buildings where Thomas Quinn waited for them.

The undercover pilot cocked his head at Vreeland and lightly gripped his shoulder. "All right," he said. "Get this done right and you earn your stripes." His grip tightened just enough to make sure Vreeland got the message. "Get it done wrong and you'll be wearing stripes."

"Hey, man," Vreeland said, "my wrong days are over."

Vreeland pushed down on the yoke and angled the Beech King toward the desert airstrip. He worked the controls with casual but precise movements until the Beech King softly touched down on the runway with a sudden rapid droning of the wheels.

The airstrip was long, and he had plenty of time to slow down, gently braking the wheels until he rolled up parallel to the second warehouse, the one with the weapons for sale.

The other warehouse would be stocked with men holding weapons in case anything went wrong.

As soon as the Beech King came to a stop, the corrugated-metal doors of the second warehouse rolled up and several men came out of the shadows. Three forklifts clanked out of the open bay, churning up a cloud of smoke behind them.

The heavy rattling tines were loaded with long crates that were stacked three to a tier, heavy enough to cause the forklifts to rock up and down as they covered the sandy ground.

"These guys don't waste time," Gavin observed, watching the crew descend upon the plane.

"Just as long as they don't waste us," Vreeland said, and pushed open the door.

CHAPTER TWENTY

Thomas Quinn stood in front of his jagged phalanx of mercenaries. They'd spread out in groups of three and four to cover both of the planes, looking almost like a firing line.

The men from Federico Mescone's Sabreliner met them in kind. They rolled open the cargo door, threw down the metal ramp with a loud, shuddering thud, then trooped down onto the sunbaked strip.

The cartel gunmen spread out in a gauntlet formation, an honor guard for the man who stood in the open doorway.

Federico Mescone looked down at Quinn and nodded curtly at him. Then he studied the weapon-laden forklifts with satisfaction. His gaze swept slowly across the complex and lingered on the warehouses where another three more lifts were rolling into the open.

His eyes moved on, squinting at a pair of empty semitrailers parked on struts between the warehouses, as if he were looking for snipers.

"Is this everybody?" Mescone asked.

"It's enough for what we have to do," Quinn replied, "so if you don't mind...let's get it done."

"By all means," Mescone said, gesturing toward the interior of the plane. "Come aboard and make your counts. We'll look at the weapons, then we'll make the exchange.''

Quinn signaled two of his men to inspect the cargo of the Sabreliner and sent another two to the Beech King, where Melitta Caporra's men had filed outside.

As a trio of cartel soldiers started to open the crates to inspect the goods, both Mescone and Colonel Navarre headed over for a personal look at the weapons.

"Beautiful," Mescone said as he hefted an ICW rifle from one of the crates. "Truly a work of art. We'll make good use of these.''

His pilot grunted. "If you get the right men.''

"That will be your department," Mescone replied. He turned to Quinn, who'd drifted over to their side.

"Everything all right?'' Quinn asked. His voice made it clear that there was only one answer.

"Of course. Just as you promised. This more than makes up for the, eh, difficulties. I think, Thomas, that we'll be doing regular business again.''

Quinn smiled. "No need to let a misunderstanding come between us. We've done well in the past. We'll do well in the future.''

The head of ISS found it easy to be polite, especially since his men outnumbered and outgunned the Colombians. After all, this was Quinn's territory. His men kept a close eye on the cartel soldiers, who did their best to return their intense stares.

Both sides had already picked out their targets in case things got out of hand.

But the transaction was going smoothly, and Quinn expected no trouble. His men were satisfied with the currency count and the quality of the contraband in the Sabreliner. The count was almost finished.

Quinn headed over to the Beech King, where Gilberto Vicente and Melitta Caporra were talking like old friends while the two other ISS men examined their cargo.

Nicholas Vreeland stood in the shade of one of the wings he was holding on to. A scruffy man with greasy hair stood beside him. He looked formidable, but nothing like the one who'd accompanied Vreeland to the meeting in Boca Raton.

"Where's your military adviser?" Quinn asked.

"He's taking care of some other things for me," Vreeland replied. "I've got other things happening, you know. Besides, there's nothing to worry about here. You and the Mescones are friends again, right?"

"Friends, no," Quinn said. "Business partners, yes."

It took about ten more minutes before the count was finalized and the discussion of the off-load-reload began. Like diplomats wrangling over small-points protocol, they finally came to agreement.

The Beech King would be unloaded first. Half the weapons would be loaded on board, then the Sabreliner would be unloaded and the rest of the weapons handed over.

Both sides would go their own way.

BOLAN PUT DOWN the imager when the officer working the battle-staff console in the EC-130E airborne command center called him on the radio.

"Belasko, this is ACC-1, we've got intruders in the southeast sector. Four ground vehicles moving in the direction of the airfield. Are they part of your mission?"

"Negative," Bolan replied. "Are there any markings? Maybe local law enforcement picked up on the operation."

"No insignia. Two Jeeps, one station wagon, one pickup. They're hidden by a ridge now but should come into view soon. They're moving fast."

"They're not mine. Check with the others, then check back with me."

It was possible the vehicles were connected to a sheriff's office in the region, Bolan thought. But it was unlikely they had tumbled onto the operation.

He doubted they were part of the ISS force. Quinn already had his people all lined up. What good would it do having more of them roar in at the last moment?

That meant they were most likely connected to the Colombian crew.

But for what?

An ambush? It didn't make sense. Quinn's people could handle that amount.

More off-loaders?

But the Colombians had enough men to do it themselves, the Executioner thought. The Beech King was loaded with their allotment of crates, and the Sabreliner was empty. It wouldn't take much for them to load the rest of the weapons onto the second plane.

But maybe the weapons were going somewhere else, and Federico Mescone was playing a wild card.

One way or the other the cartel kingpin planned on coming out of this deal with his ICWs.

Bolan radioed the EC-130 and told the command-and-control team to assume that the intruders were hostile, probably a faction working with the cartel. They'd find out soon enough, Bolan knew, when he gave the word everyone had been waiting for. They couldn't afford to let any of those weapons get out of the zone.

"Call in the choppers," Bolan said. "We're going in."

MELITTA CAPORRA WAS the first one to see the four dust clouds on the horizon. "What the hell is that?" she shouted.

"Good question," Quinn said, unholstering his 9 mm automatic and holding it at his side. "Anybody got an answer?"

Caporra shook her head. "I'm the one who told you," she said. "I don't know what it is."

Vreeland stared at the dust clouds. Gavin frowned.

A half-dozen ISS mercenaries appeared from the shadows of one of the warehouses and started running down the airfield. Each man carried an ICW smart rifle. They knelt on the airstrip and focused on the oncoming vehicles.

Claude LeBrun appeared beside Quinn and raised a pair of binoculars toward the stretch of desert in the south. "Couple of dark-glass Jeeps, pickup, old wagon. Nobody we know."

Quinn clapped LeBrun on the back, directing him toward the other commandos. "Tell them to smoke them at five hundred yards."

"Wait!" Mescone shouted as he stepped in front of LeBrun. "You can all relax. Those are my people!"

"They're about to become dead people," Quinn said, "unless you tell me what's going on."

"Of course. It's just a precaution. We're not taking all of the weapons by plane."

"What?" Caporra said.

"Too much of a chance moving them all by air,"

the cartel chief stated. "They'll go overland instead. We'll drive them across the Rio Grande. Or walk them across. It's no problem."

"You didn't tell me," Caporra said.

The cartel leader cocked his head toward her. "You work for *me*. I tell you what you need to know."

"But I put the plan together."

"And I improved upon it," Mescone said, not bothering to hide his anger at being questioned by a subordinate, especially a woman, in front of all of these men. There would be a harsh payback in her future. "It's done." He looked at Quinn. "So if you'll tell your men not to shoot, we'll go ahead with the deal."

Quinn shrugged, amused at the bickering between the cartel confederates. "We'll go ahead," Quinn said, nodding toward the vehicles. "But with a gun trained on every man in that convoy. If one of them says the wrong thing or moves the wrong way, they all go down. So do you."

Mescone raised his hand in a pacifying motion. "I understand your anger. But you must understand my caution. There'll be no trouble here. We just want to send some of the crates by land."

"How you do it is your business," Quinn said, "as long as you get them out of here."

Vreeland had been watching the exchange with controlled panic and started to edge away. The undercover pilot picked up on Vreeland's growing fright and walked him back to the plane.

"Gavin," Vreeland grated, "what's going on? We were supposed to move out, then Belasko and his crew would move in. But now—"

"Now we got a situation," Gavin said, glancing

back at Quinn's people and the cartel soldiers who were still distracted by the approaching vehicles. "Get in the plane, get ready to take off, or at least roll this thing out of here when the shooting starts."

"If the shooting starts."

"No," Gavin replied, "*when* it starts. We planned for everything on this operation. No one's getting out of here with those weapons. Just get in the plane and get ready to fly."

"What about you?" Vreeland asked. "What'll you do?"

"Whatever I have to." Gavin headed back to the group of cartel soldiers clustered around the station wagon that had slowly driven up to the Sabreliner and parked near the ramp. He kept on moving until he had a chance to catch Caporra's attention and question her with his eyes.

She raised her eyebrows and darted a look at Mescone, trying to communicate that it was all his doing.

It made sense to the undercover pilot. If she'd given up Gavin or Vreeland, they'd be dead by now.

But it didn't make much of a difference. Things had changed. The controlled operation was about to go out of control.

MACK BOLAN WAS ALMOST at the foot of the escarpment when he heard the telltale whup-whup signature of rotor blades slicing through the air.

Armand Cane was a few feet behind him, scuttling down the rock-and-sand ridge. The other two-man teams that had been scattered along the ridge were also working their way down to the valley floor.

They'd been moving slowly at first, relying on their stealthy descent and the sand-colored fatigues to avoid being seen from the complex.

But the time for stealth was almost over now.

It was time for speed.

The Aérospatiale HH-65 and Sikorsky UH-60A Black Hawk helicopter squadrons were flying in single formation down the canyon, staying hidden until the last possible moment.

The first three Sikorskys that rose over the ridge carried lightweight Desert Patrol Vehicles on their slung-load hooks. As the choppers beelined toward the valley, the DPVs hung from steel cables like descending spiders.

The Executioner ran out to a level patch of open ground and raised both arms vertically over his head to get the pilot's attention, then signaled him to move off to the right.

Rotor wash kicked up a cloud of topsoil as the Sikorsky hovered over the desert and lowered the DPV to the flat terrain that Bolan had directed him to.

As soon as the wheels of the stripped-down dune-buggy battle wagon touched the sand, one of the men from the chopper dropped onto the DPV's roll bar.

He wore a lightweight bulletproof helmet with clear protective visor and was carrying two more by their straps. He tossed the high-tech helmets to Bolan and Cane, then unhooked the cable and signaled to the pilot that the load had been released.

As the helicopter banked to the left, the man dropped into the driver's seat and switched on the ignition.

There was no time wasted, no need to talk. They all knew what they had to do.

Bolan jumped into the seat beside him while Armand Cane clambered up to the caged gunner's po-

sition on the rear upper deck and slid behind the
.50-caliber machine gun that was mounted on the
rooftop.

The driver hit the gas, thick-ridged tires dug into
the sand and the DPV shot across the desert. Wind
and sand rushed through the glassless windscreen,
beating a steady tattoo on their protective visors as
the vehicle picked up speed.

It could reach speeds up to eighty miles per hour,
and the driver was doing his best to prove it as he
headed to Quinn's complex.

By the time they were halfway to the target zone
there were five other DPVs screaming across the desert on both sides of them. The lightweight buggies
looked like tanks without armor.

When the driver angled toward the airstrip, Bolan
grabbed the 7.62 mm M-60 machine gun mounted
on the forward weapons platform. He trained it on
the warehouse where several of the ISS operatives
were preparing for their attack, firing automatic rifles
into the desert.

But the DPVs were hard targets to hit. They
moved fast and low to the ground.

The real danger came from the ICW rifle team that
had originally trained their weapons on the Mescone
ground vehicles

Now they were running toward the warehouse to
join the other ISS gunmen. The laser-guided air-burst
munitions could do a lot of damage to the open caged
vehicles, but in order to fire the ICWs they had to
be able to see. And right now it was raining fire and
smoke from above.

It came from the first wave of Black Hawks that
had soared across the desert and circled behind the
warehouse complex before swooping overhead and

unleashing a brimstone barrage onto Quinn's mercenaries.

Brilliant yellow streaks seared from the sky and burst into high-explosive halos that dug into the ground near the warehouse. Smoke rounds dropped a cloud of chemical blackness onto the airfield, making it impossible for the defenders to see the approaching vehicles until it was too late.

By the time the billowing smoke started to clear, Bolan's driver was skidding in front of the Beech King and looping back to make a broadside pass in front of the warehouse.

The Executioner swung the M-60 to the right and ripped off a sustained burst that pounded into the ground and kicked up spouts of dust. It took only a second for Bolan to correct his aim. Ten men dropped as the M-60 found its range and strafed the ISS commandos.

Only a couple of them were wounded. The rest were dead, weighted down with 7.62 mm rounds. At that range the heavy cartridges were devastating to the human body. Blood, bone and suddenly soulless corpses flew across the killzone.

Bolan maintained his fire, relying on his instinct to guide the M-60's barrel across the massed mercenaries.

Some of them managed to return fire before they fell, but they'd been so disoriented by the helicopter assault and the broadsides from the DPV that there'd been no time to gather their wits.

Right behind Bolan came the sound of the .50-caliber machine gun as Cane pounded away at the warehouse.

The heavy rounds chopped into the clusters of mercenaries and ripped a couple of them off their feet. More of them would have been hit, but the DPV suddenly dropped into a depression and bounced several feet into the air. Cane held on to the heavy gun as the vehicle swerved left and right, but his kill fire went high, drilling holes though the warehouse walls as the driver fought to regain control.

Their first run was over.

Another DPV immediately picked up the slack and pinned down the ISS gunmen with more machine-gun fire. While they were running for their lives, a third DPV roared by and caught them in a cross fire.

THOMAS QUINN HAD LOOKED hard at Federico Mescone at the first sign of the attack. He saw that the cartel leader was as surprised as Quinn at the arrival first of the helicopters, then the dune buggy battle wagons crisscrossing the desert.

Mescone was staring back at Quinn as if *he* suspected the ISS man of a double cross. The Colombian chieftain raced toward him and bellowed in his face. "What have you done? You set us up!"

At Mescone's side was Colonel Navarre, who looked prepared to shoot anyone, even though Quinn still had a cluster of ISS commandos with their weapons at the ready, waiting for their orders.

"It's not me!" Quinn shouted back. "Look over there." He pointed at the warehouse, where his men were falling beneath endless volleys of machine-gun fire. "You think I'd kill my own people?"

Mescone shook his head and swore.

Then he looked around him, calculating the best method of escape. Right now the choices were limited. The skies were full of fast-moving helicopters that droned overhead, seemingly coming out of nowhere to fire smoke, flares and chaff onto the airfield complex.

Then the buggies came in to select their targets, make their hits, then move away before any of the return fire could zero in on them. While half of the DPVs engaged Quinn's men in battle, the others drove along the full length of the airstrip, firing smoke grenades from launchers mounted on weapons platforms, paralyzing the joint forces of Quinn's ISS and the Mescone cartel.

Even with the high-tech air-burst ICWs at their command, the traffickers were outmaneuvered and outclassed.

It was one thing to take careful aim and fire the ICWs when you were with a raiding party or practicing on a target range. But it was another thing entirely to fire them when helicopters were droning overhead and their rotor wash was stirring up volcanic blasts of smoke and flame that seemed to erupt from every inch of the battlefield.

Even Quinn's well-trained mercenaries were overwhelmed by the assault. When they were facing so much immediate destruction, their main thoughts were to get out of the way before they got eaten alive by chain-gun fire.

Most of the men who'd been stationed near the warehouse had been eliminated. The others were drifting back to the planes to regroup or were moving across the desert.

Amid the chaos Quinn saw the station wagon streaking across the desert with its tailgate open and wooden crates of weapons bouncing up and down. They wouldn't make it far, Quinn thought, catching a glimpse of one of the helicopters swooping down on it like a hawk from the sky.

He knew the Colombians wouldn't make it out of there, and his own force was disintegrating all around him. So was his empire. The deal was dead and so was he unless he moved fast.

Quinn turned his attention to Melitta Caporra, who had been inching toward the Beech King. And then it all made sense. The planes hadn't been targeted during the assault. That meant that the attackers had confederates aboard.

"You!" Quinn shouted, stabbing his finger at the woman. "It was you the first time. In the Bahamas..."

"No," she said. "I had nothing to do with it—"

"And you came back to finish me off," Quinn accused.

Caporra ran for the open cargo door of the Beech King when Quinn gave the order to LeBrun. "Do her," he shouted.

LeBrun stepped forward and extended the Heckler & Koch subgun in a swift movement that tracked Melitta Caporra. She was two feet from the door and wasn't going to make it.

It gave Quinn a moment of satisfaction. But it was only fleeting, as fleeting as the brief appearance of Vreeland's shaggy-haired adviser from just inside the cargo door. In that glimpse Quinn knew that the man was the genuine article, not some drug runner with a gun.

Gavin's right hand held a 9 mm SIG-Sauer P-228 automatic with an extended magazine, and he was squeezing off rounds with a controlled aim. The first shot hit LeBrun in the temple, dropping the man to the ground.

The next shot took out Colonel Navarre. He slumped against Mescone and grabbed the cartel leader's shoulder for support. Mescone flung him off and raced toward the Sabreliner.

Quinn fired one shot from his automatic, then dived to the ground to escape the 9 mm blasts from the P-228 tracking him. Two shots rang out from the direction of the Sabreliner, and Gavin fell back inside the cargo door. One of Caporra's Colombian crewmen took his place and fired toward Quinn.

That brought an immediate response from two of Quinn's mercs, who drilled the gunman with full-auto subgun bursts.

Then it was open season. After the Colombians saw Quinn and his gunners fire on Caporra and her cartel soldier, they figured Quinn was in on the ambush. They turned their weapons on the ISS commandos, who opened fire at the same time.

So much gunfire ripped through the air that it was a lead-filled lottery. Bullets thudded into the ground, into dead and dying bodies, into the thin metal fuselages of the Beech King and Sabreliner.

And then suddenly three of the dune buggies were in their midst, soldiers climbing out, firing subguns into the cartel gunmen and Quinn's now retreating mercenaries.

One of the dune buggies exploded when an airburst munition struck the gas tank. The caged machine blew apart, and shards of metal cut through the air like shrapnel from a fragmentation grenade.

The driver and the gunner were half-disintegrated in the blast. The third man from the DPV was almost out of the explosive range, but he ran into a burst of 9 mm lead and collapsed to the ground.

A quartet of Quinn's mercenaries had made it out into the field behind the warehouse. They had enough room to move and a clear view of the battle zone, and knelt to home in on a low-flying Sikorsky with their ICWs.

Two laser-locked rounds ripped into the chopper's armor plating. A third went off through the glass. The fourth exploded right in the cockpit, blowing the pilot and copilot out of the fiery cabin.

The stricken Black Hawk dropped from the sky like a rock and flattened on the ground below, a mass of smoking metal with landing struts sticking into the air like splintered bones.

Two DPVs kicked up dust in the sand as they rocketed across the desert toward the four-man rifle team, paving the way in front of them with machine-gun fire.

Another DPV whined across the airfield and headed for the Beech King. Bolan was leaning out of the passenger seat, trying to balance the Beretta 93-R in his right hand.

Federico Mescone saw the DPV heading his way but he ignored it as long as he could and ran after the Beech King on foot, intent on putting a bullet into the woman who had betrayed him. And he knew that the DPV gunners couldn't fire at will, not without risking a hit on their own collaborators in the aircraft. As the aircraft wound its way through the body-littered airstrip, the glowering cartel chief kept up with it and fired several shots from his automatic into the open cargo door.

When the DPV was almost upon him, Mescone finally turned toward the desert battle wagon, dropped into a crouch and fired at the driver.

Two rounds bounced off of the man's ballistic helmet and jarred him senseless. His hands spun on the wheel and caused one of the DPV's tires to drop into a rut that had been blasted out of the ground. It was deep enough to trap the chassis, tipping the vehicle onto its side and spinning it end over end in a cloud of dust.

Federico Mescone moved in for the kill.

He expected to find his prey dazed and damaged, crawling away from the wreckage.

Instead he found himself standing face-to-face with the Executioner, who materialized from the smoke and dust and triggered a 3-round burst into the kingpin of the Mescone cartel.

Mescone squeezed off one last round before his knees dropped into the dirt and he fell onto the remnants of his bullet-pocked face.

Bolan helped pull Cane from the DPV cage so he could look after the driver. Then the Executioner caught up to the Beech King where Vreeland had brought it to a stop. The pilot had seen the firefight and figured his best move was to wait for Bolan.

Inside the cargo area, Bolan saw Gavin lying wounded on the floor, blood soaking through the cloth Caporra had wrapped around his wounds. She was sitting in shock, her back resting against the cabin wall. It wasn't shock from the wound, but shock that she might get out of the situation alive.

"I thought we were all dead back there," she said.

"We made a deal," the Executioner replied. "You did your part, and I did mine."

Bolan moved up to the cockpit where Vreeland was holding on to the control yoke as he taxied farther away from the battlefield. He dropped into the seat next to him. "Where's Quinn?"

The ISS head had vanished during the combat chaos.

Vreeland nodded toward the right where Quinn's corporate jet was rolling down the far end of the runway. It was picking up speed as it rocketed along the level desert.

"Last I saw he was heading for the Windstar," Vreeland said. "That thing can do four hundred, maybe five hundred miles an hour. Twice as fast as the choppers. He'll get away."

"It can do 450," Bolan said, totally familiar with the speed and specs of the corporate jet. The specialists from technical services had given him the crash course he needed to bring Quinn down to earth. "And it won't get away," he added.

Not only had the dirty-tricks specialists provided Bolan with the details of the plane, but they'd also made a site visit to the airport where Quinn's prestigious corporate jet was kept. After a surreptitious entry into the Windstar, they made sure it would perform as expected.

Vreeland looked skeptical. As a veteran flier, he thought Bolan's confidence was misplaced.

Most of the helicopters had flown south to head off the Colombian convoy and the remnants of Quinn's mercenaries who were fleeing in anything that moved. With the DPVs hot on their heels and the stopping power of the choppers, nothing was going to get out of that zone.

But Quinn looked as though he was home free.

Bolan picked up the handset and contacted the EC-130E and the HH-65 that had been specially outfitted at Fort Bliss under Hal Brognola's authority. The HH-65 had been hovering in the nearby canyon, held in reserve for a rescue mission.

Or a special mission.

Bolan called in the HH-65.

The utility helicopter appeared over the ridge, then

swooped toward the taxiing Beech King, landing about fifty yards in front of it.

Vreeland tapped the brakes and brought the Beech King parallel to the HH-65. Bolan hopped out and sprinted to the waiting chopper, grabbing the arm of the copilot, who pulled him up into the cabin.

Then the HH-65 was airborne, trailing far behind the corporate jet as the Windstar began its climb over the ridge.

THE DESERT FLOOR RECEDED as the Windstar jet streaked across the sky. Thomas Quinn sat comfortably in the cockpit and watched the ground below as the pilot flew them away from the combat zone.

He saw vehicles tracking across the sand, helicopters hovering above them and men running everywhere.

Gilberto Vicente was somewhere down there, maybe running for his life, maybe already dead. One way or the other, he was gone forever. Too bad. But there hadn't been time to wait.

As the plane reached higher elevation, the men and machines became like ants from an anthill.

They would be crushed just as easily, Quinn thought. But it was no longer his concern.

He'd made it to the jet. Now he'd make it out of the country. True, he might have to go underground for a while, but with his contacts he'd find suitable clients soon.

He leaned back into the seat and relaxed, savoring every little shudder in the jet's body as the twin engines boosted the speed even more.

But then he noticed the panicky expression on the pilot's face. The man had gone pale. He was obviously frightened and just as obviously trying to hide it from Quinn.

"What's the matter?" Quinn demanded.

"The controls have seized up. We're flying on autopilot, but I didn't put us there."

"What are you talking about?"

"I can't control the plane anymore!" he shouted. "Someone else is flying it. There's a helicopter tailing us. I think it's locked on to us and is overriding the controls somehow."

"That's impossible!"

"Yeah, it is," the pilot replied. "But it's happening. I don't know how—"

"I think I do," Quinn said, his voice sinking. It came to him then. It came full circle. The antinav gear he'd tried to smuggle out of the Bahamas hadn't been destroyed after all.

It had been confiscated by the same people who were now in pursuit of him, the people who orchestrated the ambush in the Everglades and in Saint-Denis...the people who turned Melitta Caporra and Nicholas Vreeland against him.

No, he thought, not people. Person.

He remembered the hard-edged man who'd come to his office with Vreeland, posing as his military adviser. It wasn't a pose. The man was real. Dead real. He'd been leading Quinn to this war front all along.

The last one.

The Windstar corporate jet suddenly nosed downward and headed toward a high ridge of jagged rock.

The pilot screamed.

Quinn stared at the wall of rock that rushed up to meet them as the jet streaked toward it like a ten-ton bullet, a jet-speed air-bursting bullet fired by the man in black.

He opened his mouth to curse the man, but all that came out was an ungodly howling as he passed through an eternal doorway of pain.

Brief white light enveloped him, then there was all-consuming darkness.

The aircraft practically disintegrated on impact, momentarily transforming Quinn and the pilot into compressed bits of metal, flesh and bone before scattering them across the barren landscape in one last searing flash.

MACK BOLAN PUT the black box on the floor of the cabin. It had taken only a slight push of the control yoke on the box—a miniature high-tech doppelgänger of the controls in the Windstar—to send Thomas Quinn to oblivion.

The HH-65 had been transformed into a flying control tower, packed with the antinav gear components that had been snatched out of Quinn's hands. But now it had been given back to him with interest.

Bolan signaled the pilot to take them down to the desert where the rest of the strike team was rounding up the survivors of Quinn's covert empire.

This war was over.

Stony Man turns the tide of aggression against
the world's most efficient crime machines

STONY MAN™ 32

LAW OF
LAST RESORT

The playground of the Caribbean becomes a drug clearing
house for an ex-KGB major and his well-oiled machine
handling cocaine and heroin from the cartels and the
Yakuza. But turquoise waters turn bloodred as Mack Bolan,
Able Team and Phoenix Force deliver a hellfire sweep that
pulls the CIA, international mafiosi and Colombians together
in an explosive showdown.

Available in January 1998 at your favorite retail outlet.

**A violent struggle for survival
in a post-holocaust world**

JAMES AXLER

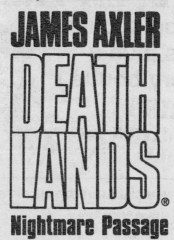

DEATH LANDS®

Nightmare Passage

Ryan Cawdor and his companions fear they have crossed time lines
when they encounter an aspiring god-king whose ambitions are
straight out of ancient Egypt. In the sands of California's Guadalupe
Desert, Ryan must make the right moves to save them from another
kind of hell—abject slavery.

James Axler

OUTLANDERS™

SAVAGE SUN

A reference to ancient mysterious powers
sends Kane, Brigid Baptiste and Grant to
the wild hinterlands of Ireland, whose stone
ruins may function as a gateway for the alien
Archons.

But the Emerald Isle's blend of ancient magic
and advanced technology, as wielded by a
powerful woman, brings them to the very brink
of oblivion.

OUT3

Don't miss out on the action in these titles featuring THE EXECUTIONER®, STONY MAN™ and SUPERBOLAN®!

The American Trilogy

#64222	PATRIOT GAMBIT	$3.75 U.S.	☐
		$4.25 CAN.	☐
#64223	HOUR OF CONFLICT	$3.75 U.S.	☐
		$4.25 CAN.	☐
#64224	CALL TO ARMS	$3.75 U.S.	☐
		$4.25 CAN.	☐

Stony Man™

#61910	FLASHBACK	$5.50 U.S.	☐
		$6.50 CAN.	☐
#61911	ASIAN STORM	$5.50 U.S.	☐
		$6.50 CAN.	☐
#61912	BLOOD STAR	$5.50 U.S.	☐
		$6.50 CAN.	☐

SuperBolan®

#61452	DAY OF THE VULTURE	$5.50 U.S.	☐
		$6.50 CAN.	☐
#61453	FLAMES OF WRATH	$5.50 U.S.	☐
		$6.50 CAN.	☐
#61454	HIGH AGGRESSION	$5.50 U.S.	☐
		$6.50 CAN.	☐

(limited quantities available on certain titles)

TOTAL AMOUNT	$
POSTAGE & HANDLING	$
($1.00 for one book, 50¢ for each additional)	
APPLICABLE TAXES*	$ _____
TOTAL PAYABLE	$ _____
(check or money order—please do not send cash)	

To order, complete this form and send it, along with a check or money order for the total above, payable to Gold Eagle Books, to: **In the U.S.:** 3010 Walden Avenue, P.O. Box 9077, Buffalo, NY 14269-9077; **In Canada:** P.O. Box 636, Fort Erie, Ontario, L2A 5X3.

Name: _____

Address: _____ City: _____

State/Prov.: _____ Zip/Postal Code: _____

*New York residents remit applicable sales taxes.
 Canadian residents remit applicable GST and provincial taxes.

GOLD
EAGLE®

GEBACK19